What Are the Odds?

A Sandi Webster Mystery

by

Marja McGraw

To Dorothy,
You have become one of my dearest friends. Thank you!

Marja McGraw

Other Books by Marja McGraw

The Sandi Webster Mysteries

A Well-Kept Family Secret
Bubba's Ghost
Prudy's Back!
The Bogey Man
Old Murders Never Die
Death Comes in Threes

The Bogey Man Mysteries

Bogey Nights
Bogey's Ace in the Hole
They Call Me Ace
Awkward Moments

First Edition, July, 2014
Cover by Marja McGraw

This is a work of fiction. Names, characters, places and incidents either are the product of the author's imagination or are used fictitiously. Any resemblance to actual persons living or dead, events, or locales is entirely coincidental.

DEDICATION

To Sherri and Bill, long-time special friends who loaned me their home as an inspiration for *What Are the Odds?* Their hard work and tenacity has paid off in ways they never imagined. Ain't life grand?

ACKNOWLEDGEMENTS

Thank you to Dorothy Bodoin, Judy B. and Diana Perry –
close friends, excellent critiquers and women whose
encouragement and support seem never-ending. Good friends
mean more to me than they sometimes realize.

Special thanks to Sherri and Bill, more close friends, for the
loan of their house for this story – the house that just keeps
giving.

Chapter One

A woman's wedding day is supposed to be a day she'll remember for the rest of her life. My special day won't be a problem. I have to admit, I'll never forget a single moment – from walking down the aisle of the church next to Felicity (it was a double wedding) to watching Pete, Frank and Stanley try to revive the preacher to seeing the ambulance take Pastor Walker away.

The widow-maker had taken him so fast he never knew what hit him. A heart attack. At my wedding.

"What are the odds?"

I didn't realize I'd spoken aloud until Pete's closest friend, Rick Mason, opened his mouth and closed it again without saying a word. He considered me a body magnet because everywhere I go it seems like a dead body turns up.

Pete and I started our new life as husband and wife with him trying to revive someone who was probably dead before he hit the ground. Yes, it was truly a day I'd never forget.

My sigh was big enough to blow up a balloon, and for once my mother didn't chastise me about my bad habit. I had a feeling she was holding in her own sigh.

Pete stood in front of Stanley. "I'm telling you, he said

'I now pronounce you man and wife.' Sandi and Felicity said, 'I do', you and I said, 'I do', and the preacher said, 'I now pronounce you – "

"That's not what I heard," Stanley insisted. "He said, 'I now pronounce you man and w...' He said *woo*, not wife. I don't think we're legally married."

"We're legally married," Felicity said. "He signed all the papers before the ceremony, and he had us sign them, too. He was supposed to officiate at another event and he was in a hurry."

"*Woo* is not wife. I think we should consult an attorney." Stanley was insistent.

"Are you wishing we hadn't gone through with the ceremony?" Felicity looked like she was ready to cry. Her lower lip quivered.

Stanley realized his mistake. "Oh, my little peach, of course I'm glad we were married this morning. I just want to be sure it's legal."

"It's legal. Trust me, pal. And stop whining." Pete turned to me and rolled his eyes.

I turned away from him and spoke to the small group who'd attended our wedding. "It's been a rough morning, but we're married. I'm sorry my regular pastor couldn't be here. He had a family emergency. I feel bad about Pastor Walker, but there's nothing I can do.

"For the rest of the day we're going to celebrate our little hearts out. Got it?" I looked directly into Stanley's eyes.

He averted his gaze. I think he might have been embarrassed because he'd made a scene.

My friend and neighbor, Dolly, moved to stand by Stanley. She patted his back and *tsked* at him. "I've been around for over eighty years, Stan, and I've seen a lot. This is minor. *Woo* is the same as saying *wife*."

I smiled at Dolly and turned to my itty bitty mother. She nodded, taking hold of my step-father's hand. Frank put his arm around her.

Rick stood and held his hand out to first Pete, and then Stanley. "Congratulations! I think Sandi's right. We need to move on and celebrate. Heart attacks happen, and the minister wasn't someone any of us knew. There was nothing anyone could do to save him. We tried, but it was too late."

Again, my mother nodded.

Rick turned to her. "Livvie, Jessica and I will do whatever you need help with today." He'd brought his long-time girlfriend to the wedding. They were good people, both together and individually.

Mom nodded.

I squatted down in front of her. "Mother? What's wrong?"

Pete stood next to me. "Yeah, Livvie. It's not like you to be so quiet."

Tears started to slowly make their way down her cheeks. "First your pastor dies, although at least he finished the ceremony – God rest his soul – and just to make things worse, none of you get to take a honeymoon. And it's all *my* fault." She dabbed at her nose with a tissue.

"You certainly didn't have anything to do with the minister's heart attack, and we'll get to take a honeymoon," I said, "just not now. We said we'd help you after the wedding and we will. It's not a big deal, Mom."

She cried harder. My little pixie of a mother is under five feet tall and she keeps us all on our toes. She's menopausal and when she forgets to take her hormone pills, she's out of control. Her emotions are all over the charts. I hoped she hadn't missed them today.

"Mother, did you…"

"I took my pills, *Sandra*. Now let me feel guilty in peace."

Uh oh. The dreaded use of my proper name.

Pete took hold of my hand and pulled me away. "I

never got to kiss the bride." He pulled me to him and gave me a wedding kiss I'd never forget.

When we separated, Stanley turned and kissed Felicity. His face turned a bright shade of crimson when we applauded.

I watched my mother and found our antics had pacified her feelings of guilt. She couldn't watch our happiness without feeling some of her own.

The church secretary walked in, shaking her head. She hadn't met Pastor Walker until the morning of our wedding, but she somehow seemed to feel like she'd let everyone down. His death had happened on her watch. She waited while we gathered our belongings and locked the door behind us when we left, never saying a word.

I held back and watched people head for their cars. Besides Pete and me inviting my parents and Rick, Felicity had invited a photographer and a couple of other models to the wedding. Pete's parents had been waylaid by the flu and couldn't make it from New York to California. I had yet to meet them and had looked forward to that event. Of course, my neighbor Dolly was there along with her granddaughter and great-granddaughter.

Felicity is a model, although she's not a runway model. You might see her hands or her face in magazine ads. She's too small for a runway job. Her long, almost black, hair hung down her back for the wedding. She has deep dimples that set off a beautiful face. She reminds me of a little China doll. And she makes my mother look almost tall. I feel like a giant next to her, and I'm only about five foot three.

On the other hand, Stanley Hawks is very proper and a little nerdy. When we met him, his job had been as a writer for greeting cards. He's around forty, but he never would share his actual age with us, and he's gone through some major changes since meeting Felicity. He changed his appearance and tried to be more down to earth. Sometimes it works for him. He was one of our first clients and now works with us at the agency.

You might ask: What agency? My name is Sandi Webster and I'm a private eye. Pete Goldberg is my partner, and now he's my husband. By the way, don't let the name fool you. Pete is one hundred percent Italian. Long story. Oops. My name is now Sandi Goldberg.

Your next question might be: Why don't we get to go on a honeymoon?

That would be because my mother and step-father have acquired a thirty-acre ranch with what will be a gorgeous house after a lot of work, and they're turning it into a bed and breakfast. The house has a checkered history and it's been vacant for several years.

Pete and I, along with Felicity and Stanley, decided to forego our honeymoons in order to help fix up the tri-level house. My mother can be very persuasive, and the house needs plenty of manual labor.

The two things I'm leaving out are that there were murders committed in the house – and the neighbors think it's haunted.

I don't believe in ghosts.

Chapter Two

*P*ete and I combined households during the week before the wedding. I own my great-great-great-grandmother's old house and we decided to live there. It's a grand old house, even though I've had more regrettable situations than I care to remember under its roof. Although, how can one forget being threatened and almost murdered in one's own home – more than once. I tell myself it comes with the territory. I've always wanted to be a private investigator. I got my wish and then some. On the bright side, I have a new husband thanks to my choice of professions, and things are never dull.

After the wedding we met at my house. It was a small but happy group.

Bubba greeted us at the door when we arrived and Dolly's great-granddaughter immediately went outside to play *fetch* with him. Bubba is my dog, although he resembles a small bear in size. He's half wolf and half Golden retriever, and he frequently smiles, which sometimes puts people off because they think he's baring his teeth at them.

Felicity and I changed out of our wedding dresses, giggling like school girls while we discussed the fact that we were now both married women. Our giggles turned to a sigh when we talked about Pastor Walker's death.

My mother and Felicity helped me put out food and a small wedding cake. Pete had already passed out drinks, and a bottle or two of champagne chilled in the refrigerator.

I finally sat down and took a deep breath.

Jessica sat next to me. "So tell me about this bed and breakfast your mother and her husband are opening. Rick said there were murders in the house? Does she think people will stay there regardless of the place's history?"

Before I could open my mouth, my mother the drama queen, who sat on my other side spoke loudly. "Let me tell the story. It's a tale of murder and jealousy. Or so I've been told. Frank and I sold our house in Bullhead City. That's in Arizona, you know. Escrow closes in about thirty days, and I think we'll move to the llama ranch now instead of waiting."

The room fell into silence and all eyes were fixed on Livvie Brewster, my loves-a-good-story mother.

"This happened, oh, probably twenty years or so ago. It's a thirty-acre ranch and it used to be a llama ranch. An elderly man and his daughter ran the place, along with one ranch hand. It's said – "

"You're enjoying this, aren't you, Mom? 'It's said'?"

"Hush and let me tell the story. Actually, this would be better told over a campfire on a dark night."

She laughed at her own little joke.

"A neighbor gave me the scoop, so this should be pretty accurate, although he didn't give me any of their names. He said the ranch hand had a thing for the daughter. So did a man from a neighboring property. The men were constantly trying to outdo one another. The daughter wasn't a young woman and she'd never been married, so she was thrilled by all the attention.

"Her father told her to be careful because it was all going to backfire on her. He said she needed to make a choice between the men and put an end to their competition. But she wouldn't listen."

My mother actually leaned forward as though it was Halloween night and she was stirring a pot of scary information.

"Well, the father was right. It backfired. She finally chose the neighbor, and the ranch hand went nuts. One stormy afternoon he stealthily entered the house and found the daughter in the living room, kissing the neighbor. The ranch hand had a gun in his hand and he shot the daughter where she stood, in the head. The neighbor ran out the front door. The ranch hand ran after him and killed him, too, before returning to the house. You can still see a bullet hole in the screen door.

"The father, hearing the shots, came running in with a shotgun. Before he could shoot, the ranch hand shot him. He didn't die, and he raised the gun and killed the ranch hand."

"What neighbor told you about this?" With four deaths, I couldn't help but wonder if the neighbor had all the details straight. Time and memory often change things from fact to exciting fiction.

"An old man who lives down the street in a mobile home. I'm sure he's reliable."

One of the models sat in a chair across from us and leaned forward, studying my mother's face. "What happened to the father?"

I could see my mother mentally rubbing her hands together. She had everyone's interest. "He died before the police got there." She sat back and looked very pleased with herself. "And that's the short version of the story."

Felicity smiled at my mother. "And a neighbor says the house is haunted by these people?"

"Only the ranch hand. Well, he told me someone said they saw the daughter once, too."

"Interesting story," Rick said. "Are you sure people will want to stay in a house where murders were committed?"

Frank decided it was his turn to speak. "Their curiosity will get the best of them, and they'll want to see the house.

Some of them will hope to see the ghost while they're there. And others simply won't care. We're turning it into kind of a dude ranch with horses. There are plenty of places to ride and we're at the base of a small mountain. It's unusual because it's flat desert surrounded by mountains, and then there's this small mountain right in the middle of the valley. We're going to have chickens, too."

Rick looked at Stanley with a sparkle in his eye. "Are you sure you're up to going all the way to Arizona and working on a haunted house?"

"You can tease me, but I'm going along. I'll do whatever my talents allow me to do." He seemed to realize Rick's question was good-natured.

"Mother," I said, "you don't know anything about farm animals, do you?"

"I can learn." She said this with finality, not leaving room for arguments. "Besides, Frank was raised on a farm. He knows what to do."

"I see." I knew there was no sense in arguing with her. Her mind was made up.

Pete seemed to think it was time to change the subject. "How about some champagne and wedding cake?"

Conversations picked up where they'd left off, and I heard a few people discussing the llama ranch, soon to be the dude ranch. I heard one of the models say she'd never stay in a place like the llama ranch, or any house with ghosts. She even demonstrated with an exaggerated little shiver.

Rick approached my mother. "Uh, Livvie, I guess you'll be the first to find out, but Jessica and I are getting married, too. In about six months. We'd like to be one of your first boarders, if the bed and breakfast will be ready by then." He raised his eyebrows, waiting for a response.

My mother threw her arms around Jessica, who still sat next to her. "Oh, but of *course* you can be our first boarders. We're planning on opening in about six months, so the timing is perfect." She took Jessica's hand and reached for Rick's. "Congratulations! As I recall, you were one of Sandi's first clients, Jessica. Isn't that how you and Rick met?"

Jessica smiled, a bittersweet distant look in her eyes. "Yes, you have a good memory. My stepson and husband were killed and Rick was on the case. I'd hired Sandi and Pete to help me find the killer."

Dolly stood and put her hands on her hips. "Good grief! Has everyone here been involved in a crime? Even my granddaughter was involved in a murder. Well, I mean she wasn't *involved*, but it happened in her basement and she was the chief suspect for about a minute. Well, I guess she was involved, but she wasn't the killer." With her permed hair and glasses sliding down her nose, she looked like a typical grandmother. If you saw her, you'd never imagine she'd been involved in some of my cases.

One of the models held her hand in the air. "I've never been involved in a crime."

Stanley looked from Felicity to me and back at the model. "If you're hanging around with Felicity, give it time."

"You've become very cynical," Pete said. "I guess you have every right to feel that way though."

"Hey! This is a celebration of two weddings," Felicity said. "We don't need to go over past history. Let's have a toast."

Rick picked up his champagne glass. "Here's to the two most beautiful brides I've ever seen, and to the lucky men they'll be sharing the rest of their lives with, God willing."

Everyone laughed and we each took a sip of champagne.

Rick glanced at my mother. "And here's to Livvie and Frank Brewster and their llama ranch, ghosts and all."

Chapter Three

*E*veryone was gone by eight o'clock and Pete and I shared a glorious wedding night. It was everything I'd hoped for, and more. The stuff dreams are made of. I hoped he felt the same, and in the morning I was pretty sure he did, judging by the smile on his face while he slept.

Knowing Bubba would need to go outside, I dragged myself out of bed and headed for the stairs.

"Mrs. Sandi Webster," I said to myself. "Dang! Old habits die hard. Mrs. Sandi *Goldberg*." I descended the stairs slowly, humming to myself.

Bubba sleeps at the foot of my bed at night, but I'd made him stay downstairs. He and Pete seem to have drawn a line in the sand, each daring the other to cross it. They could both be territorial when they wanted to be. My favorite dog wasn't too happy and when I entered the kitchen, he snubbed me.

I looked him in the eye before reaching for the back door to let him out to do his doggy business. "Pete lives here now and you're just going to have to get used to it. Understand? We're a family. It's not just you and me anymore. It's the three of us. Got it?"

Sometimes I could swear my dog understands most of

what I say to him. He looked up at me knowingly and seemed to be searching my face before he scratched at the door and lumbered outside like big dogs tend to do. That is, big dogs tend to lumber. He glanced back at me before putting his head in the air and sniffing. Letting out one deep *woof,* he turned away. He was definitely in a snubbing mood. I was pretty sure that would pass when I put his breakfast out for him.

"Considering you were talking to a dog, that was quite a little speech." Pete stood in the doorway to the kitchen, watching. He walked through the room, closed the back door and gave me a morning kiss.

"I'm ready to get used to this." I smiled up at him, brushing back the hair on his slightly graying temples. Pete was close to six feet tall with dark brown, almost black hair. He wasn't what I'd call handsome, but he had a unique man's man look that women couldn't resist. He was rugged looking. There was a tiny scar at the right side of his mouth which turned white when he scowled. At the moment he was smiling, not scowling.

"Wanna go back to bed?" he asked.

Before I could answer, the doorbell rang.

"Guess not." He turned and headed for the living room.

I wanted to make him a special wedding breakfast and I began pulling things out of the refrigerator and cupboards.

"Have you two had breakfast yet?" I could hear Pete talking to someone as yet unidentified.

"We have." Stanley's voice carried to the kitchen. "We thought maybe we should get an early start to Arizona. Are you and Sandi packed?"

"Stan, give Pete a break. Can't you see he just got up?" Felicity's tinkling voice carried to me, too. "Cute jammie bottoms, by the way."

Pete laughed. "Good thing I put them back on."

The doorbell rang again and I began putting everything

back in the refrigerator and cupboards. It didn't look like I'd have time to make the special wedding breakfast.

I filled Bubba's bowl with dog food and opened the back door. He took his time coming in, even though I knew he was hungry. He'd just have to adjust.

I heard my mother's and Frank's voices and decided I'd better go join the crowd.

"Good morning," I said. "What's everyone doing up so early?"

My mother gave me a hug. "Frank and I are leaving to get things ready at the llama ranch. Did I tell you a friend loaned us their motorhome to use while we work on the house?"

My stomach did a small lurch. "A motorhome? What do you need that for? Won't you be staying in the house?"

"Oh, no. There's no electricity or water yet. Didn't I tell you? While the house was vacant someone scrounged around and stole everything they could. They ripped out wiring, took sink faucets and swiped some of the lighting fixtures. They took copper pipes."

Frank frowned. "They even took the well pump. There's a hole in the ceiling where someone was trying to steal more wiring and fell through. They must have been injured because they didn't go back to get their wire cutters."

"This place is on well water?" Pete sounded interested, even if I, on the other hand, had a sinking feeling. "It must be a lot farther out in the country than we thought."

"It's about thirty miles north of Kingman, off a dirt road. We're going to be roughing it for a while."

Frank looked happy, Pete seemed intrigued, and I had major reservations. Stanley looked almost panic stricken. Felicity was simply Felicity, ready for any adventure. As small as she was, she never let her size get in the way.

"Mother? *You're* going to be roughing it?"

"Yes, dear, I can rough it with the best of them. Besides,

we'll be in a motorhome, so it won't be that bad. Just be sure to bring lots of bottled water with you. Oh, and a sturdy pair of boots. You never know when you might run into a rattlesnake or a scorpion. There's a hoard of black widows, too. We've set off four bug bombs and you should *see* the dead bugs. Piles of them. But the house should be fairly safe by now."

I glanced at Stanley and saw a horrified look on his face.

"Rattlesnakes?" His voice wasn't much more than a squeak.

"Honey bun, we don't want to miss all the fun. We'll be just fine. Remember, we'll watch out for one another." Felicity was excited, which seemed to flummox Stanley even more.

"What did I get *into?*" he asked.

Felicity's smile disappeared. "I certainly hope you're not talking about our marriage."

Stanley took a step toward his wife and looked horrified, once again. "Oh, my precious, absolutely not. I'll revere the day we married for the rest of my life. I mean – "

"Okay, dumpling, I get it." Her smile was back in place. "And let's save the pet names for when we're alone, if that's okay with you."

I silently thanked her because the names were so gooey. They were hard to take on an empty stomach. I looked at Pete and had a feeling he felt the same way, although he was chuckling.

"You two are going to have an interesting marriage," he said, grinning at Stanley. "However, now you're going to have to show us what you're made of and help out at the ranch. Right?"

"Right. How much harm can a snake or two do?" Stanley choked on his words and Felicity patted his back.

"Has everyone had breakfast?" Mother asked.

Pete and I shook our heads while everyone else

nodded.

"Well, move along so we can get on the road." Uh oh. My mother was in Supervisor mode. I was glad we wouldn't be taking the long trip in the same vehicle. "I was going to go ahead and set things up at the ranch, but I've been thinking we should caravan out there."

"So we need to bring sleeping bags and tents?" I asked.

"If you want a place to sleep, that would be a good idea. Just sleeping bags though."

"Pete, why don't you start getting those things together and I'll fix something we can eat on the road? I'll get Bubba's food and a few toys to take with us. How am I going to teach him to stay away from snakes? He'll think they're toys. Oh, good grief. Stanley's right. We had no idea what we were getting into."

Frank patted Bubba's head. "I'm not sure, but I have a feeling dogs may have an instinct about these things."

"I don't know," I said slowly. "Remember when he thought there was a ghost in this house? Oooh, yeah, I guess if he's afraid of ghosts, maybe he'll be afraid of snakes."

Ghosts? Too much ghost talk, and I was making it. Too much snake talk, too.

"Don't worry, sweetie, I'll protect you." My mother said that, not Pete. "The ghosts would never dream of bothering you with all of us around."

I don't *believe* in ghosts. Not now, never did.

Chapter Four

We'd already packed our suitcases, and after hearing about the living conditions, or lack thereof, I added a lot of items. I still remember the time Pete and I were stranded in a ghost town so I thought about what I'd wished we had with us but didn't. I headed for the candy drawer in the kitchen and filled a bag with chocolate bars. Chocolate was high on my list of priorities, right up there with food and water. I knew there were stores in Kingman, but the town was thirty miles away from the llama ranch.

While we were loading the car, Pete opened the bag and laughed. "Of course." He threw it in the back seat of the Jeep.

"Careful with that," I said. "You know how I can be if I don't have my chocolate fix." It was kind of like my mother without her hormone pills.

Stanley and Felicity made a trip to the sporting goods store and picked up a few things while we packed. Neither one had ever gone camping, so they were sorely lacking in supplies. When they pulled up in front of the house, Stanley was wearing a camouflage baseball cap.

I bit my tongue because it was sooo not Stanley.

"Frank already took the motorhome out to the ranch, so we won't have to stop in Bullhead City. Is Bubba in the car?" Mother glanced in the back seat and smiled at him. He grinned back.

She put her hand in the air and walked toward their car. "Onward, troops."

Pete rolled his eyes and started the car. "I know we're going to follow them, but do you have directions in case we lose each other?"

"Yes. Mother gave them to me before the wedding." I reached into my backpack. "Oh. Don't leave yet." I opened the car door and ran to the house, keys in hand.

Pete honked the horn to get everyone's attention while I ran into the house to find the forgotten directions.

Dolly stood on her porch with her little family and waved when we finally drove away.

I leaned my head back on the headrest. "It's been a crazy few days, but we're finally married and we're on our way to a supposedly haunted house."

Pete smiled. "How much better can it get?" He reached over and patted my knee. "Sandi and Pete are on another adventure."

It was a long drive to the llama ranch. We'd have to call it something else since there weren't any llamas there anymore. That would be up to my mother and Frank though.

We talked about our future during the drive. We had plans to enlarge the agency, but that would have to wait. The national economy was in the dumpster at the moment. Still, it wouldn't hurt to have plans ready when the time came.

I was hoping at some point we could open a satellite office and move away from Los Angeles. I loved the city, but I was ready to put down roots in a smaller community. Pete felt much the same way.

"Have you given any more thought to kids?" he asked, coming at me from out of the blue.

Oh, we'd talked about children, but we both had mixed feelings about the timing. I wanted to wait a while, and yet neither of us was getting any younger. I was pushing my mid-thirties and Pete was a couple of years older than me.

"I'm still on the fence about it."

"We're not getting any younger, you know."

"Now you're mind reading? I was thinking the same thing. But we just got married yesterday, so let's put our decision on the back burner, at least until after the honeymoon."

"Of course. I'm just making conversation." Pete glanced at me before turning back to the road. I noticed he was grinning.

Our route took us through a lot of desert. There wasn't much scenery to watch so I finally tipped my head back and fell asleep. The lack of scenery made me feel lethargic. I hoped it didn't have that effect on Pete, since he was driving.

I awoke when we drove over a big bump in the road. "Are we almost there?"

"Nowhere near the ranch yet."

"Oh. How are your leg and ankle? Do you want me to drive for a while?"

Pete had been in an accident and broken his right leg and left ankle several months earlier.

"I'm fine. I think if I had to use my left foot more it might be sore, but right now it's not."

I turned in my seat and checked to be sure Felicity and Stanley were still behind us. Felicity saw me turn and waved. Stanley still wore his camo hat. I waved back.

"Do you think there really are rattlesnakes?"

I kind of hoped he'd say it was all a joke.

"You can count on it. I talked to Frank and he said they already killed one they found in the barn. There are a lot of black widows, too."

"How much farther do you think it is?"

"We should be there in about another hour and a half."

The scenery whizzed by and practically hypnotized me. I nodded off again. After all, we hadn't had much sleep. Wedding nights are like that.

Waking again just before we reached Kingman, I began to feel unusually excited. Pete was right, we were heading for another adventure. I didn't have any doubts. My bones were practically rattling with excitement.

We stopped at a store in town and stocked up on more food and water. Pete found a little outdoor stove that ran on propane. It even had burners and a small oven. We oohed and aahed over it before storing it in Frank's car. He still had some room left. We were loaded to the gills.

It took us over another half hour to reach the llama ranch. We turned off onto a dirt road and followed it to the road where my mother and Frank turned. It was a bumpy ride.

Frank pulled up to the property and climbed out of their car to opened a large gate before he climbed back in the car and pulled forward, driving to the right side of the house and parking.

We stopped in front and I looked around. There was a stand of trees in front. They looked forlorn and were in need of a long drink of water. Past the trees I saw what would one day be an amazing house. The plaster was peeling off the walls, but it had once been beautiful. It needed some tender, loving care.

There was a large front porch with columns on each side of the steps leading up to it. The security screen door was white and rusting. It sure hadn't done the past residents any good. I could see a small dark spot that would probably be the bullet hole my mother had mentioned.

Off to the side I could see something that looked like a workshop, and behind that was what I thought might be the barn.

I was chomping at the bit. I couldn't wait to get out of the Jeep and explore.

My mother said this was a tri-level house, but it looked like it was two stories to me. I tipped my head and considered the building. I must have misunderstood.

Pete pulled around and parked beside the house.

I could see the motorhome sitting next to the workshop type building. There was an attached garage on the side of the house which opened on the yard side of the lot, and when Frank opened the door I saw they'd already stored a lot of their things at the ranch.

I walked around to the front of the place with Bubba at my side to get a better look. Glancing at the second floor, I thought I saw someone watching us from the window. I opened my mouth to say something, but the figure disappeared in a heartbeat.

Bubba blinked and hurried back to the cars.

I *don't* believe in ghosts! Period, end of story.

Chapter Five

We decided to do a little exploring before unpacking the cars.

There was a door leading from the garage to stairs descending to a basement. We carried flashlights because there wasn't any electricity yet. It was huge, and it looked like at one time it might have been a game room or something. The floor was covered with dust and dead bugs, and the walls were stained, but it didn't look like water stains. I wasn't sure I wanted to know what the stains were.

Pete immediately got rid of the resident black widow spider who greeted us. At least, I hoped it was the only one around the house.

My mother was enjoying being the tour guide. "Let's head upstairs and look at the main floor."

"Mom, didn't you say this is a tri-level house? Didn't you mean a two-story house with a basement?"

"No, dear. You'll see it all." Although in her fifties, she ascended the stairs with the steps of a teenager. She was excited.

Bubba sniffed all the corners and I had to call him away. I think the only reason he listened to me was because there was more to explore.

Mother's excitement was catching and I hurried up the stairs with the others trailing in our wake.

In the living room, the old carpeting had been pulled up. "Did you and Frank already start working on the house?" I asked.

"No, sweetie, this room was already bare. See that big yellow circle painted on the floor? We think someone painted over the blood stains to hide them." She sounded so blasé about it. I guess she had to be or she wouldn't want to live in the house.

Bubba headed straight for the yellow paint, lowering his head and sniffing intently.

There were two bay windows at the front of the room. The windows were both wide and tall. It was a large room with a stone fireplace.

To the right were two huge front doors. I opened them and came face to face with a bullet hole in the screen door. "Oh." After studying the hole for a moment, I returned to the group.

"Bubba, come." He ignored me and kept sniffing. "Bubba! I said to come." He turned his head slowly, and reluctantly followed me.

We traipsed through the kitchen, which was fairly large and included a walk-in pantry. Bubba found the pantry quite fascinating, so I left him to explore.

Looking over my shoulder, I didn't see Stanley or Felicity, so I reversed my steps and found them in the living room. Stanley was staring at the paint.

I didn't want him to obsess about it. "Come see the kitchen. It's got lots of possibilities."

"Come on, love bug, let's see the rest of the house." Felicity pulled on his arm.

He shifted his eyes away from the spot on the floor. "Yes, sugar lump. I'm coming."

I heard Pete groan behind me. "I thought you were

going to save the sappy talk for private moments."

Felicity laughed. "We've decided to come out of the closet. We're just sappy at heart."

Back in the kitchen, I saw someone had tried to pry up the ceramic tiles on the sink top. Apparently it was too big of a job and they'd given up. Thankfully, the thieves left the tiles they'd managed to pull up on the sink or my mother would have to buy all new ones. The sink was there, but the faucets were gone.

On to a family room which was behind the living room. There was another fireplace. The two sat back to back. A bright blue ceiling fan hung at an odd angle. I could see why the thieves hadn't taken it.

"If this tragedy occurred around twenty years ago, shouldn't the house be in even worse shape than it is?" It needed a lot of work, but so much of it seemed to be cosmetic.

"There was a caretaker out here for a long time," Frank said. "I think he might have been a cousin or something like that. He only lived in one part of the house, a little apartment we'll get to later. Anyway, he couldn't keep it up and the bank finally took it over. It's only been *completely* empty for a couple of years."

"I see."

There were three bedrooms and two bathrooms on the main floor. They were just ordinary bedrooms, but I noticed someone had removed all of the rods for hanging your clothes on out of the closets. Odd.

We continued through the house. Climbing up a short flight of stairs, we found two bedrooms and a bathroom. One of the bedrooms was quite large, obviously meant to be the master bedroom. With no electricity, we couldn't see much in the main bathroom, but it looked like there was a nice large shower. There was no toilet. Some people will steal anything.

Pete stood next to Frank. "When was this house built?"

"In the sixties. We're going to leave it as close to

original as possible, with just a few alterations."

"Come on, we're wasting daylight," my mother said. "It's getting late and I want you to see as much as possible." She waved her hand in a *come hither* movement.

I smiled at her. "We're coming."

We descended the stairs to the mail level, but instead of staying on the main floor, my mother opened a creaky door and I saw another set of stairs leading down to... Ah, the third level.

The lower level was a small apartment. It had another kitchen, a living room, two more bathrooms, three bedrooms, and a smaller walk-in pantry.

Bubba *woofed* from upstairs and I soon heard him padding down the stairs. He headed straight for the pantry.

I did a mental count. "Okay, so there are eight bedrooms. I know you wouldn't want anyone to stay on the upper level in the bedroom next to yours, so you'll have six rooms you can use for the bed and breakfast. Right?"

Mother nodded. "Yes. I'm going to turn the bedroom next to ours into an office."

There was a sliding glass door off of the living room. I peeked outside. It led to a huge swimming pool and an outdoor kitchen. I felt someone behind me and looked over my shoulder. Pete, Stanley and Felicity were looking past me.

"Amazing," Stanley said.

Felicity nodded. "The place needs a lot of work though."

Pete sighed.

I turned to my mother. "This is going to be a showplace when you're done fixing it up."

My mother beamed. "You don't think we made a mistake?"

Frank put his arm around my mother's shoulders and gave her a slight squeeze.

"It's going to cost a lot of money to get it up and

running." I sounded like her conscience warning her.

"We sold some property Frank owned back in Chicago and our home in Bullhead City. Plus we have a pretty hefty savings, thanks partly to my inheritance and partly to Frank's investments." Mother had inherited a tidy sum a few years earlier. Frank had been an investment counselor and took his own advice, investing wisely and getting out when the getting was good.

"I could get lost in this place," I said. In addition to everything else, there were built in nooks and crannies all over the house. The short flights of stairs seemed out of place. There was no single staircase, and the stairs seemed to be located in the middle of the house.

"I did." My mother touched my arm.

"You did what?" I asked.

"I got sort of lost the first time we came out here. A black widow scared me and I lost track of my surroundings."

I heard boards creaking upstairs and did a quick count to see who was missing. Everyone was accounted for.

Bubba ran out from the pantry and sat, looking up at the ceiling, obviously listening.

"*Who's there?*" Frank called up the stairs.

There was no answer.

I nodded my head while I said, "It's just the house settling."

Stanley stood next to my big lug of a dog and stared at the ceiling. Bubba believed in ghosts, and so did Stanley, if I could go by past behavior.

I didn't.

The noisy boards continued to creak.

Chapter Six

I let out my breath when a voice coming from upstairs hollered, *"Hello? Anybody here?"*

Bubba stopped watching the ceiling and raced up the stairs.

"Told ya," I said, poking Stanley's arm. "No ghosts."

"We'll be right up," my mother yelled.

Felicity took her new husband's arm. "Safety in numbers. No one would dare confront our little group."

He didn't look convinced, but followed along anyway.

We didn't see anyone at the top of the stairs and headed for the living room, where we found a young man standing very still and holding his hand out to Bubba. I watched as he slowly took a step forward and let my mangy mutt sniff. About six feet tall with dark hair and glasses, he was a good looking man. He wore jeans and a light blue shirt, and his work shoes were covered with dirt.

He looked up once Bubba finished sniffing. "Hi. I'm your neighbor, Tyler Hansen. My wife and I live on the little farm across the road and down a ways. I've seen you here before, and when all the cars pulled in I thought I'd come introduce myself." He smiled. "I heard the place had finally sold."

He held his hand out to Frank and they shook.

"Well, it's so nice to meet you." Mother looked around the room. "Where's your wife?"

"Racheal will be along shortly. We know what a wreck this old place is and... I'm sorry, I didn't mean that the way it sounded." He looked embarrassed.

Mother smiled at him, trying to set him at ease. "It *is* a wreck, but it won't be by the time we're finished with cleaning, repairing and renovating. We have big plans for this house."

He glanced around. "I haven't been in this place since I was a kid, before the, uh, incident happened. You know about that, right?"

"We know. A neighbor from down the street told us." Frank stood with his arms folded across his chest. He looked like he was sizing Tyler up, and he finally dropped his arms to his side.

I stepped forward and waved my arm, taking in the small group. "We all came along to help get the work started. Maybe while we're here you can tell us what really happened. All we've heard is what the neighbor told my mother."

"Ah, you must have talked to Brad. He's the neighborhood... Uh, he's a character. Barbara and her father, Harry, didn't deserve... We'll talk later." He glanced out the window. "Here comes Racheal now."

I followed his gaze and saw a young woman with long sandy blonde hair walking toward the house, carrying a large paper bag. She wore jeans and a plaid shirt, and I could see boots on her feet. She was a small woman, but not tiny like my mother and Felicity.

"So you two have a farm here?" I asked.

"We do. Actually, I have a job that allows me to work at home, so between that and the critters, we keep busy."

Pete stepped forward and introduced himself, holding his hand out for a shake. "What kind of critters do you have?"

"Cows, chickens, and a couple of goats. We grow a lot of produce, too."

Mother watched Tyler with interest. "How rude of me. Let's wait until your wife gets here and I'll introduce you to everyone. Where *are* my manners? You say you grow vegetables?" It sounded, if I knew her well and I did, like she was already thinking of him as a food source for the bed and breakfast. I could practically see the wheels turning in her head.

"Hello?" Racheal stepped into the house and her gaze settled on her husband for a moment. "Ah, there you are."

She set her paper sack down next to the front door and walked straight over to Bubba, giving him a scratch on the head. He immediately turned to putty in her hands, throwing himself on the floor and rolling over on his back, waiting for a belly rub.

True to her word, mother introduced everyone. She kept glancing at the bag and I knew her curiosity was getting the best of her.

Apparently Racheal noticed it, too. She smiled and retrieved the bag, handing it to my mother.

"Livvie, I brought you some goodies from our garden. I saw you move the motorhome onto the property a few days ago and figured you were going to be staying out here. When I saw the other cars follow you in today, I thought maybe you could use some extra food."

She followed Mother out to the kitchen and they set everything on the counter. Felicity and I followed while the men talked in the living room. Bubba was front and center, hoping there was something he could eat.

My mother made a shooing motion with her hand.

He ignored her.

"This is so nice of you." Mom gave Racheal's shoulders a little squeeze. "I can tell we're going to enjoy our new neighbors."

While the two women talked, Felicity and I decided to do a little exploring. We opened a door off the kitchen and found a laundry room with another bathroom off of it. Past that was a screened in room. My mother and Frank had swept it out and stored more of their belongings there. A door led outside to the patio, and another door, when I opened it, led back to the garage. We'd come full circle.

"I love this place," Felicity said. "It's got so much potential. I wish Stanley and I had found it." There was wonder in her voice. "It's going to take a lot of work though."

A door slammed somewhere in the vicinity of the garage.

"It must be one of the boys," I said.

"Of course."

A scraping noise reached our ears. Not one to let things pass while I ignored them, I threw open the door to the garage and looked into every corner. It was beginning to turn dark, and I couldn't see much. I didn't have a flashlight, of course.

"Let's go back inside." Felicity was no Chicken Little either, but the prudent thing at the moment seemed to be spending time with the group. Besides, we could see if anyone had gone outside or to the garage.

Back inside the house, everyone was where we'd left them. Felicity and I glanced at each other.

"I'm sure it was nothing," she said.

"Probably just the wind blowing a door shut." I glanced out the front window, unconvinced. There wasn't any wind.

"It's not a big deal. Just don't say anything to Stan. You know how jumpy he can be."

"Not a word," I said.

Pete left the men talking and came to stand beside me. "What are you two whispering about?"

"We found another room," I said. "While we were out there we heard a door slam in the garage. But you're all in here, so I don't know who it could have been."

"I'm sure there's a logical explanation."

"Sure there is. And there's a logical explanation for the scraping sound we heard, too."

"I'll go take a look. Show me where this room is."

He followed me through the house and out to the screened in room, limping just enough to tell me he was tired. I pointed at the door leading to the garage.

"This is called an Arizona room," he said. "Frank told me about it. Kind of like an indoor patio, huh?"

"Okay. Now what about the garage?"

Pete pushed the door open and stepped into the garage.

I grabbed hold of the back of his shirt and followed him. "You know, if this house didn't have a reputation for being haunted, I never would have given the sounds a second thought."

"Uh huh."

"Even though I don't believe in ghosts, someone was out here. I know it could have been an animal, or maybe another neighbor, but something… I mean, someone, was out here."

"This isn't like you, babe. Don't let it bother you."

"Maybe it's because we're so far from town. You know, no police, no fire department, no nothing. It's just us and the neighbors. And remember, the neighbor told my mother that everyone around here believes the house is haunted."

"I'll ask Tyler about that."

I don't believe in ghosts, I've *never* believed in ghosts, and I wasn't going to start now. But I had a feeling something was going on at this house. Strange. Maybe it was because of the face I thought I'd seen at the window.

I'd get to the bottom of it no matter what it took. If my mother and Frank were going to live here, I wanted to make sure they were safe.

Chapter Seven

"See anything?" I asked.

"It's too dark and there are too many shadows. Why don't you go inside and ask Frank for a flashlight?"

Before I could do so we heard voices coming from the front of the house. My mother stepped into the garage. "What're you two doing in here? A little newlywed tryst?"

I rolled my eyes at her even though she probably couldn't see what I was doing. "We *could* use a little privacy while we're here."

"You'll have it. I'm putting you two in the master bedroom."

"Oh, great. Us and all the bug bodies."

Pete chuckled over that one.

"I'll put Felicity and Stan in the little apartment on the lower level. They'll need some privacy, too."

Frank joined us. "Come on, you two. Let's get these cars unloaded. It's getting dark and we need to get you set up."

Mother put her arm around Frank's waist. "Sweetie? Why don't you go get that cordless vacuum so we can get rid of the bugs in the two bedrooms everyone will be using?"

He nodded. "I charged it before we left home. It should

last long enough to do that."

We walked out to the yard and found Tyler and Racheal looking around and waiting to say their good-byes. "If you need anything while you're here, just let us know." He pointed toward a small farmhouse. "If I've got time, I'll be over tomorrow to see if I can do anything to help y'all. There are so few of us in this valley that we help each other whenever we can."

"If you need to put a few things in my refrigerator, let me know. I've got a little extra room." Racheal seemed like such a sweet person.

"My brother and his wife are coming out tomorrow for the week. I'm sure they'd be happy to help, too." Tyler took hold of his wife's hand and waved with the other one as they left.

Frank carried an oil lamp and the cordless vacuum into the house while we began unloading the cars.

We took cases of water to the garage while my mother stored our food in the motorhome. Pete unloaded two suitcases, two sleeping bags (they could be combined into one) and a couple of pillows. I helped him carry them in.

Felicity and Stanley stood ready to carry their things to the little apartment. "Too bad we don't have running water," she said.

I nodded and returned to the car to see if we'd missed anything.

Mother brought two more oil lamps from the motorhome, passing them out to Stanley and Pete. "I'm afraid this is as good as it gets for now. I have an electrician coming out tomorrow to start restoring the wiring. Maybe by tomorrow night we'll have some light. A plumber is coming out, too. Hopefully we won't have to wait too long for running water."

Frank returned and after we took our things upstairs, he and Pete set up a picnic table. Mother put out cold chicken, potato salad and cold barbeque beans. A bag of potato chips rounded out the meal. Dinner was served.

Cold or not, it tasted wonderful. As I once heard a friend say, hunger is the best sauce, after all.

"This is going to be quite an adventure," Stanley said, dabbing his mouth with a napkin. "I'm sure it won't be like your stay at the ghost town, but still, it's going to be fun."

I wondered if he realized how much work we'd be doing. Fun? I guess it was all a matter of perspective.

While I listened to everyone talking over dinner, I decided maybe he was right. It could be an adventure, if we'd only look at it in that light. I smiled to myself and took another bite of potato salad.

Bubba was so good about not begging while we ate that I gave him a little more kibble than I normally would and dropped some shredded chicken on top. He gobbled it down and threw himself on the ground.

"Sandi, you might want to get him up. This place is overrun with big black ants. I'm going to spray tomorrow." Frank reached over and pulled on Bubba's collar. "And keep him with you for now. Don't forget about the rattlesnake we killed."

"He can stay with us," Stanley said, sounding hopeful. "You know he can be very protective."

Felicity patted his knee. "So can I, love muffin."

Pete groaned and reached for my hand, giving the Hawks a taste of their own medicine. "Come on, *sugar lump*. It's been a long day and we need to get things set up inside."

Felicity's little tinkle of laughter followed us to the porch.

After we set up our room, not a lot of work, we walked down to the little apartment to see how Felicity and Stanley were doing.

She turned in a circle with her arms extended, taking in the empty living room. "Who needs a five-star hotel for a honeymoon when we've got all of this?"

"Now, pumpkin, we'll have a honeymoon." Stanley looked at her with adoration in his eyes.

She laughed. "I'm serious, Stan. I think this is great. I can't wait to get started fixing this house up. We've got our own little apartment and we're with the people we care about the most. How much better can it get?"

Stanley slowly shook his head. "What did I do to deserve such a wife? I never thought I could be this happy." He meant it, too. I'd never seen him so happy.

All of a sudden Bubba stood and growled, looking toward the sliding glass door. It had grown dark and all we could see was the reflection of the oil lamp in the window.

Pete walked to the door and tried to slide it open, but it was stuck. He pulled with a vengeance, just about pulling his shoulder out of place.

It turned out it was locked, and the lock still worked. Quite well, apparently.

Bubba stood behind him and continued to growl.

"Uh, Sandi, would you mind if Bubba sleeps down here with us?" Stanley's eyes were glued to the glass doors. "I think it might be prudent to let him guard the doorway."

By that time Pete had unlocked the door and he slid it open, stepping outside. "I don't see anything out here. Back in a minute." He disappeared from view.

"I'd better go with him," Stanley said, hesitantly, "just in case he needs help."

Neither Felicity nor I tried to stop him. Sometimes you just had to let a man be a man, even if he'd rather not take that road. He disappeared out the door and turned to the right, following Pete.

"I wonder what was out there," Felicity said.

"Honestly? If it was something to worry about, I think Bubba would have done more than growl. Look at that dopey dog. Now that he's sent out an alarm, he's perfectly happy to stay here with us."

He was lying on the dirty floor near the kitchen, grinning at us.

I sighed and the dog's tail began banging on the floor.

We heard Pete and Stanley talking, outside. "It was nothing," Pete said. "Probably just a little critter passing by the door."

"You're sure?" Stanley didn't sound at all convinced.

"If the boogey man gets you tonight, we'll know for sure."

"Oh, you!"

"If not the boogey man, then maybe a big black widow."

"You're still joking, right?"

Pete laughed and thumped Stanley on the back.

I've thought it before, and I thought it again. I'd never understand how these two totally different men had become such close friends. Their personalities couldn't possibly be any different. Stanley didn't seem to have many friends before coming into our lives, so I was glad things had worked out the way they did.

After making sure the door was relocked, Pete and I decided to go back upstairs and get some sleep. Or, with any luck, maybe we'd have a post wedding night celebration. I smiled to myself.

"Bubba, you stay here with the Hawks."

The name was a new word to him and he watched me, trying to figure out what I meant.

"You stay here with Felicity."

He knew *that* name and turned his big head to grin at her.

"Will he stay out here?" Stanley asked.

Pete nodded. "Sure. Just close the bedroom door and he won't bother you."

"Although he does like to sleep at the foot of my bed," I

added, grinning. "Be sure to put out some water for him."

Sometime during the night I heard Bubba padding through the house, exploring and watching over us, too.

Thank heaven for small favors, he never sent out another alarm.

Chapter Eight

We were up early the next morning. The sleeping accommodations didn't exactly promote sleeping in. I picked up my watch and saw it was six o'clock. Way too early after the long day we'd had driving from California to Arizona.

I really wanted to take a shower so when we met my parents outside I was thrilled to see a truck with the plumber's name on it. Instead of taking time to meet him, I rushed into the motorhome to take care of more important matters, like finding a working toilet. After all, there are priorities, and the house was short on the amenities.

Bubba was following my mother around like a lovesick puppy. I noticed she'd already fed him for me, and she was obviously carrying treats in her pockets because the dog would take tentative sniffs when she wasn't looking. She liked giving him little rewards, or treats, no matter what he did. She spoiled him rotten, although she frequently referred to him as my mangy mutt, a description I'd started using, too.

The electrician showed up while we were eating. Thank goodness we had a stove in the motorhome, so meals weren't an issue.

He spoke to Frank, who explained about the wiring being ripped out. Shaking his head, not a good sign, the electrician entered the house to begin his inspection and work.

In the meantime the plumber returned to talk to Frank.

"Those thieves took the pump from your well, along with a lot of copper tubing. I'll have to replace the pump before I do anything else."

Surprisingly, Frank took the news in stride without getting upset. "We knew what we were getting into, more or less. I'll work on installing the sinks and faucets that were stolen while you take care of the rest of it. In fact, we need to install a new toilet, too. Guess I'd better run into town."

"I'll bring one back from the shop." The two men talked about color and type before the plumber left to round up a well pump.

Frank motioned Pete and Stanley over. "Why don't you two take care of the sinks and faucets first? I'll work on repairing the damage to the walls and that hole in the ceiling. Livvie can tell the girls what she wants them to do."

They walked off toward the garage where Frank had stored the parts and tools they'd need.

"Mother? What do you want us to do?"

"I hate to do this to you, but there's an awful lot of cleaning to be done in the house before we can paint and start repairs. Are you up to it?"

Felicity threw her paper plate in the trash and stood with her hands on her hips. "Of course. We *girls* are the strong ones in this group. I could even help put in the sinks if I needed to. Men underrate us, don't they?"

As tiny and cute as she was, my friend could pretty much do anything she set her mind to. So could I, for that matter.

Mother led us to the garage where we found brooms, rags and all kinds of cleaning supplies. She took two buckets back to the motorhome and filled them with water. We lugged everything inside and began our assigned tasks.

Since the house was empty, it was full of echoes. I could hear the men talking in the bathroom. Their voices carried and I listened to Pete patiently explain the process for putting in the faucets. Stanley didn't say anything and I had a feeling he was probably nodding. After that, things were quiet while they worked, other than the sound of a few clinks and clunks.

Felicity and I began our work in the living room, sweeping away cobwebs and dead bugs. Apparently those bug bombs really work, judging by the number of tiny bodies we found. My mother headed upstairs with a bucket, a mop and more rags.

We started by breaking off the baseboards along the edges of the room. They'd have to be replaced anyway, and we wanted to sweep all the way to the walls. A screwdriver and a hammer helped us pry them off before we began sweeping.

Frank was in and out of the rooms, using spackle to repair nail holes in the walls.

As Felicity swept, all kinds of things went flying into the corner. She took a dust pan and began sweeping the mess into it. I worked toward the other corner, humming to myself. I looked up when I realized my friend had stopped working and had squatted down by the pile of trash.

"What'd you find?" I asked.

"Come here, Sandi. Come see this."

Frank, paying no attention to us, headed outside.

I leaned the broom against the wall and walked across the room, wondering what she'd found. Bending over, I studied the dirt. Something glimmered, slightly.

Felicity picked it up and held it out to me. "This must have ended up under the loose baseboards or something."

"That's an engagement ring," I said, taking it from her, holding it gently in my hand. "I can't imagine where this came from. Oh. It must have – "

"It must have belonged to the lady that was murdered here." She sounded in awe of our discovery. "Can you think of any other explanation?"

"No. It's been here a long time, too. Look how the dirt has crusted on it." I scratched some of it off with my fingernail.

"She must not have been a big woman. That's a tiny ring. Why, I'll bet it would fit me." Felicity had very small hands.

It actually looked too big for her, but too small for me.

I couldn't seem to take my eyes off the ring. "It's too small for me, that's for sure."

The floorboards creaked in the next room and we looked at each other. Mother was upstairs, Pete and Stanley were in one of the bathrooms, and Frank was out in the yard talking to the plumber, who'd apparently returned. I could see them through the window.

The boards creaked again as though someone was walking through the family room, and I heard a soft *whooshing* sound.

"I wonder if we set something off by finding the ring." Felicity grabbed it out of my hand and hid it in her pocket.

I gave her my best *get real* look. "Bubba?" It had to be the dog.

The footsteps stopped.

"Bubba," I called again, a little louder.

He scratched at the screen door, standing outside on the porch.

Felicity and I walked to the door.

"I think I'll just let him in." Felicity giggled nervously and reached out, turning the door handle. "Come on, boy. You can keep us company."

"Oh, for crying out loud. I'm a private investigator. I'm not going to let some creaking noise scare me."

I turned around and headed for the family room, where the sound had come from. Maybe it was Pete or Stanley. They'd been working in one of the bathrooms, but they could have changed locations. Maybe Tyler was back.

I stepped around the doorway, and…

"*BOO!*"

Grabbing my chest, I fell to the floor.

"Sandi? Sandi? Oh, my dear Lord. I've killed my little girl."

Bubba came running and began licking my face.

Pushing him away, I sat up. "Mother, I thought you were upstairs. What are you doing sneaking around down here?"

"I wasn't sneaking, *Sandra*." She looked relieved and amused, although she'd used my given name once again. "Since everyone seems to think this house is haunted, I thought I'd play a trick on you and Felicity. That's all."

"Oh, brother. Well, as you've seen, two can play at this game."

"How did you know it was me?"

"Just before I came around the corner I saw the toe of your shoe."

"Oh. Guess I'll have to be more careful next time."

We looked up at the sound of laughter. The electrician's face hovered over the hole in the ceiling. "You two are a crack up. I can't wait to get home and tell my wife about this." His face disappeared. I could still hear him chuckling as his footsteps grew faint.

"At least we're entertaining *someone*," my mother said.

"Come on out to the living room and see what we found."

"You gave me quite a start, you know. Don't do that again." She patted her chest.

"Then don't try to scare *me* again."

Yes, this was going to be quite a little adventure, if my mother had her way.

Chapter Nine

*F*elicity grinned at my mother while she dug in her pocket for the ring. "Why, Livvie, I've never seen this side of you before. You tried to scare us."

"It worked, too," I said. "You were ready to cut and run."

Mother returned Felicity's grin. "I have my moments. Now let's see what you two found."

My friend held the ring out for my mother to examine. Mom took it out of her hand and walked to the window where she studied it in the light. I saw her scratch at it with her fingernail, just as I'd done. "Where did you find this?"

Felicity followed her to the window and stood next to her. "It was in the dirt I swept up. We tore down the baseboards, so I think it must have slid underneath or the police would have found the ring."

"I wonder if it means anything. Sandi?" Mother held the ring out to me.

"I have no idea. If I were to venture a guess, maybe the day the woman... Wasn't her name Barbara? Maybe the day she was killed the neighbor asked her to marry him. Who knows? That could be what set the ranch hand off. I can picture him watching through the window when the neighbor showed it to her."

My mother patted my hand. "You have such a vivid imagination, sweetie."

"I *said* it was just a supposition. Don't you think it makes sense?"

"Yes, dear, it does. But after all is said and done, it's still just a guess."

Sighing, I turned back toward the trash I'd swept into the corner. Before I made a move to finish sweeping, I suddenly turned and yelled, "*BOO!*"

Mother dropped the ring and Felicity jumped.

Feeling satisfied, I went back to work and finished sweeping the corner.

I could hear them discussing the ring, and it was gratifying to hear them coming around to my way of thinking. Really, why else would there be an undiscovered ring in the room?

I stopped sweeping and leaned the broom against the wall. "Unless," I said, "the ranch hand had the ring with him and *he* was going to propose. Picture him walking around to the front of the house, filled with anticipation about proposing to Barbara, and looking through the window to see her kissing the neighbor." I spoke slowly, putting my thoughts in order. "Maybe he saw them together and stormed back to his apartment. He grabbed his gun and returned to the house, killing everyone in a fit of rage. Somehow that makes more sense."

I began sweeping in front of the windows.

"That makes the most sense. Good job, honey. I knew a private eye could figure this out." My mother watched me with pride in her eyes.

"I think your mother's right, Sandi. And after he murdered everyone, he was so upset he killed himself."

"End of story," I said. "Who needs police detectives

when we're on the job?"

"You do." Pete stood in the doorway, listening to us. "Everything you've said is just a guess. I'm sure the police department did a thorough investigation out here. I don't think it would have made a bit of difference if they'd found that ring. Everyone involved was dead. They knew who the killer was and they knew the circumstances. They were here right after the murders, for crying out loud. This is supposed to have happened something like twenty years ago? You were a mere child at the time, and you certainly weren't here to know what was happening. You're putting the whole crime together and coming up with suppositions. Believe me when I say they did their job."

This wasn't like Pete and I stopped sweeping to listen to him. He sounded like he was upset with me. "Pete? What's this all about?"

Stanley stepped around from behind Pete. "We've been discussing the case while we worked. Pete came at it from a policeman's perspective. He *was* a police officer, you know."

Mother chuckled. "I get it. We're having a boys versus girls challenge to figure out if all the facts came out at the time of the murders. We can get a copy of the police report, I'm sure. It should tell us exactly what happened."

"*Is* this a challenge?" I asked.

"It wasn't, but I guess it could be. Let's see who can come up with the real story behind the crimes. Let's see who's the better investigator."

Now that I thought about it, Pete didn't sound angry or upset. He sounded tired. It had been a few very busy days, and here we were, working in a haunted house when we should be relaxed somewhere on our honeymoon. He was tired enough that his limp was more noticeable. Breaking his leg had really done a number on him.

Uh oh. Had I just referred to this as a haunted house? It couldn't be.

"You're on," I said. "Three women and three men, and then we'll get a copy of the police report and see who's got it figured out. Next time Frank goes to town he can ask for it."

"At least this time we're not working on an unsolved murder," Stanley said, "and what perfect timing. It's October and Halloween is coming up soon. It's the right time for our little challenge."

The front door opened and Frank came in followed by Tyler and Racheal, and another couple.

Tyler! Just the man I wanted to talk to.

Racheal carried a cake plate and paper plates. "Tyler said you were recently married so I brought a cake to celebrate." She smiled widely, showing perfect white teeth.

"What a sweet thing to do," I said. "Thank you so much."

Tyler stepped forward, pointing to the other couple. "This is my brother, Micah, and his wife, Zoë. We thought maybe we could help out. Frank says he could use a hand putting up corrals for the horses. The girls thought they might be able to help inside."

Micah was a taller and more muscular man than his brother but he had the same deep brown hair. Zoë was tall and slender with dark auburn hair, the kind that some women would pay big bucks for at a beauty shop.

Micah and Zoë held out their hands.

"Congratulations! I hope your marriages are as happy as ours," Zoë said. "Just remember to keep your sense of humor, even when you think it's impossible, and you'll always be able to work out your problems."

"Problems?" Stanley looked taken aback.

"I'm sorry. I didn't mean to put a damper on things. All marriages have problems from time to time," she said. "It's a given. But most issues aren't insurmountable." She was a wise woman, and reminded me a little of myself. The twinkle in her eye somehow seemed to tell me she'd already recognized

Stanley as a slow-moving target, and I had a feeling she might be a tease. There was something in her tone of voice. I liked her.

"Don't worry, pumpkin pie, we'll get through anything that comes our way." Felicity smiled encouragingly at her new husband.

"Pumpkin pie?" Racheal looked surprised. "Oh, sorry."

"Don't be," I said. "They're trying to drive us crazy with cutesy little pet names. This isn't the way they normally talk to each other."

While my mother spoke to the newcomers, I called Tyler aside. "Say, Tyler, are there any neighbors around who lived here when the murders were committed?"

He didn't look surprised. "I had a feeling you might want to know more about what happened. I started to tell you yesterday, but Racheal showed up. Yes, as a matter of fact, there are two families who lived here at the time. Want me to introduce you to them? Well, I was here, too, but I was pretty young. My brother was staying with a friend for the night, so he didn't know much about what happened, except what he heard."

"Yes, please, I'd like to meet the neighbors. And would you mind not mentioning this to Pete? We're having a little competition."

"No, just let me know when you want to talk to them. I think I mentioned that I work at home? Well, I'm a mystery writer and I've been thinking about doing a book based on this house. I understand you're a private investigator. Maybe we could collaborate a little. Would you mind answering a few questions for me after you talk to the neighbors? It might encourage me not to mention our agreement to your husband." His grin told me he was happy to join our game.

"I love a good mystery. You betcha. I'd like your input, too, since writers seem to have such creative minds."

Pete had been watching us and finally decided to join

us. "What's going on over here?"

"Nothing, sweetums. We're just having a little talk. Did you know Tyler is a mystery writer?"

Tyler laughed. "Sweetums? So you two are playing the name game, too?"

Pete didn't reply. "Don't tell me, he wants to know if we've seen the ghost yet."

"Why, Petey, you know I don't believe in ghosts." Did my tone sound innocent enough?

"What ghost?" Tyler played dumb quite well.

Chapter Ten

With Micah and Tyler's help, Pete and Stanley finished installing sinks and faucets in record time. They found Frank outside, beginning to put up fencing for the corrals, and jumped right in.

In the meantime, the plumber installed the toilet in the bathroom on the upper level. Now if we only had water.

When I walked out to the garage to grab a couple of extra buckets I could hear Micah's booming voice talking about farming. From what he's said earlier, it sounded like he and his wife had a large place somewhere in New Mexico.

In comparison, Tyler was very soft-spoken. He and Racheal's farm was quite small.

In the meantime, Zoë and Rachael took a tour of the house before picking up brooms and helping us clean.

"This place is going to be quite a showplace by the time you're through with it," Zoë said. "I heard you're going to turn it into a bed and breakfast and bring horses in. Kind of a dude ranch, huh?"

"That's the plan," my mother said.

"Do you already have your horses?" Zoë asked.

"Frank is looking into it."

"Talk to Tyler. He knows everyone around here and I

think he can fix you up with a mare and maybe a stallion. Do you know what breed you want?"

While my mother and Zoë talked about horses, Felicity, Racheal and I worked our way around the house pulling off more baseboards. After we got the floors as clean as we could, we wanted to start painting.

Mother wandered through and explained she was going to fix lunch for all of us. Felicity and I offered to help, but she said she had everything under control.

"So, Racheal, what more can you tell me about what happened here?" I tried to sound casual, but it didn't feel like I quite pulled it off.

"I only know what Tyler's told me. Barbara Stockholm was a nice woman, but maybe a little scatterbrained. Although, she kept the llama ranch going. Her father was up in years so she took things over. Let me back up a little. Barbara was all business when it came to the ranch, and she knew exactly what she was doing. It was a going business, believe it or not. But she was a scatterbrain when it came to men.

"Both the ranch hand and the neighbor were in love with her and she played one against the other. From what Tyler said, I'm not sure she really *meant* to pit one against the other, but still, that's the way it worked out. One of the neighbors said she'd never had time for a social life and at her age she was waaaay flattered about the attention."

"How old was she?" Felicity asked.

"I understand she was in her early fifties. She'd been some kind of hotshot attorney who lived and breathed her career until settling down with the llama ranch."

"Hmm. She was older than I'd imagined," I said.

"Tyler told me when he was a boy she'd invite him in for cookies and milk, and in return he'd help clean out the barn. Somehow I think my husband got the short end of the stick."

Felicity chuckled. "Yeah, I'd say so."

"Anyway, the story goes that Barbara's father told her she was making a fool out of herself and needed to make a choice. Long story short, she chose the neighbor, the ranch hand went nuts, and the rest is history. He killed them all."

"Well, that's short and sweet." I was hoping for more detail.

Racheal looked thoughtful. "You know, something about the story never quite set right with me."

My ears perked up.

"Tyler said the ranch hand never struck him as crazy, and what he did was nuts. In fact, the ranch hand befriended my husband because there weren't any other kids living nearby. The only time he saw other children was at school." She smiled. "Maybe that's why he's quiet and such a computer nerd. Oh, he's not really a nerd, but he spends an awful lot of time working on his books. Sometimes he barely comes up for air."

"What about his brother?" I asked. "Didn't they hang out together?"

"Not really. Micah is eight years older than Tyler. They've only become close as adults. When they were kids, Micah was always off somewhere with his friends from school. He had a car. He's definitely the more outgoing of the two boys."

Felicity stood by quietly, taking in the conversation. "If the father shot the ranch hand, then that seems to clinch his guilt. Why doesn't it set well with you?"

Racheal chewed on her lip for a moment before replying. "Those murders are the biggest thing that ever happened in this valley. The neighbors still talk about them from time to time. Every one of them says they never would have guessed Clyde Stipple would turn out to be a killer. They still have trouble believing it, even when you think about him feeling jealous. Yes, it's a motive, but they all say Clyde was more the type to walk away with his tail between his legs and write it off."

"Hmm. The name Clyde makes me think about someone with strength of character, not someone weak enough to commit murder." Felicity looked around the room thoughtfully.

"But, Fel, you don't have to be weak to kill someone. You just have to be angry or conniving enough to do it." My experience so far had been that greed, relationships and... Well, yeah, sometimes there really wasn't a good reason.

Felicity and I looked at each other and smiled.

I spoke first. "Maybe there *is* more to this than meets the eye. How many times have hunches paid off? If it doesn't set right with Racheal, then it doesn't set right with me. We just might beat our husbands to the answers on this one."

Racheal looked at us with questions in her eyes.

I explained. "We don't know the whole story about what happened here. My husband and I..." I smiled. "I love saying *my husband.*" I shook my head, getting back on track. "We don't know the whole story, and our husbands have challenged us to see who can come up with the answers first. I should explain. My husband and I, and Stanley, are private investigators."

"Oh! Does Tyler know that?"

"He does, and he wants to pick my brain while we're here. In return, he said he'd introduce me to some of the neighbors so I can get their take on what happened here twenty years ago."

Racheal grinned. "Can any outsiders get in on this competition?"

I nodded. "But you have to keep quiet about it. We don't want our husbands to know you and Tyler are helping us with this."

"Zoë," she yelled, "*come on back here.*"

While we waited for Zoë, Racheal moved closer to us.

"You know about the ghost, right?"

Felicity and I glanced at each other.

"No. Tell us." I wasn't about to admit I'd heard ghost stories about the house.

"Lights have been seen in the upstairs bedroom – "

"Which room?" I asked, remembering the sight of a face at the window when we pulled into the driveway the day before.

"Front left. It's the only bedroom window you can see from the front of the house. The other window is the bathroom, and the master bedroom is at the rear. Why?"

"Have I mentioned, I don't believe in ghosts?"

Racheal turned her head and looked at me out of the corner of her eye. "You might change your mind about that after staying here for a few days."

Chapter Eleven

We explained the challenge to Zoë while we worked.

"I don't know what I can do to help, but it sounds like fun."

While we continued sweeping, Racheal told us about the few neighbors who'd lived in the area when the murders were committed.

"Zetta and Bill Ellison have lived here for something like forty years. They're old people, I think maybe in their sixties. Although, it seems like Tyler mentioned them being in their eighties once. I'll have to ask him."

I laughed. "Don't let my mother hear you calling them old. She and Frank are in their fifties, not that far away from the Ellisons, unless they're in their eighties."

Racheal nodded. "Oh. Maybe that's not really old, but it seems like it to me. Anyway, they bought their property around the same time Harry Stockholm and his wife bought theirs. They were good friends until Harry's wife died. Zetta said after that Harry was kind of like a hermit. He didn't want to be social anymore. Barbara was an attorney and she lived back east somewhere and hardly ever came to see her father until she took over the ranch."

"Just out of curiosity, what was Mrs. Stockholm's name?" I asked. If I was going to do this, I needed to do it right. That meant knowing who all the players were, past and... Well, they were all in the past.

Racheal closed her eyes and thought for a moment. "I don't think I've ever heard it. I'll ask Tyler, if it's important. She died even before he was born, but he might know."

"I guess it's not that important. Like I said, I was just curious."

"Shirley and Jeff Shaw have lived here forever, too. They moved in not long after the Stockholms and Ellisons. Before Harry's wife died, they all hung out together. Their kids all played together, too.

"There was another couple, but I don't know their names. The neighbor that fell in love with Barbara bought their house and he lived here for about five years before Barbara came back."

"Do you know what his name was?" I asked. "The neighbor, I mean."

"Mike Hamilton. Tyler remembers him. He might be able to tell you some stuff, too."

Before we could talk more, my mother called us for lunch. She invited the plumber and the electrician to join us, too, but they'd brought their own lunches.

Mom had cleaned off the outdoor kitchen countertop and set up sandwich fixings, along with paper plates. While we brought chairs, she walked out to the men and told them to come eat.

"I'm going to have to get a dinner bell or something." She paused for a moment. "You know, that's not a bad idea, now that I think about it. The guests might get a kick out of having me call them to dinner with a bell. I'll have to look for something big and loud."

"Look no farther," Racheal said. "We've got two of those triangle things at our place. You know, you run a thingy around them and they call everybody in."

"You have such a way with words," Zoë said, laughing. "The triangle thing that you run the thingy around to make noise. You're priceless, Racheal."

Racheal smiled at her sister-in-law. I could see it was good-natured banter by the way they looked at each other. "Yeah, you're a real wordsmith compared to me, Zoë. So what's the triangle thing called?"

"A triangle dinner bell."

"Oh. That was too easy."

Felicity and I started to laugh. The sisters-in-law looked at us to see what was so funny.

"It's just that you sound like Felicity and I do sometimes," I explained.

That seemed to satisfy them and they started preparing sandwiches, adding leftover potato salad to the plates. When Micah and Tyler joined us, the women handed them their plates and started making their own sandwiches.

Taking note of the wifely thing to do, Fel and I glanced at each other and made sandwiches for Pete and Stanley.

"I hope they don't expect this kind of treatment all the time," I said. "I have a feeling our husbands could get used to us doing everything for them."

"Yeah, we could." Pete tapped my shoulder and reached for his plate.

Stanley took his plate and uncharacteristically gobbled up his food. He was usually so slow and careful about eating, making sure he didn't drop any crumbs. "I don't think I've ever been so hungry," he said. "We've been doing manly man's work, and it sure is different from sitting at a desk."

He dropped his napkin. Felicity and he both bent to pick it up at the same time and knocked heads, which was interesting because that's what had happened when they first met each other. My two favorite people were somewhat accident prone, and I loved them all the more for it. Lifting their heads, they looked adoringly at each other.

"Sorry, little dumpling," Stanley said.

"That's okay, pookey bear."

Micah looked at them and when I thought he'd say something about their pet names and how silly they were, he turned back to his food instead.

"We were newlyweds once, too," he said softly. "It's okay to be silly when everything is new."

I was impressed with his thoughtfulness. He could have made fun of them, but chose not to. I liked the Hansen boys and their wives.

I chewed and swallowed a bite of sandwich before turning to my mother. "So what's next?"

"More sweeping, sweetie. If you're going to paint while you're here, we need to get the floors as clean as possible."

"More sweeping. It figures."

Frank dropped his empty plate into a trash bag. "These boys are something. We're almost done with the corrals already." He smiled. "Even Stan has done a full day's worth of work."

Stanley beamed. "I can come through in a pinch. I know our time here is limited. We need to get as much done as we can."

"Good job, Stan, my man." Pete slapped Stanley's back.

For just a moment I had an overwhelming sense of love for my family and friends. My heart felt as full as it ever had. I had a strange desire to cry, but I swallowed, willing the feeling to go away. I wasn't a crier, and never had been. I wasn't about to start being a weepy woman now.

I stood and blinked a few times before dropping my plate in the bag. "Back to work," I said. "Lots to do and not much time to do it."

Mother watched me with a look on her face that made me feel like she might know exactly what I was feeling. She smiled and winked at me.

The house beckoned to me and I returned to the bedroom I'd been sweeping before our lunch break. While I worked, I thought about Barbara and Harry, father and daughter, dead for some twenty years. I'd bet they loved this old house. It had character. Even in disrepair, I could see so much potential.

I saw something move in my peripheral vision and glanced up, expecting to see anything but what my eyes met.

There was someone outside the window. I blinked and the person was gone. Running to the window, I looked out. No one. I tried to open it for a better look, but it wouldn't budge. The face lingered in my mind. While I didn't have a good look at it, I'd still noticed two things. It was a woman, and she had long blonde hair. The window was so dirty. It made the woman's face look almost ethereal.

"What are you doing, Sandi?" It was my mother's voice.

"Nothing, Mom. I just wanted to let some fresh air in, but the window's stuck." I didn't want her to know someone had been peeping in. I turned and smiled at her.

"Are you okay? You look like you've just seen a ghost."

I swallowed. "You know I don't believe in ghosts, Mom."

Chapter Twelve

$\mathcal{A}$ moment later I heard voices. The other women joined us and we worked with renewed vigor. I debated about the face I'd seen for no more than a split second. We had a job to get done, but frankly, I wanted to go outside and explore that side of the house. Maybe whoever had been there had left footprints, or maybe she'd dropped something. So much for split second thinking.

I swept like a mad woman for about five minutes before I decided I'd simply take a break. No one would care.

"Potty break," I said, leaning my broom against the wall.

No one even acknowledged me.

In my rush, I took a wrong turn and had to stop to get my bearings. If I wasn't careful, I'd end up in the dank basement. I found the correct stairway and hurriedly descended to the apartment Felicity and Stanley were staying in. Out the back door, left turn, and around the house. Up a grade and within moments I was outside the bedroom where I'd seen the face.

Not wanting anyone to know what I was doing, I crept to the edge of the window frame. I studied the ground, looking for footprints. Bending at the waist, I continued looking for signs that someone had recently walked under the window.

That's when things went terribly wrong.

Bubba ran up behind me and playfully knocked me down. At the same time, someone finally got the window unstuck, threw it open, and poured out a pail of dirty water – I groaned. No point in trying to keep the secret now.

I stood up with water dripping from my hair and face. Bubba seemed to think it was a game and he pranced around me, trying to get me to include him. My shirt was soaked and stuck to me. I didn't even want to think about what might have been in the dirty water.

My mother's head popped out of the window. "Sandi? What the heck's going on out there?"

"Nothing. Just nothing. I'm going to your motorhome to use the shower. I don't care if I use up the last of the water or not." I sulked as I walked away from the window. One last look over my shoulder and I was annoyed. All of the women stood and laughed. It was a big window. I saw four faces watching me.

Bubba still pranced around me, grinning his stupid doggie grin.

"Get out of my way, you big dope."

My ire didn't even faze him. When I entered the house, I slammed the door in his face.

I made my way, by some miracle, to the right stairs and found the room Pete and I were staying in. Clean clothes and a shower would renew my formerly good mood – I hoped. I gathered dry clothes and shampoo and headed back outside.

Reaching the motorhome, I took the quickest shower I could, including washing my hair, since I knew the water supply was limited. When I walked outside wearing clean clothes and with my hair pulled back in a ponytail, I found my mother was waiting for me at the picnic table.

"What were you doing under the window?" she asked.

"You won't believe me, Mom."

"Try me."

"Before the rest of you came into the room, I saw someone watching me through the window."

She looked alarmed. "Do you mean someone other than one of our group?"

"I do. The window was too dirty to see much, but it looked like a woman with long blonde hair. I wanted to see if there were footprints outside the window without telling everyone I'd seen something."

"You were afraid it was a ghost."

"Nooo, don't be silly. But why would someone watch us through a window? The private eye in me just couldn't let it go."

"And what did you find?"

"Not a thing. There weren't any footprints."

"Okay, in all fairness, Sandi, the dirt out there was hard, wasn't it?"

I pressed my lips together for a moment before replying. "That's the thing. There were no footprints and it was soft, thankfully, since I landed hard after Bubba pushed me. If someone had been outside, there should have been prints. Speaking of the big lug, have you seen him?"

"Yes, and I think you hurt his feelings. He was headed toward Pete with his tail between his legs. He was just trying to play with you."

Great! Just what I needed – guilt. "I'll make it up to him."

She handed me some doggie treats. "Take these and go find Bubba. Then come back inside and help us. That is, if you're through fooling around."

"Fooling around? Someone was peeping. Don't you want to know who it was?" I was almost, but not quite, incensed that she'd think I was goofing off.

"I'll ask Racheal if there's a woman with long blonde

hair who lives around here. Now *I'm* going back to work. See you upstairs. We're done with the room we were working on when you..." She laughed and walked away without finishing her sentence.

I sighed before going in search of Bubba. Calling his name brought immediate results. He'd been lying at the front of the motorhome and approached me slowly, probably wondering if he was in trouble.

"Come here, Bubba," I said softly. "You're a good boy. I know you were just playing." I held out a treat.

He glanced into my eyes before taking it, and his tail began waving like a flag in a windstorm.

"Yes, you're my good boy."

I'd be devastated if anything ever happened to him. He'd been my friend for a long time now. He was a throwaway who'd adopted me. It didn't matter if I wanted him or not, because he'd made up his mind he was going to live with me in my big old house. We made a pretty good team.

I scratched his head and he threw himself on the ground, rolling onto his back. He was ready for some attention.

I didn't have time. "Come on, you can spend some time inside with us. My *mother* will baby you while we work, not me."

We walked through the garage and the Arizona room to enter the house. Before we got halfway through the kitchen, Bubba sat down with his head up and began listening. To what, I had no idea, but he was listening intently. I stopped and watched him. His nose twitched a few times. I listened, too, but I couldn't hear anything.

Suddenly, he stood and continued through the kitchen, as though nothing had happened. I figured he must have heard the women working upstairs, even though I couldn't hear them.

They'd moved up to the top floor and I found them hard at work.

"You made quite a picture," Zoë said. She pointed at Felicity. "She did it."

Felicity's face turned red. "I didn't know you were out there. How could I?"

I laughed. "It wasn't your fault. I should have let you all know I was outside."

"What were you doing?" Racheal asked.

I glanced around the room, avoiding the question. "Where's my mother? Didn't she come back?"

Felicity shook her head. "No. I haven't seen her since we were downstairs, working on the other room. Is something wrong?"

"I'm sure everything is fine. I'll go look for her." I didn't feel as confident as I sounded.

She should have been back before me.

Chapter Thirteen

Since our volunteer cleaning crew was working in the room next to the one Pete and I were using, I could only go downstairs.

Bubba followed me down one set of stairs to the main floor.

"Mother?"

She didn't reply.

Bubba sniffed the air.

I walked through the rooms looking for her, realizing we'd hopped from room to room. We hadn't swept the other two bedrooms on the main floor – just the one where I'd seen a face at the window.

I descended again, to the apartment on the lower level.

"Mother?" I called again.

She didn't reply, so I searched each of the rooms with Bubba dogging my steps. No Mother. I was beginning to worry until I realized she must have gone to see how the men were doing. I hurried out through the sliding glass doors of the apartment, walked past the swimming pool and outdoor kitchen, through the Arizona room and the garage and out to the corrals. Bubba raced ahead of me.

My mother wasn't there.

"Pete?" I motioned him aside. "Have you seen my mother? I can't find her. I'm a little worried because someone was peeping in at one of the windows earlier."

"Someone was doing what?"

"I saw a woman watching me work through one of the windows. Now I can't find my mother."

"She hasn't been out here since lunchtime. Do you want me to help you look?"

"No. This is such a big place, she could be anywhere. If I can't find her I'll come back for help."

"Are you sure?" My husband looked concerned, mirroring my own face.

"I'm sure. I'm probably just being silly."

"Let me know if you find her. Or if you don't. Why is your hair wet, and why do you smell so clean?" He leaned forward and sniffed.

"Long story. I'll tell you about it later."

I walked back to the house with my canine friend still following me, searching the horizon for a small figure with soft brown hair. Nothing. The only place I hadn't searched yet was the basement, and I couldn't think of any reason she might be down there. Nevertheless, I picked up a flashlight someone had left on the countertop in the kitchen and headed for the door leading down to the dank space below.

Opening the door, I saw a light in the far corner.

"Mother?"

"I'm here," she replied.

With relief flooding through me, I thought about all the exercise I was getting from climbing up and down stairs while I went to meet her. "What are you doing down here?"

"I can't really explain it. It's the weirdest thing, but since you mentioned the face at the window, all I can think about is this cellar. Well, it's certainly more than a cellar.

Obviously this room was used as a game room."

She pointed her flashlight at a light fixture hanging from the ceiling.

"That would have hung over a pool table, don't you think?"

I nodded. "What made you think of the basement?"

"I have no idea." She aimed the flashlight at several different areas before walking to the block wall I'd noticed earlier – the one with the stains on it. She studied it, moving the light from corner to corner.

"What are you looking for?" I asked.

"Nothing in particular. You know, if this room was in a movie, there'd be a dead body hidden behind those blocks. I mean, really, why put up a block wall down here? It doesn't seem to serve any purpose."

"Are you trying to scare me again?" I asked.

She followed the outline of the stains on the wall with her flashlight. "No, but now that I think about it, let's get out of here."

"It won't seem so spooky once the lights are working." I followed her up the stairs with Bubba leading the way. "Really, Mom, there's nothing out of the ordinary in the basement."

"But why does the wall have stains on it? It's an inside wall so there's no roof to leak."

"Let's see what's over the wall upstairs. Maybe there was a leak in the kitchen or something. Or maybe it's under the laundry room. A washer could have broken and flooded the room, leaking to the basement."

"No, the block wall isn't near any of those things."

She wasn't hooking me with her hair-brained suspicions. There was no body behind the block wall, and there was a logical explanation for the stains.

I left her and Bubba in the family room while I ran outside to tell Pete I'd found her. I yelled, "*Pete! I found her,*" across the yard.

Looking up, he waved before going back to work.

Once again, we climbed the stairs to the bedrooms on the top level. Felicity, Zoë and Rachael had finished the smaller room and were carrying Pete's and my belongings out of the master bedroom so they could start cleaning it.

With five of us, we'd worked out a system. While two of us swept, the other three washed down the floors. We switched off because washing the floors was hard on one's back.

The men came in to see how we were doing. They'd finished the corrals, which consisted of pre-made panels that simply had to be assembled. Of course, they had to cut down brush and smooth the ground out a little before they could assemble them.

Stanley was beginning to look sunburned, so Felicity got some lotion from their luggage and made him put it on. He sputtered something about "real men" not needing lotion, but she stood her ground.

The men left us to our work while they began another project. Frank wanted to fix the hole in the ceiling while the others began working outside again.

After finishing the upper floor, including bedrooms and the bathroom, we gave up. It was late afternoon and everyone was exhausted. We plopped our behinds on the floor in the family room.

There was a knock on the front door and my mother groaned when she pulled herself up to answer it. The plumber and the electrician were checking in before leaving. She walked outside and talked to them while the rest of us sat like vegetables in a patch, too tired to even speak.

She returned shortly. "The plumber said he's got the well working. He'll hook up lines tomorrow and we'll have running water. He said the water out here is full of minerals and all kinds of things, and we might want to consider putting in a water purification system, but at least we'll all be able to take showers tomorrow night. And the electrician has part of the power working, including a new hot water heater, so we'll even be able to shower in hot water."

"The whole house will be hooked up that soon?" I asked.

"No, not the whole house. Just the little apartment and part of the main floor. They said it will be a few days before everything will be up and running."

"It sounds like quite a job," Zoë said.

"Someone broke in and stole a lot of the wiring and copper pipes," my mother explained. "They're having to replace a lot of equipment, too."

"I wish we'd seen what was going on." Racheal shook her head. "Unfortunately, unless we're outside we don't see what's going on over here. And they must have come during the middle of the night when everyone was sleeping."

Mother *tsked*. "The things some people do are shameless. Let's go outside where it's cooler. I sure hope they can get the air conditioning working soon."

"Me, too." Felicity was far beyond wilted.

My mother took her hand. "Come on. I've got iced tea out in the motorhome. We can all relax out on the patio."

"Where did you two disappear to earlier?" My little friend raised her eyebrows at us. "It's not like you to walk away from hard work."

"Well, we certainly weren't ghost hunting," my mother said a little too quickly.

I sighed, deeply but quietly.

Chapter Fourteen

Felicity's eyebrows dropped and she looked stunned. "You weren't *what?*"

"Mooother, why would you even say that?"

"Well..."

I briefly explained the face I'd seen at the window. "Racheal, do any of the women around here have long blonde hair?"

"I can't think of anyone, other than me, and I was with the other women when you saw the face." She grinned and fluffed her hair. "I have naturally blonde hair. The desert sun seems to bleach hair, so the other women don't try to dye their hair blonde. Besides, most of the folks out here are old."

Before I could stop her, my mother asked, "What about Barbara? What color was her hair?"

"I saw a picture of her once, and her hair wasn't blonde. It was closer to black. Of course, she could have dyed it."

"Okay, maybe I imagined I saw the face." I knew what I'd seen, but there was no reason to keep this conversation going. "After all, those windows are so dirty, and we're all tired."

That seemed to satisfy everyone, except maybe Felicity. She knows me too well. And, of course, my mother knew better.

"Well, we'd better get going." Racheal stood and stretched. "I've got some animals to feed and veggies to water. By the way, we won't be able to come over tomorrow because we're driving to Las Vegas to do some shopping, and maybe a little gambling. I might come back the next day though."

"Oh, Racheal, I can't thank you and Zoë enough for your help." My mother stood and hugged the two women, in turn. "This was far and above the neighborly thing to do. I didn't expect this much help, but I sure appreciate it. Please, don't feel obligated to come back though."

Zoë smiled and bent over to return my mother's hug. "Livvie, as hard as we worked, I still had a good time. Micah and I will be here for a few more days, so we'll be back."

We walked outside with them while they told their husbands they were heading back to the little farm.

The men were studying a large cement area in the back, outside the Arizona room. It was near the pool and outdoor kitchen.

Micah and Tyler broke away and left with their wives.

"I can't imagine what purpose this served," Frank said. "I think we need to break it up and get rid of it, and maybe put something else in here."

Pete nodded. "Yeah, it looks so out of place. We can work on that tomorrow." He rubbed his back and I knew he was tired. I could see he was favoring the leg he'd broken several months ago, too.

Stanley nodded, trying to look like one of the guys. Actually, he looked like he was dreading the new job.

Bubba sniffed around the cement, seeming to understand it was the subject of the moment.

My mother jabbed me in the arm, speaking behind her

hand. "Looks like another good place to hide a body."

Not only did I sigh, but I rolled my eyes.

"What?" Felicity asked. "What about a body?"

"My mother was joking," I said. "She seems to be seeing hiding places for bodies everywhere she looks. You know how she's been trying to scare us."

Felicity looked relieved. "Let's have some of that iced tea you mentioned, Livvie. My back is killing me."

"I've got some salve in the motorhome that should take care of your back pain. I'll give it to you at dinnertime." As usual, my mother had come prepared.

I hadn't given any thought to bringing something like that. "Speaking of dinner, I'll do the cooking tonight. I'm thinking wieners and beans."

"Sounds good to me. I bought some macaroni salad at the store yesterday, and some fresh fruit salad that should go well with wienies and beans." Felicity rubbed her back and sat on one of the chairs we'd brought to the outdoor kitchen. "Wouldn't it be nice if everything was working and we could cook here on the patio?"

I nodded. Looking up, I saw Tyler opening the front gate and heading our way, motioning me to meet him. "I'll see what he wants. You stay here and relax."

By the time I met him, he was halfway up the driveway. If you came in at the side of the property like we'd done when we arrived, it was almost like a little road in front of the lot. If you came through the front gate, it was merely a longish dirt driveway. He'd come in through the front.

"I wanted to let you know I'm going to call the neighbors tonight to let them know you're coming to talk to them. We'll be gone all day tomorrow, and I had a feeling you wouldn't want to wait."

"Thanks!"

He pointed at two houses across the dirt road. "The one on the left is where Zetta and Bill Ellison live. On the right is where Shirley and Jeff Shaw live. Racheal said she told you about them already. None of the other neighbors lived here when everything happened." He looked thoughtful for a moment. "Brad lived here back then. He lives in the beat up old mobile home down the street. He kind of keeps to himself, most of the time."

"Tyler, what did Barbara look like? I'm just curious. You know, having a description of the people involved helps me keep it straight in my head."

His look said he didn't quite believe me, but he wasn't sure why I wanted to know and he wasn't curious enough to ask. "Barbara was in her early fifties at the time of the killings. Her hair was what I think they call salt and pepper, part grey and part black. She wasn't really pretty, but I think some people would call her a handsome woman."

"Ah, there's the writer in you coming out. A handsome woman is a good description."

He grinned. "I'll have to bring you one of my books to read. Anyway, for a woman her age she had a good figure. Working here on the ranch seemed to keep her in shape. Let me think." He paused. "Salt and pepper hair, good figure, handsome woman, and... Oh, yeah. I don't know how I could forget. She had a faint scar that ran down the right side of her face. She was in a bad accident when she was still lawyering, but it didn't leave a mark except the faint scar. I guess that's about it."

"How tall was she?" I was honestly trying to picture the woman in my mind.

"Oh, I'd say about five foot six or so. She wasn't dinky like you and your mother. Oops. Sorry, I didn't mean to offend you."

I laughed. "I sometimes forget I'm kind of short because I spend so much time with women who are shorter than I am. Like my mother and Felicity. I have an elderly neighbor at home who's pretty dinky, too."

"You and that dog of yours crack me up," he said. "He's almost as big as you are, and yet he seems to know who's the boss."

I hadn't given it much thought. Bubba *did* listen to me when I gave him commands. Huh! I guess I was the alpha dog in his mind. Or, maybe he was playing me.

"I may have to include him in one of my books."

I smiled. "I'd like that. The big lug *should* be a character in a book. I'll have to tell you more about him before we leave for home."

"We'll talk." Tyler had a faraway look in his eyes and I had a feeling he might be thinking of a storyline for one of his books.

I brought him back with a question. "What did Harry Stockholm look like? I might as well get this straight in my head before I talk to the neighbors. It helps when I can put a face on a victim."

"Harry was a tall, skinny, cranky old man. He was never the same after his wife died. I had a feeling maybe he wished he'd died with her. Although, to be honest, he was cranky before she died, too."

"What did she die of?" Now I was just being nosey.

"Funny thing. He never told anyone. I was too young to remember her, but my dad said Harry told everyone she'd gotten sick in the middle of the night and he took her to the hospital, and she died on the way. There was no funeral. He told my mother he didn't like that kind of thing."

"That family saw more than their share of tragedy." I had a sudden thought. "Do you know what she looked like?"

"I don't remember. I'll take a look at some of the old family photos. I know she was in some of them."

I hoped she didn't have long blonde hair, because I've never believed in ghosts, and I didn't want to start now.

Chapter Fifteen

"*B*y the way, Sandi, I should probably mention that the neighbors are in their late eighties now, so you may want to be careful with them."

"I'm glad you mentioned it, Tyler. I hadn't even thought about their age. It makes sense though, since the murders took place twenty years ago and these people bought their property at the same time as the Stockholms. They were young at the time, from what I can gather. I'm surprised they've all stayed out here since it's so far to town and medical services."

"That's why my parents left. They didn't want to stay out here in their old age, although they're not really very old. Racheal and I bought the farm from them when they moved into town."

"Are they still in Arizona? Do you think I could talk to them, too?"

"They live in Kingman. I'll speak to my dad. Okay, I've gotta go. And don't forget, I want to get some insider stuff from you about being a private investigator."

"Let me know when you're ready to sit down and talk.

Besides, it'll give me an excuse to stop cleaning."

He laughed before turning around to head home. I liked Tyler and his brother and their wives. They were down-to-earth people, and hard work didn't seem to scare them off.

Remembering I'd said I'd fix dinner, I headed for the motorhome. Pete had set up the outdoor cook stove we'd bought and I thought I'd try it. I bought plenty of wieners and beans at the store, so I put the beans in a large pot and dropped the wieners in before setting the pot on the stove to start heating.

I reminisced for a moment, remembering when I'd fixed wieners and beans in Wolf Creek. Since we'd been stranded in the ghost town, we hadn't had a lot of food choices. We were supposed to be going camping, so we only had what we'd brought for our vacation. Those franks and beans had tasted like manna from heaven.

Pete joined me and plopped himself onto a lawn chair to watch what I was doing. He leaned forward and rubbed his ankle.

"Is it bothering you very much?" I asked. "Maybe you should rest for a while."

"It's fine. A couple of minutes and I'll be good as new."

I knew Pete well. He wasn't about to let his ankle or leg stop him. He didn't care that he had a plate and screws in his ankle; he was going to do whatever he wanted to do. Even so, he sat and continued to rub the spot.

"So where did you find your mother earlier today?" he asked.

"She was in the basement, looking it over." I laughed. "Do you remember that block wall by the stairs? She said it was a good place to hide a body."

"What an imagination."

"Yeah, but she keeps me laughing." When she wasn't in the throes of menopause, my mother could be pretty funny. "I'm going to have to get even with her for trying to scare me though."

"Uh oh. I have a feeling the rest of us had better stay out of the line of fire."

I smiled mischievously. "Probably a good idea."

I set a chair by the stove and sat down while I stirred the beans. Although this was a stove, it was small, about two feet tall and maybe three feet wide. It even had a little oven. It would come in handy when we next went camping.

Frank joined us. "Believe it or not, I can smell those beans cooking all the way over by the pool. I hope you made plenty, because I'm hungry. By the way, did you hear your mother say she thought that cement slab would be a good place to hide a body? What a character. Life with Livvie is never dull."

I stood and gave him a quick hug. "You're good for my mother, Frank. You make her happy, and you seem to understand her. Or, at least you put up with her."

He hugged me back. "She's worth the time and effort."

Pete looked up at him. "When do you want to break up the cement and prove there's no body there?"

"Tomorrow is soon enough. I think we've all had enough for one day. Besides, she doesn't really believe there's a body under the cement."

I glanced back toward the corrals and noticed they'd also cut down a lot of weeds. Good. No place for snakes to hide, at least the slithering kind. Now why had I added that? Probably too many thoughts of ghosts and bad guys who were snakes in the grass.

Before long everyone joined us. Felicity brought out the macaroni salad, fruit and drinks, while my mother and Stanley set the picnic table with paper plates and plastic utensils. Another blessing – not many dishes to do after we ate.

While we waited, I fed Bubba and listened to everyone talk. They seemed quite pleased with what we'd accomplished.

Before long I put dinner on the table and things were quiet while we filled that empty spot in our stomachs.

Something didn't feel right and I looked around for Bubba. He should have been lying by my feet, waiting for a handout. "Anybody seen Bubba?"

"He's over there, sitting and watching the corrals," Felicity said. "I don't know what he's doing, but he won't take his eyes off that place."

Frank stood. "I'll be back in a minute." He hurried into the motorhome and came back with a gun in his hand.

"What – "

Bubba stood and growled, his hackles standing at attention.

"Call your dog, and everyone stay where you are." Frank slowly headed toward Bubba.

"Bubba, *come!*" Something was wrong. I didn't know what it was, but apparently Bubba was in danger, or at least that was the feeling I got from Frank.

"Snake," Mother said, not too calmly. "That's Frank's snake gun. He uses snake shot."

"*Bubba, come now!*" I stood up, but Pete pulled me back down.

"Stay here," he said.

Bubba ignored my command, but at least he stayed where he was.

Stanley jumped out of his seat and stood in front of Felicity with his arms out from his sides, looking very protective – and very pale.

All eyes were on Frank. He moved slowly and methodically, finally raising his gun. The shot made us all jump.

"*Got him,*" Frank yelled.

Stanley practically deflated. His shoulders sagged before he turned and hugged his wife.

"What was it?" Pete stood and walked toward his new father-in-law.

I followed.

Frank was shaking when we reached him. "I wasn't really sure it was a snake, but I thought I heard rattling just before your dog growled."

Bubba slowly approached the snake.

"Stop him," Frank said. "Now! They're dangerous even after they're dead."

Pete took a step forward. "Bubba, come here!" I'd never heard him sound quite so authoritative before.

Bubba hesitated before returning to us.

Mother joined us. "Was it a rattler?"

"It was a Mohave Green rattler," Frank replied. "They're worse than a diamondback rattler; more poisonous. Wait here while I take care of him."

I grabbed Bubba's collar and tried to pull him toward the motorhome, but he was being stubborn and wouldn't move. I even offered him a treat, but he wouldn't take his eyes off the snake.

Pete gently pulled my hand off Bubba's collar and took hold of the dog. "Come, boy."

Darned if that stupid dog didn't follow Pete, and they left me standing there.

My mother put her arm around my shoulders. "This is the desert, Sandi. We knew what we were getting into. Cutting down all those weeds must have ticked off the snake. Or maybe it was looking for food."

"Ghosts, snakes, Bubba listening to Pete instead of me? What's next?"

Some days just don't take the direction you want them to.

Chapter Sixteen

*I*t was October and the sun was going down earlier every day. My mother commented that it was cooler here than in Bullhead City because the llama ranch was at a higher altitude. Although there were mountains nearby, it wasn't mountainous in the area of the llama ranch, other than the one small mountain that sat by itself. She said Kingman usually got at least a dusting of snow during the winter months. While it wasn't cold at the moment, it was cool enough that I went inside and got a sweater.

My mother set lanterns around the motorhome and we sat outside talking until around eight o'clock. There was no TV, no radio and it was kind of nice. We heard coyotes howling off in the distance, and after a while they began to sound closer. Bubba would definitely stay inside at night.

You're not in Los Angeles anymore, Sandi, I thought to myself. I could get used to the quieter life – maybe. There were no traffic noises or sirens, sounds that I'd become accustomed to in the city. However, there were snakes and coyotes, things I'd rather *not* become accustomed to.

Frank cut off the snake's head and buried it to keep Bubba's curiosity from getting him in trouble. He'd hung the snake's body across the top of a fence, intending to work with Bubba to make him realize this wasn't something he should go near. I had a closer look at the snake after it was dead, and sure enough, it had a green tinge to it. Mohave Green was a good name for it.

Felicity and Stanley left us not long after eight and retired to their little apartment. I heard her say, "You're so brave for protecting me from the snake, love muffin."

I could see Stanley straighten his back before he put his arm around her waist.

Pete heard her, too, and made a gagging noise.

"Oh, Pete, you know they're just doing that because they're newlyweds. Besides, it drives you crazy and they know it." I understood what they were doing, even if he didn't.

"But *love muffin*? Really?"

My mother laughed. "At least she didn't call him her stud muffin. They make quite a pair, don't they?"

"They do," I said. "Mother, you don't really believe there's a body hidden around here, do you?"

I wanted to know if she'd been joking, and I could see Pete beginning to fidget. I knew he was ready to go upstairs.

"No, they found all the bodies when the murders were committed. But you have to admit, until we get this place fixed up, it's kind of spooky. There really are some unusual things, like the block wall and the concrete. Neither one seems to serve a purpose."

Frank sat forward. "I'll take a look at the wall. Maybe it's a weight-bearing wall."

My husband looked skyward. "Okay, babe, let's go upstairs and get some sleep. We've still got a lot to do tomorrow. It looks like clouds are moving in, too."

I glanced up and saw he was right. The moon had almost disappeared.

Mother yawned before standing and giving Pete and

me a hug. "I'm ready to call it a night, too. We'll have plenty of time to talk more tomorrow."

That was the end of our day. We'd only been married for three days, and I was too tired to even think about wifely duties. If I hadn't been so tired, I never would have thought of them as duties. Sweeping, mopping, looking for my mother, ghosts, and snakes. What a day.

I glanced up at Pete and he was watching me intently. The corners of his mouth slowly turned upward, and suddenly *duty* didn't seem like the right word. In fact, I raced him up the stairs, giggling expectantly. Pete didn't let me down.

Once again, I awoke during the night to hear Bubba roaming around the house. I heard the stairs creak under his weight when he came upstairs and finally settled outside the bedroom door.

~ * ~

Early the next morning, Bubba scratched at the door. I heard him snort, which is a sign he's ready to go outside and I'd better hurry. I pulled on a pair of jeans and a sweatshirt and quietly opened the door, trying to let Pete get a little more sleep. It was still dark out.

I took a flashlight and checked my watch before I made my way downstairs. It was four in the morning.

"Bubba," I whispered, "you're a city dog. You shouldn't be up this early."

I followed him and he led me through the house to the front door. The security screen was wide, with two doors. I noticed the day before that they'd apparently bent a little. One side made a horrific screech when I tried to open it. I was careful to pull the door to the side before exerting any pressure, but it still made a noise.

My friend, the dog, made a beeline for the nearest tree while I waited on the porch. I wanted more sleep, but Bubba began sniffing every tree, bush and weed, looking for just the right spot to take care of business.

"Would you hurry up?"

It was a pointless request. I knew he'd ignore me. He took his morning trips outdoors quite seriously.

I descended the stairs and sat on the bottom step. With my elbows on my knees, I rested my head in my hands. It was so quiet. Other than the dog moving around there wasn't a sound.

Bubba finally joined me, sitting on the ground in front of me. I could see him grin by the light from the flashlight. He was happy and relaxed, and unfortunately, I was wide awake. Leaning forward, I hugged him. He was warm and soft and loved having me make over him.

There was no kitchen where I could make coffee or heat a kettle of water for tea, and no microwave to heat water, either. I'd just sit on the steps for a while. I snapped my fingers, remembering the little stove Pete and I bought.

Bubba turned and looked toward the end of the house where the garage sat just about the same time I heard muffled footsteps. I turned off my flashlight to hide myself in the dark, but I wasn't worried because the dog hadn't reacted. Besides, I had no doubt he'd protect me with his life if it came to that.

I waited and the footsteps continued to make their way in my direction.

"Who's out here?" It was Frank's voice, and he spoke softly.

"It's Sandi." I turned on my flashlight.

He walked over and sat next to me. "What are you doing up so early?"

"Bubba needed to go outside. Now I'm wide awake. What about you?"

"I always get up early. Livvie just ignores me and turns over."

A sudden gust of wind whipped the tree tops back and forth.

"Where did that come from?" I asked. The wind was chilly and I rubbed my arms.

Frank chuckled. "We've learned over the past few years that the desert winds are unpredictable. The calm disappears in a flash and the winds attack with gusto. Come on, we'll go around and sit in the garage. I'll get a lantern and some coffee for us."

I followed him to the garage and pulled a chair over to sit on while he disappeared into the motorhome. Bubba stood by the open garage door for a moment, and finally dropped to the floor, ready for a nap.

"Dumb dog. You woke me up and now you're going to sleep?"

A soft snore was his only reply. It sure didn't take him long to drop off.

The wind picked up even more. While I waited for Frank, I decided to explore the garage a little. With flashlight in hand, I shined it around the walls. I saw a box had fallen off a pile, so helpful little stepdaughter that I am, I worked my way between pieces of furniture to replace it.

I set the flashlight on top of a container and pushed the box back onto the pile. I knew it had to contain something heavy because it had knocked a hole in the wall. Curious, I picked up the light and shined it on the hole.

"Uh oh."

Chapter Seventeen

The hole in the garage wall was at eye level, and when I lifted the flashlight I could see something behind the wall. I carefully studied the edges, making sure there weren't any spiders or other bugs. Not seeing any black widows, I leaned forward and shined the flashlight through the hole.

You could have knocked me over with a feather. I could see *stairs*, and they'd been walled off.

"Sandi?"

I jumped. "Frank, you're as bad as my mother. You scared me."

He laughed. "Sorry. What're you looking at?" He set down two coffee mugs and carried his lantern closer.

"One of the boxes fell and knocked a hole in the wall. Come look at this. You're not going to believe what I found."

He squeezed between the furniture and boxes and stood at my side. Bending, he was a lot taller than me, he peered through the hole. "Well, I'll be a son-of-a-gun. Stairs." He glanced upward, but our view was blocked. "I wonder where those lead to. And why did they close off the stairs?"

"This house has surprises at every turn. You know my

mother is going to figure there's a body at the top of the stairs, don't you?"

"You're probably right." He sounded resigned. "I have a feeling part of the reason your mother wanted this house was because of its history. Thanks to you," he said, looking directly into my eyes, "she sees mysteries everywhere."

I shrugged, uncomfortable about encouraging her. Well, in all fairness, I never truly encouraged her. However, she sometimes had an almost unnatural interest in my cases.

"I think I may cover this over for now. I can stack boxes in front of it. If your mother sees it she'll want me to knock out the wall so she can follow the stairs."

I shrugged again and smiled at him. "That might not be a bad idea."

"I'm glad she was still asleep when you found this."

"You're glad who was asleep when you found what?" My mother's voice carried across the garage, and she sounded sleepy, but very curious.

I grinned. "Can't keep anything from her," I said softly.

"I just can't seem to get a break." Frank waved at my mother.

"Well? What did you find?" She was tenacious, I'd give her that.

"Just a minute, Mom. There's not much room back here. Let me squeeze out and you can take my place."

Frank poked my arm like I'd said too much and I laughed.

Whatever you didn't want my mother to overhear, she'd hear. Whatever you didn't want her to see, she'd find. She was an enigma.

She took another of Frank's lanterns even though I held up my flashlight.

I worked my way out of the corner and barely got out of her way before she was following the trail I'd made into the corner.

The wind whistled through the garage. There were plenty of nooks and crannies that needed to be sealed. Wood shrinks, glass cracks, and they both leave open spaces for the wind to travel through.

"*Sandi!* Did you *see* this?" She sounded excited, incredulous, and all sounds of sleepiness were gone.

"Yes, Mom, I saw it." Of course I'd seen it. I *found* it.

"How much do you want to bet there's a body at the top of the stairs?"

Frank started to laugh and I joined him.

Mother had a one-track mind.

Frank worked his way past her and back to the front of the garage, sitting on a chair next to me. "Do I know my wife or what?"

"You're a quick study. After only a few years of marriage you know exactly how she's going to react to any given situation." I took a sip of my now cold coffee. "Ick. I'm going to go heat this in the microwave in the motorhome. Do you want me to heat yours, too?"

"Please." He held out his mug.

"Back in a minute."

Bubba snorted in his sleep when I walked past him.

The wind whipped my hair in my face, half blinding me, and I hung on to the mugs tightly. I was amazed at how quickly the wind was picking up.

I brought back a cup of coffee for my mother, too. She was sitting in my vacated chair and reached for the mug.

"Thank you, sweetie." She'd set her lantern on top of some boxes.

"What a way for the morning to start," I said, handing Frank his mug and pulling up a third chair.

"Yeah, this is the house that just keeps giving." He didn't actually sound too happy. "Your mother wants me to take out the wall."

I understood his lack of enthusiasm all too well.

"Gosh, *I'm* surprised." My sarcasm wasn't lost on my mother.

"Now, Sandra, you know there has to be a reason for those stairs to be there."

I hated it when she used my given name. In this case I knew it was because she didn't like my smart aleck attitude.

I tried to smooth things over. "It could be as simple as the builders needing temporary stairs while they worked on other things, or maybe they started something there and then the owners changed their minds. I'm sure there's no body at the top of the stairs."

"Weeellll… You never know about these things. Maybe there's a skeleton." I could almost hear the wheels spinning in her head. She sounded too hopeful and looked too serious.

I opened my mouth to speak, but thankfully I was interrupted before I could say a word.

"Here's where you are." Pete stepped into the garage, looking groggy and rubbing his eyes with his knuckles. "I woke up and you were gone. I waited for you to come back, but you never did."

I handed him my coffee. "Have some of this. It might wake you up. Bubba had to go out and while we were in front, Frank showed up. I knew I'd never get back to sleep so we came to the garage."

"And wait until you see what we found." Mother looked like the cat that swallowed the canary. She was so proud of our discovery. "This really is a mystery house."

I glanced at my watch when I realized the horizon wasn't as dark as it had been. Had I really been up for two hours? It was going on six o'clock.

"What'd you find?" Pete took a big swig of coffee and made a face. "It's cold."

"Must be the wind cooling things off," I said. "I'll get you some fresh."

Mother pointed toward the back of the garage and

handed Pete my flashlight, which I'd set on the boxes next to the lanterns. I saw him heading that way before I left to get him something to drink.

"Wait for me." My mother followed in my tracks. "I'll put on a fresh pot of coffee. It won't be long until Stanley and Felicity are up, too."

I glanced up at the sky. "Now that the sun is coming up, I can see a storm is moving in. Look how black those clouds are."

Mother glanced up and nodded. "We may be working inside all day today, from the looks of it."

"You don't really believe there's a body at the top of the stairs, right?" Whether or not she really believed there were hidden bodies around the house was becoming a common question.

"No, dear, but I would like to know where the stairs go. Really, don't you think it's kind of odd that there are stairs hidden behind the wall?"

"There could be any number of reasons for them. Although, I have to admit, I'm curious, too. I don't think we should make Frank tear down the wall though."

"Well, how else will we find answers?"

"Answers to what?" I asked.

"Answers to what's up there, of course."

"Oh. Do we have to find out? We need to work on this house. Don't forget, we'll be leaving in a few days."

"You'd leave your mother in the midst of chaos? With questions that need to be answered?"

"In a heartbeat." Guilt trips didn't always work on me. "Besides, what are the odds that we'll find *anything* of interest up there?"

Returning to the garage, we found Pete and Frank standing in the back of the garage talking and pointing at the hole in the wall.

"And she actually said she wonders if there's a body

up there?" Pete sounded dubious.

Frank nodded.

I cleared my throat.

My mother did the same.

And Pete looked sheepish.

Chapter Eighteen

We finally sat with cups of hot coffee, relaxing and talking about our plans for the day. Pete frequently glanced at my mother to see if she might be miffed at him, but she was fine.

Felicity and Stanley joined us before too long. While we told them about our morning, my mother brought out more hot coffee.

"I want to see the stairs. This is turning out to be the most interesting house I've ever seen." Felicity's eyes searched the garage, looking for any other anomalies.

"Now, my little button nose, why don't we drink our coffee first." Stanley tapped Felicity's mug.

Pete couldn't take it anymore. "If you two don't stop with the cutesy names, I'm going to... I don't know what, but I'll do something. You're driving me nuts."

Stanley and Felicity looked at each other and started to laugh.

Stanley spoke first. "That was the idea, to drive everyone crazy." He grinned. "And it seems to be working."

"Why would you do that?" Pete asked.

Stanley's grin widened. "Just a lark. Will you ever forget Mr. and Mrs. Hawks' wedding day? Well, I guess it's turning into a wedding *week*, isn't it?"

Pete gave Stanley a look I couldn't read. "How could I ever forget our wedding day? The minister dropped dead after pronouncing us man and wife, and man and wife."

"So we're just adding a little color to an already colorful day."

I watched Pete and Stanley for a moment. "Personally, I think it's kind of cute, as long as it doesn't last for the rest of your marriage."

"Me, too," my mother said.

Felicity glanced at Stanley. "What do you think, lovey, should we stop?"

Stanley, still grinning, shook his head. "No, Mrs. Hawks, let's keep it going for a while. I'm having fun."

That effectively ended the conversation.

"Now show me the staircase," Felicity said.

I picked up the lantern and motioned for her to follow me. A lantern would make the stairs and the hole in the wall just a bit more mysterious than my flashlight.

"It's amazing to think you even *found* these stairs." She took the lantern from me and gazed into the hole in the wall, seemingly studying what she saw.

"What do you think?" Stanley called from the front of the garage.

"I don't know what to think." Felicity's voice echoed through the garage. "They're not regular stairs like the ones inside the house. They're more like planks nailed to a frame. Very rustic. Either the builder used them for something or someone put them together in a hurry to use for who knows what? I think we should see where they lead."

"You'll have to talk to Frank about that," I said. "He may not want to tear into the wall. I doubt if I would."

"But you're a P.I. It seems to me you should be dying to

see what's up there."

"Oh, come now. You're not thinking there's a body up there, too, are you?"

"Who else thinks that?"

"My mother. Who else?"

Felicity turned and glanced at my mother, who was busily trying to look as innocent as a newborn baby. "Of course. Why did I even ask?"

I took the lantern from Fel and suggested we move back to the group. "I don't want you to encourage my mother and her fantasies."

She nodded and we moved away from the hole in the wall.

Although I hadn't heard the vehicle, I saw lights as a truck turned in and parked just outside the garage. It was the electrician, and the plumber pulled in right behind him. They exited the trucks and approached the garage when they saw us sitting and talking.

"Mornin'." The electrician ran his fingers through his windblown hair. "I'm going to take care of the initial hookups, and then I'm outta here. Big storm coming this way. You won't get rain out here very often, but when you do it'll be a gully washer. Since all the roads around here are dirt, it's gonna be a mess. I'll be back tomorrow though. Yep, it's gonna be one big ass mess."

The plumber joined us.

"Do the roads really get that bad?" My mother stood and approached the electrician.

Before he could reply, lightning split the sky and thunder boomed.

Bubba's head jerked up, but he didn't bother to move from his spot.

The electrician glanced up at the sky and tipped his head, smiling. "Yes, ma'am. You're gonna wanna keep the food well-stocked when storms move in. Well, you've got those big walk-in pantries anyway. I have a feeling you're gonna get a taste of a big storm today. You'll probably wanna work inside all day."

The plumber followed suit and glanced skyward. "I'll get some running water for you, but you won't have it in the whole house yet. I can get things working in the little apartment, but that'll have to do for now. And I'll be back tomorrow to finish up the job. Like John said, you're roads are going to be like a running river." He chuckled and returned to his truck, shaking his head.

What had my mother and Frank gotten into, living so far out of town with nothing but dirt roads? Oh, well, other people lived out here and dealt with the weather.

"Works for me," my mother said. "I can use today to work inside, and maybe I'll do a little exploring, too."

"At least we won't have to worry about snakes." Stanley smiled, looking relieved.

"Maybe we can work inside the stable," Pete suggested.

"Good idea." Frank looked thoughtful.

My mother turned to him. "Honey, maybe Sandi and Felicity and I could pull down the wall – "

He put his hands on her shoulders and gave her a very serious look. "No pulling down the wall today. No breaking of the cement slab in the backyard. And no knocking out the block wall in the basement. Today we work on the house. Understand?"

My mother had a look of surprise on her face and nodded, not saying a word.

Frank motioned to Pete and Stanley to follow him. "Come on. Let's take a look at the stable and see how bad it is." He turned to my mother with a pointed look on his face. "With any luck the women will fix breakfast while we're gone."

"Yes, dear." My mother spoke softly.

The three men walked out with the electrician, leaving

us standing in the garage.

Mom smiled, watching them walk away. "He's not forceful very often, but once in a while it's kind of nice. Let's start breakfast." She glanced at the sky. "I think we'd better cook inside the motorhome this morning."

Right on cue there was another boom of thunder, and on its heels came a downpour. The electrician and plumber ran for the house while our husbands – how I love calling Pete my husband – took off for the stable.

My mother picked up a sheet of plastic from some furniture it covered and pulled it over her head, motioning Fel and me to join her. We did, and we ran like the wind to the motorhome.

An hour later we'd eaten breakfast and cleaned up the dishes. While we were eating, the electrician and the plumber had done their magic and there was hot water in the little apartment. I cleaned the shower as much as I could under the circumstances, let the water run for a few minutes in case there was any rust, and we each took very quick showers so we could get to work. It seemed to leave everyone feeling refreshed. Of course, my mother and Frank had used the shower in the motorhome.

The workers left and our husbands returned to the stable. We three women finished sweeping and washing the floors in the two remaining bedrooms, hoping to be able to start painting.

"You know, this house is kind of creepy right now," Felicity said.

"You're right." I couldn't help but agree with her.

"It's just the wind blowing through the place," my mother explained. She held up her hand indicating we should be quiet. "Listen. You can hear the wind whistling through the cracks and crevices. I mean, it's actually whistling."

"Like in a haunted house," Felicity said. She whistled a scary theme song from a scary old television show. I recognized the tune, but I couldn't remember what show it was from.

"All we need now is a creaking door." My mother turned and leaped in our direction. "*Booooo!*"

Felicity jumped and rubbed her arms.

I didn't react. I was beginning to expect the unexpected from my mother.

She looked disappointed, and somehow I knew she'd try harder to scare me in the future. She just cracked me up sometimes. I'd have to scare *her* before she could scare *me*. We were turning it into a game, which I guess is kind of nuts, but to each his own.

Chapter Nineteen

Glancing out the window, I saw it was still raining. In fact, it was raining harder than I'd ever seen before. Thanks to the wind it was blowing sideways. Interesting.

There was a loud clap of thunder that shook the house.

I jumped and grabbed Felicity's arm just as she was reaching for mine.

The three of us looked at each other and started to laugh.

"Maybe I couldn't scare you, but the thunder sure did," my mother said. "It's directly overhead right now."

As if to confirm her statement, a big bang shook the house again.

"I wonder how long this is going to keep up." I glanced outside.

"Get away from the window," Mom said. "You're just asking to be struck by lightning."

I moved away quickly. She was right.

"There's paint in the Arizona room. Let's get started. At least it'll keep us busy. Besides, the kitchen in the apartment is relatively small."

I rolled my eyes. "Yeah, like room size is an issue. Where do you want to start?"

"Like I said, the kitchen in the little apartment. You haven't been listening to me, have you? If we're going to have electricity in the apartment, we might as well clean things and paint so we can use it."

"Good idea," Felicity said. She turned and headed for the screened room with us on her heels.

"I can't believe I didn't notice these paint cans before." I bent and started reading the colors on the cans. "What color are you going to use?"

"Pale yellow. It's such a cheerful color, especially in a kitchen. I'll decorate with... I don't know. I'll figure out what looks best with it. Maybe some curtains over the window with yellow and other colors will work. Blue might work, too, or maybe green."

"It sounds cheerful to me," Felicity said. "At least it'll wake me up in the morning." She smiled at my mom.

We carried paint cans, trays, brushes and paint rollers downstairs with us, walking through the house when walking outside would have probably been easier and faster. However, staying indoors would keep us dry.

After mixing the paint we poured some into a roller pan and started working. Mother and Fel painted with the rollers. I came along behind them with a brush and began doing the areas where the rollers wouldn't work.

There was almost a rhythm to our working together. We became so engrossed in what we were doing that we stopped talking, which is when I began to hear noises.

"Did you two hear a creaking noise overhead?" I asked.

"It's just the electrician moving around in the crawl space, or attic, or whatever it is," my mother replied.

"They already left. Remember?" Felicity stopped painting and held her roller still. Yellow paint dripped onto the counter top. She quickly grabbed a rag and wiped it clean.

I heard the creak again, along with a kind of smacking sound. "Mom?"

"It's just the storm causing the house to settle."

"Uh huh. Sure. I think I'll go check it out." I set down my paint brush and wiped my hands on the rag Fel had used, and my hands immediately turned yellow. Sighing, I grabbed a clean rag and wiped off as much paint as I could.

I heard some faint creaking and figured whoever, or whatever, was up in the crawl space was moving away.

"Wait a minute," I said, reality breaking into my thinking. "The crawl space is on a different level, not over the apartment. Something must be on the roof."

Mother and Felicity both stopped and stared at me.

"A coyote?" Mother dropped her roller into the pan.

"A bear?" Fel's eyes were wide.

"We don't have bears here," Mom said.

"Thank goodness!"

"At least, I don't think we do. Besides, I doubt if they crawl on roofs."

I heard thunder, but it was farther off, no longer directly overhead. "I'm going to take a look."

"We'll go with you." My mother took hold of Felicity's hand and pulled her toward the sliding glass doors.

Fel's face had a look of trepidation. "You're sure there aren't any bears?"

Mom nodded.

I tipped my head and studied them for a moment before turning toward the glass doors. Yes, I wanted them to go with me.

Walking outside, we looked up and realized we couldn't see what might be on the roof.

I looked around and saw there was a fence I could climb on at the other side of the pool. It would give me a good view of the apartment roof and a lot of other things.

"Wait here," I said.

Climbing the fence was tricky because it was wet, dirty and slick, but I made it with only a couple of splinters to show for my efforts. I could clearly see the roof of the apartment, even with rain drops running down my face, but I had to hang on or the wind might blow me over to the other side.

I waved at Mom and Fel. "It's okay. There are a few loose shingles and that's probably what was making the noise."

Not wanting anymore splinters, I jumped off the fence. Just as I leaped I glanced to the side of the apartment and I could have sworn I saw the back of a blonde head. It disappeared around the corner of the house before I could be sure my imagination wasn't playing games with me.

There were huge puddles everywhere and I landed in a deep one, soaking myself, my clothes and my shoes.

My mother and friend began to laugh from where they were standing, under an overhang.

Ignoring them, I ran along the side of the house and out to the front yard. It was pouring rain again and the wind blew my hair in my eyes. I came as close as I'd ever come to growling. I was, needless to say, frustrated. I pushed my hair back and looked around, but didn't see a woman with long, blonde hair.

I ran to the back and discovered my mother and Fel had gone back into the house. While they went to work, I ran upstairs to find dry clothing. I was shivering between the rain and the wind, and an unheated house.

When I returned to the apartment kitchen, they'd begun painting again. Without a word, I picked up my brush and began working on the places they couldn't reach.

After a moment, I asked, "What were you two laughing at a while ago?"

Felicity fought a smile. I could see her struggling. She didn't say anything.

On the other hand, my mother seemed delighted to answer me. "It seems that you just can't stay dry the past few days. From a bucket of dirty water to rain and mud puddles, you're doomed to be wet while you're here."

"I see." I waited a moment before walking outside.

I could hear the two of them mumbling, apparently wondering what I was doing. I was picking up an old bucket that had quite a bit of rain water in it. I carried it inside.

"Uh oh." Felicity backed away from me.

"Yep," I said.

"Young lady, you keep that water away from all this fresh paint." My mother sounded somewhat panicky.

"Then move," I said.

Not knowing what else to do, they did.

I scooped up a handful of water and threw it at Felicity. Even though she had a good idea about what I was going to do, she sucked in her breath in surprise.

Mom took a couple of steps away from me. "Sandra..."

I scooped up more water and threw it at her before setting down the bucket and picking up my paint brush. I should have known better and taken the bucket back outside before I began painting corners.

"Noooo," I squeaked when someone dumped water down the back of my shirt.

Turning around I found Mom and Fel standing behind me, each one holding onto the sides of the bucket full of rain water.

"Never try to get even, Sandra. I'll always be right there to do the same." My mother set the bucket on the kitchen floor.

I bit my tongue before I started to laugh. "You two are crazier than I am."

The bucket belonged outside, and that's where I deposited it before going back to the painting.

"By the way, I meant to ask you," Felicity said. "Why

did you run off, down the side of the house?"

"Interesting story," I replied.

"Let's hear it," my mother said.

Chapter Twenty

"I know you both think I have an overactive imagination, but I swear I saw someone with long blonde hair at the side of the house, walking in the rain. I don't know if she could have been on the roof or not and I don't know how she would have climbed up there. I guess that would be kind of silly. Why would she climb up on the roof?" I was trying to work things out in my mind while I spoke. I wasn't having much luck.

My mother looked skeptical, but she didn't say anything while she went back to painting.

Felicity appeared thoughtful.

Did either one believe me?

Mom set her roller down and turned to face at me. "You realize, of course, that no one else has seen the blonde?"

"Well, sure, but – "

"And I haven't seen Bubba take out after her."

"He wasn't around when I saw her. I asked Pete to take him to the stable while they worked. Besides, no one else has been watching for her. Although I have to admit, I haven't really been keeping an eye out for her. She just turns up, uninvited, when I least expect it."

"I want to see this woman so I can describe her to Tyler and Racheal. Maybe she's a nosey neighbor." Mother picked up her roller again

Surprisingly, we were almost done working on the small kitchen.

I painted some of the window trim in the kitchen with a different type of paint that came in a smaller can. "I noticed something interesting about the woman."

"What was that?" Felicity turned on the water faucet and confirmed we now had running water in the kitchen.

"Although it was pouring rain, the woman's hair didn't look wet. I didn't notice her clothing because I was trying to get a look at her face. I'd really like to see what she looks like."

"Okay, I think we should tell the men about this woman," my mother said. "It could be a neighbor who's wearing a wig or something. Maybe she's a snoop and doesn't want to be recognized. I think our husbands should keep an eye open for her, too."

I sighed happily over her reference to *our husbands*. Felicity grinned. I briefly wondered when we'd get to spend more time with them.

Shaking my head, I tried to bring my thoughts back on track. "You're probably right, but what does this woman have to do with anything? *That's* what we need to figure out." I dipped the brush in the paint can once more. "I have a suspicion someone is trying to scare us, but I can't understand why."

"I can't imagine why anyone would want Frank and me to leave this house. That just doesn't make any sense. Scare us? I don't think so."

"Think about it, Mother. You're expecting to see a body behind every little nook or cranny, or under a cement slab in the yard. I'm surprised *you're* not the one seeing the blonde."

"Yes, sweetie, but I'm mostly joking when I mention finding a dead body. Although, the block wall in the basement has me wondering."

I had no reply for her, so I finished the trim and washed my paint brush. "Let's go see what the men are up to before we figure out which room we're going to paint next. We can mention the blonde, too."

My mother nodded. "Let's do the walk-in pantry when we come back." She turned and entered the small room. "We can start bringing food in and store it in here. I want to paint it off-white so it doesn't seem so dark."

The rain had let up, at least for the moment, but the sky was still charcoal gray and the wind was howling. We headed for the stable without wasting time.

I kept my eyes open and my head flung from side to side while I watched for the mysterious blonde.

My mother *tsked* at me. "Let it go for now, Sandi. If she wants to be seen, she'll make *sure* one of us sees her."

Felicity nodded. "I think your mom is right. I honestly don't believe this woman is spying on us. I think she wants one of us to see her. Well, in all honesty, I think she wants *you* to see her." She shrugged her shoulders as though she didn't understand the whole situation.

I shrugged back. I didn't get it either. Instead of watching for the blonde, I changed the direction of my gaze and started searching for snakes. A gust of wind gave me a shiver. Snakes probably wouldn't be out in the wind and rain, right?

Entering the stable, we saw Stanley sweeping several years' worth of clutter out the back door. Frank and Pete were measuring, presumably for stalls that needed installing.

"Hiya," I said.

Pete waved at me and watched me intently for a moment before walking over to give me a kiss. He grinned and spoke softly. "Can't wait for the honeymoon, babe."

"You mean this isn't it?" I waited for one of his bear hugs after my little joke, but it didn't come. Instead, he turned and walked back to help Frank.

"The plumber suggested we turn on the faucets and let the water run for a while before we use it," he said over his shoulder. "He's got to do a few more things, but it's useable. I mean, we all took showers. The electrician said the apartment has electricity and he'll take care of the rest of the house when he comes back. Of course, he got the hot water heater working."

"When is he coming back?" my mother asked.

"Tomorrow, weather permitting."

"I have a feeling it's going to be chilly in the house tonight. Can we use the fireplaces?"

Frank, Pete and Stanley looked at each other.

"We talked about that earlier," Frank said. "We're going to clean them out this afternoon so they can be used. Stan knows how to do it."

"Stan?" I asked. How would he know how to clean a chimney and take care of a flue?

As if reading my mind, Stanley said, "When I was growing up, I used to take care of the fireplace at my mother's house. Obviously, she couldn't do it."

I nodded, letting it go.

My mother nodded and held up her hand, calling for everyone's attention. "We finished painting the apartment kitchen and we're doing the pantry next." She glanced at her watch. "I'll fix lunch in about half an hour."

Frank pulled out the end of the tape measure and handed it to Pete. He pointed to a spot on the floor while backing toward the wall.

Pete headed for the spot Frank had indicated.

"What's for lunch?" Frank asked.

"How about ham sandwiches? Or we could have roast beef. I'll fix a few of each." She tapped her watch. "We can't eat outside, so meet us downstairs in the apartment. We'll eat there. Bring chairs."

"I'm certainly hungry," Stanley said. "We've carried out trash all morning and made a pile outside the door. It's going to be difficult to load it into a trash bin because it's all going to be soggy." He turned to Felicity. "So what's new, peaches?"

"Nothing. We've just been painting. I had to use a paint roller with a long handle." She crinkled her nose at him. "There are problems with being so short sometimes."

"Where's Bubba?" I asked.

Hearing his name, he made a soft woofing sound from the corner. Where had he been when I needed him?

Felicity grinned and quickly glanced at me before answering Stanley. "You asked what's new, sweetness. Wait until we tell you about the mysterious blonde Sandi's been seeing. It's only been a couple of times, but it's strange. We need your help."

"It's not a ghost," I said quickly.

"Who said it was?" Pete let go of the tape measure and it *zipped* as it automatically rewound.

Chapter Twenty-one

I explained my blonde sightings to the men and waited for comments.

Frank shrugged. "Maybe it's a nosey neighbor."

Stanley tipped his head and looked thoughtful. He didn't comment.

Pete grinned at me. "Reminds me of the time you thought Humphrey Bogart was following you." He scratched his chin. "Although, I have to admit, there was a remarkable resemblance between the man following you and the actor."

"All I'm asking is that you keep your eyes open for this woman. I want to know who she is and why she's watching us."

"Us?" Felicity shook her head. "It seems to me that you're the only one she's watching."

I found myself on the defensive. "She could be watching the rest of you and you just didn't see her."

Instead of arguing the point, Felicity said, "We'll keep our eyes open for her. Frank's probably right. It's most likely a neighbor."

I heard thunder off in the distance and glanced outside.

It was beginning to rain again and I had a feeling more of the storm was moving in. Another clap of thunder made me believe I was right.

"Hurry up," my mother said. "We need to get back to the house and back to work." She ran out the door.

We followed, along with Bubba.

We ran to the garage and headed for the Arizona room. Mother showed us which cans of paint she needed and we carried everything back to the apartment. After opening cans and stirring the paint, we began working on the walk-in pantry.

Mother and Fel painted the walls while I worked on the shelving. "I think it's safe to paint the baseboards in here," I said. "They're in decent condition."

Bubba was way too interested in what we were doing.

Mom looked at me. "There isn't really room for all three of us, along with that dopey dog. Why don't you relax while we paint the walls? When we're done, we'll relax while you paint the shelves. And take Bubba with you."

"Works for me," I said. "I think I'll go explore the house. Just yell upstairs when you're ready for me to come back."

Mom nodded and I took off with Bubba, heading upstairs. There was so much to explore in the house. There were so many nooks and crannies that I was sure we'd missed plenty of things. I figured I'd start in the basement and work my way up.

"Sit and stay." I held my hand out to the dog, palm facing him.

He sat, but just barely. He wanted to explore, too.

Taking a flashlight, I took the stairs down to the basement and approached the stained wall that had my mother so concerned. I knew Frank wouldn't want to tear down any blocks to find out what was behind them, so I took a different approach.

I shined the flashlight high and low, considering what might have caused the stains. Leaning forward, I sniffed the wall. If anyone had seen me, they would have thought I was nuts. But if they were anything other than water stains, there might have been an odor, even after all this time. There wasn't.

I ran my hand down the blocks. Nothing felt out of the ordinary. My curiosity got the best of me and I began knocking on blocks to see if there was a difference in the sound. Maybe there was a hollow spot behind them. There wasn't.

Unable to resist the sound of the knocking, Bubba ran downstairs.

Momentarily distracted, I scratched his head, but I had a purpose for being in the basement.

Keeping track of where the block wall was, I returned to the main floor to see what was overhead.

"Got ya," I said, finally figuring out at least part of the mystery. The wall was directly under the fireplaces in the living room and family room. "They must have used the block wall as a support for the fireplaces. I'll bet something happened with a fire and they threw water on it. The water found its way down to the basement. That's it."

Bubba nudged my leg.

"And stop talking to yourself," I said to myself.

"Yeah, stop doing that."

I whirled around to find Pete standing in the kitchen. He walked over and gave me the big bear hug I'd been waiting for. I melted in his arms.

Bubba wandered off, apparently bored with us.

"I knew if anyone could figure out the block wall, it would be you," he said. "Well, Frank or I could have figured it out, too, but we haven't had time to think about it."

Opening my mouth to answer him, he put his index finger against my lips to stop me. I closed my mouth and just enjoyed the time I spent in his arms.

He leaned down and kissed me. "We need some alone time."

"We do." I initiated the next kiss.

"Pete! We need you out at the stables." Frank's voice could be heard at the back door to the kitchen, inside the Arizona room.

Pete sighed and gave me one last hug, accompanied by a brief kiss.

"*Coming*," he yelled.

I stepped away from the loud voice.

He winked at me. "Later."

He headed for the Arizona room and I tramped back downstairs to the apartment, ready to share my conclusions with my mother. She and Felicity were sitting on the floor, chatting.

"Oh, there you are, Sandi." Mom stood and turned to me. "We're done, so you can finish those shelves now. It didn't take us very long with the rollers, and we've already touched up the corners with the regular paint brush. It's a good thing we brought in a ladder from the garage."

"I thought you'd like to know what I found," I said, and I explained about the block wall.

"Okay, I guess that makes sense. Although," she said thoughtfully and slowly, "if you're building a fire in a fireplace, I would think there wouldn't be any openings where the water could have run through to the basement."

"I'll tell you what," I said. "Later, when we've got the time, we'll pour some water down the back wall of the fireplace and see what happens."

"That's a great idea. I knew I could count on my private eye daughter." She grinned at me with pride showing on her face. "And if there is some kind of an opening there, we'll have to close it up."

It wasn't that big of a deal. If I was able, I'd *usually* test conclusions as I came to them. However, she made me feel pretty good.

After I finished the shelving we decided to get started on the bedroom Felicity and Stanley were staying in. We could open the windows to air out the room so it would be ready for them later in the evening.

The first thing I did was open the window, but I immediately closed it again. The rain was torrential. It was raining so hard it was difficult to see more than a couple of feet into the yard.

While we painted, we heard the boys come inside and stopped for a few minutes to go upstairs to see what they were up to.

"Go to the garage and look outside," Frank said. "You're not going to believe what's going on out there."

The three of us turned and walked through the Arizona room to see what he was talking about. The men followed us. I glanced back at them and noticed their legs were soaking wet, almost to their knees. Their shoes were gone so they must have taken them off because of the mud.

Pete saw me looking and his face was grim.

It was raining so hard that the yard between the house and the stable looked like a river. What I'd seen out the apartment window was nothing compared to this. It was a good thing the house and other buildings were on a slightly higher level than the yard, or dirt driveway, or flooding would be a problem.

My mother turned to Frank. "What are we going to do?"

"When the water runs off and things begin to dry we'll dig a trench. I'll figure something out from there.

"Here's the other thing, Livvie. We'd better sleep inside tonight, too, because I'm concerned about the stability of the motorhome. I'd hate to have it tip over while we're inside."

My mother sighed and put her hand on his arm.

"You're probably right, honey."

"We'll bring some food in from the motorhome along with Pete's cook stove. I'll bring some clothes, too. Now we're going to work on the fireplaces."

We women returned to the apartment and began painting again.

"At least we have electricity and water in the apartment. There's no fireplace, but we'll all be upstairs anyway."

"Think of it as a coed sleepover," I said. "Does the heater work yet?

"I don't know if it works or not," Mom said. "It hasn't been used in years. I don't think we should take a chance. The electrician needs to look at it."

She was right.

Three couples and two fireplaces, and one fireplace might have an opening down to the basement. It might be cozy, but it sure wouldn't be romantic. And it might not be safe.

"We have a couple of space heaters in the garage." Mother looked over her shoulder at us. "I guess I should have brought them in earlier, but who knew it was going to be so cold? Felicity and Stan can use them in the apartment."

I rolled my eyes at her.

"We'll stay upstairs with you," Felicity said.

"We don't have electricity upstairs yet," I said. "You'll only have the fireplace for heat."

"That's fine," she replied. "It'll be cozier and more romantic."

"Yep. Cozier and more romantic while you sleep on the floor." I don't think my sarcasm was lost on her.

~ * ~

By the end of the day we were all exhausted. I figured I'd lost at least a couple of pounds with all the work I'd been doing – with any luck.

The fireplaces and flues were cleaned and the boys brought in some wood Frank had stacked in the garage. Good thing it was such a large garage. Three cars could have easily fit inside. I found some foil and lined the back of the fireplaces, making sure sparks wouldn't fall through to the basement.

I wondered if the blonde would show up with all of us in the house.

We'd be too busy staying warm and watching for sparks to worry about her, anyway.

Chapter Twenty-two

𝔉rank proudly put some fireplace screens he'd saved from his original home in Chicago in front of both fireplaces. They weren't really big enough for these fireplaces, but they were close enough.

My mother had moved from California to Chicago to live near her sister, Martha, for a few years before getting married and moving to Arizona with Frank. She met him in Illinois and they hit it off after knowing each other for a year or two. He'd been her financial advisor.

Time to think about dinner. We heated canned stew and had bread and butter with it for dinner.

"Next time you eat stew here it'll be homemade," my mother said, taking the last bite of her food.

No one replied, but we all nodded.

Bubba ate his kibble and settled near the fireplace.

Felicity and Stanley brought their sleeping bags upstairs and settled into the family room.

Since there was nothing but block and cement in the basement, under the fireplaces, Frank didn't think the fireplaces would be an issue.

I hoped he was right.

It wasn't east coast type cold, but the storm and wind had really cooled things down. And it may not have been a romantic evening, but it was definitely cozy in front of the fire.

Thankfully, the blonde never showed up. On the other side of the coin, before I went to sleep I found myself wishing someone else had seen her.

~ * ~

I awoke to the smell of coffee. Looking around I saw that my mother and Frank were gone. I figured the aroma must be floating up the stairs from the kitchen in the apartment.

Bubba was gone, too. One of them must have taken him outside to do his business.

I reached over and shook Pete's shoulder. "Time to get up, sweetie."

"But it's still dark outside."

"It might just be more clouds. Besides, I smell coffee."

He propped himself up and sniffed the air. "Your parents sure get up early."

"Normally, so do we. There's always something for us gutsy ol' private eyes to do, and unfortunately it's often in the morning."

"Yeah." He stood up and, after pulling on his jeans, headed for the stairs and the apartment. I felt bad watching him because he was limping. The work he was doing seemed to be bothering his leg more than I realized. We'd have to have a serious talk about it.

I peeked around the corner and saw that Felicity and Stanley were still sound asleep, so I pulled on my jeans and a sweatshirt and followed Pete's lead, running my fingers through my hair while I climbed the stairs.

By the time I reached the kitchen downstairs, the sun had come out. I opened the sliding glass doors and stepped outside, taking a deep breath. Glancing up at the sky I saw the last of the clouds drifting away. The sun was bright, and it was warming me already.

I thought I remembered my mother saying the property was about thirty-five acres in size, or maybe it was forty acres. As a P.I., I should remember details. However, I was on vacation, sort of, and I didn't care about details at the moment. I walked back to the kitchen and poured myself a cup of coffee.

Bubba pranced around me, but I knew he wasn't begging for coffee. Yeah, like he'd ever want that.

"I wonder what the roads are like today. I mean, it's a dirt road that leads back here. I'll bet it's a mess," I said.

"Good morning, to you, too." My mother smiled in my direction.

I smiled back and gave her a hug. "Sorry. Good morning." I took my mother, Frank and Pete in with a sweeping gaze.

Bubba looked up at me as though he thought I could read his mind.

"I know, pal, you're ready for breakfast." I filled his bowl from a bag of dog food Pete had moved from the garage to the walk-in pantry the night before.

"What's on the agenda for today?" Pete took a sip of hot coffee. "Digging a trench for rainwater runoff?"

Frank set his coffee mug on the sink and stretched before replying. "No, it's too muddy. Maybe tomorrow. Today I'm thinking we might set up my workshop so I have a place to work on things."

"Workshop?"

"Did you see that metal building just past the stables? I'm going to make that a workshop."

Pete nodded and took another swallow of coffee.

Bubba finished eating and paced around the living room of the apartment.

I ignored him and turned to my mother. "What about

moving your refrigerator and stove inside? It would make life a lot easier."

"We can bring the refrigerator in, but we're going to have to buy another stove, both for down here and for upstairs. Ours is a gas range and it's all electric out here. There aren't any gas lines."

"Makes sense to me."

Pete and Frank were listening.

"Okay, we'll bring the refrigerator in this morning before we start on anything else." Frank was being very cooperative. I liked that in a man.

Walking back to the sliding glass doors, I glanced around the property. "The rain must have made some weeds come up. I can see dark colors across the back of the property."

Frank and Bubba joined me at the window. "You could be right, but I'd swear the weeds are moving. Must be the wind."

"Is it my imagination or does Bubba seem a little antsy this morning?" Pete asked.

"I noticed the same thing." I patted the dog's head, but he pulled away from me and ran upstairs.

"Good morning," Felicity said, descending the stairs. "Stan and I smelled the coffee."

Mother grabbed two mugs and filled them for her and Stanley.

His hair, as thin as it was, was standing on end. He saw us studying it, grinned and ran his hands through it. "A shower will help."

The men went outside to make sure the motorhome was still standing while I fixed scrambled eggs and bacon on the small camp stove which I'd outside the sliding glass doors. It turned out to be easier to use than I'd expected.

I glanced out across the property and it seemed like the weeds were closer. I figured it was the angle of sight from where I was standing.

The men came back and we ate breakfast before scattering to take showers before starting our day. Stanley and Felicity took the first shift while I cleaned up the breakfast mess which consisted of paper plates and plastic silverware. My mother brought me some dish soap and I washed out the coffee mugs.

She stood in front of the sink and watched out the window. "What is that black stuff? I'd swear it's closer than it was. I mean, there's not a lot of it, but there's enough to know it wasn't there yesterday."

"I don't know what it is. Let's go take a look after I take my shower." I laughed. "At least we know it's not snakes. They wouldn't look like that. They'd fit in more with the desert terrain."

"No, not snakes."

Fel and Stan came out looking refreshed.

"My turn," I said. "After I take out the trash." I picked up a plastic bag.

Stanley took it out of my hands. "I'll take that out for you."

"Thanks."

"Where are Frank and Pete?" he asked.

"They're out looking at Frank's future workshop," Mother replied. "I think the three of you are going to work on that today. I know Frank wanted to go into town and get some supplies for the stable, but the roads are too muddy. Maybe he can do that tomorrow."

He set the trash bag down on the floor. "I'm going to put on some boots I brought with me before I take the bag out. Then I'm going to take a look at the workshop."

Felicity stood at the sliding glass doors, watching. Her face looked like she was a hundred miles away.

"Penny for your thoughts," Stanley said.

"I was just wondering what that dark stuff is out there.

I feel like I'm standing in the middle of a sci-fi movie. It seems like it's moving."

Stanley followed her gaze. "I'll take a walk outside and look around after I take care of a couple of things."

"At least we can tell you it's not snakes," my mother said. "They'd blend in with the scenery, and I doubt they'd be so dark."

Chapter Twenty-Three

*P*ete returned to the house, stopping to talk to my mother. "Frank said he's going to take his shower in the motorhome. He asked if I'd tell you to come on out there."

She nodded and headed to the motorhome.

Bubba came flying down the stairs and whined at me. I knew he didn't need to go outside to do his doggy business. This was something different. Contrary to what some people think, dogs can often express their feelings through a look. Bubba looked frantic. I narrowed my eyes at him trying to figure out what was going on.

He turned to Pete and whined at him.

"What's up with you this morning, you mangy mutt?"

Bubba ran back up the stairs.

"Maybe he saw the blonde."

"Very funny," I said. "I know there's something wrong with him, but I can't read his mind, so let's take our showers and we can get to work. I'm sure he'll calm down. We're getting a late start this morning."

Pete headed for the bathroom and a shower while I climbed the stairs to find fresh, clean clothes.

Carrying them back to the apartment, I took Pete's clothes to the bathroom and left them on the sink. "Leave enough hot water for me," I said.

"Sure."

Remembering I'd left my brush and comb upstairs, I headed back to our room, passing Stanley on the stairs.

"I'm going to take the trash out now and investigate the black stuff."

"Okay. It's not solid black, and it's probably the wind blowing weeds, but be careful."

"I will."

"Where's Felicity?" I asked.

"She went to the Arizona room to see what other colors your mother picked out for the house."

I nodded and continued upstairs.

Bubba was pacing again. All of a sudden the hair on his back did a salute and his back hunched. I know Bubba well, and I knew something was wrong – very wrong.

"Bubba? What's going on? You're kind of scaring me."

He growled.

That's when I heard a woman scream. My mind's eye saw someone with long blonde hair flailing around in terror. The sound seemed to be coming from the direction of the apartment.

I ran down the stairs with Bubba right behind me. I almost ran into Pete at the bottom of the staircase and he was dressed in nothing but a towel. We glanced at each other for a moment before we heard another scream. The dog sidestepped both of us.

Bubba ran to the sliding glass doors, looked out and turned to run back up the stairs, leaving us to our own devices. Whatever he'd seen was something he didn't want to deal with, now or ever.

Pete ran to the door. "You're not going to *believe* this."

I stood behind him and looked around him, sucking in

my breath. I saw one of my worst nightmares coming true. A herd of tarantulas was invading the yard, and Stanley was frozen to the spot, his mouth open in terror. He held his arms in the air and I saw his hands shaking. I couldn't blame him. There were hundreds of tarantulas outside. Crawling, walking, moving – coming our way.

Pete peeled my hand off his arm. "Stan, get in the house and be fast about it."

"I *can't.*" He sounded pitiful and when he glanced down at his jeans I saw what had him rooted to the spot. A tarantula was climbing up his leg. He began making odd little guttural noises – Stanley, not the spider.

"Pete, do something," I said. "Please!"

"Hold on, Stan. Be right there." He ran to the bathroom and rushed back wearing jeans and shoes, but no socks. His lack of a shirt almost got my attention. Another place, another time. Not now.

The huge tarantula was moving slowly and getting closer to Stanley's waist. (Okay, huge to me, but really a baby.) My friend's face was pale and his eyes were wide with terror. His hands were still shaking, although they were clenched into fists.

"Here comes Pete," I called, feeling helpless.

"I think I'd faint but they'd get me," Stan said in a high, soft voice. He glanced at the ground where dozens of the arachnids were passing him and quickly raised his face to the sun, closing his eyes.

Pete ran outside, sidestepping the critters so he could help Stanley. Reaching over, he gently brushed the brown spider off the other man's leg. He reached down and actually touched it, and it rolled on its back, pulling its legs up in what looked like fear.

I wasn't sure who was more afraid; Stanley or the tarantula.

Stepping outside the door, I thought if Pete could walk

among them, so could I. That's when I realized they were babies; well, young. They were migrating to wherever baby tarantulas migrate. And I realized that, no, I couldn't walk among them. I stepped back into the house and closed the sliding screen door.

"Follow me," Pete said, touching Stanley's elbow, "but don't step on them. They're good for the environment."

"Aren't their bites poisonous?" Stanley asked, carefully stepping around them. Sweat ran down his temples and he waved his hand in front of his face, trying to cool himself off.

"Not these. These are called blonde tarantulas. Their bite wouldn't be any worse than a bee sting, more than likely. They generally only come out at night, looking for food. But these young ones need to move on. They could be looking for someplace to hibernate for the winter. I don't really know."

I was sure Pete was trying to distract Stanley with his nature speech.

Applause came from behind us.

I turned and saw Felicity, my mother and Frank watching intently and listening. Bubba stood behind them, cowering.

Felicity grabbed Stanley's arm and pulled him inside the house before making him turn in a circle to make sure no more critters came in with him.

"Where did you learn so much about tarantulas?" Frank asked.

"Since we were coming out here, I did some research on the Internet. I learned a lot of things, but I had no idea they might actually come in handy."

Stanley peeked out the door before turning to us. "This is the *scariest* house I've ever been in. First Sandi sees the blonde skulking around, even though the rest of us never laid eyes on her. Then Sandi and her mother keep trying to frighten each other, which is a little frightening in itself. Now the tarantulas. How much scarier can it be? Oh, and I almost forgot about the rattlesnake. Good grief, people, what are we going to *do?*" His voice was still high-pitched but a little less shaky.

"You forgot about the hidden staircase, lover," Felicity said.

He nodded. "There's that, too."

Looking him in the eyes, I said, "Honestly, Stan, the tarantulas seem to be on the move. It doesn't look like they're going to stick around. And to be honest, I would have been just as frightened as you were." The thought made a shiver run down my back.

Frank excused himself and ran up the stairs, only to return in a few minutes. "I watched out the front window. Those little buggers are headed across the road and out into the vacant fields looking for new homes. Just give it a little time and they'll be gone. Well, most of them. If you see any sticking around, don't kill them. They'll help Livvie and me keep the bug count down."

"They will?" my mother asked. "Are you saying that bugs mean fine dining to them?"

Frank nodded and put his arm around my mother's shoulders. "We're in the country now, Livvie. You're going to have to get used to some of these things."

She looked skeptical. "We're in the country, but the country we're in is in the *desert.*" She sighed heavily, a la Sandi. "I never thought I'd have to get used to snakes and tarantulas, but I guess you gotta do what ya gotta do."

Stanley looked even more skeptical than my mother. "I think I'll just work in the house for a while. What can I do to help?"

"While you're all talking about this, I'm going get dressed. At least I finished my shower before Stan screamed like a girl." Pete left us, returning to the bathroom.

Stanley watched his retreating back, smiling. It wasn't the first time he'd ever screamed in that high-pitched voice.

Thankfully he was good-natured and didn't mind teasing from his friend.

"Did you leave enough hot water for me," I called after him.

He didn't reply.

Ignoring Pete and me, my mother gave Stanley a hug. "You can help us paint today. By tomorrow I think the hairy little things will be gone." She paused and glanced out the window again. "They are kind of cute in an ugly sort of way."

Stanley followed her gaze and frowned.

Felicity smiled at him. "Everything will be okay, honey bun."

I'd never be able to explain it, but I had this unbelievable desire to go outside and make friends with one of the "hairy little things".

I fought the urge.

Chapter Twenty-Four

After my shower I decided to take a quick look outside, through the front window on the main level.

The tarantulas seemed in a hurry to get away from us as much as we wanted them gone. It took some time since there were so many. Frank headed out to his workshop. I saw him bend over in the doorway and carefully pick up a spider, setting it outside. Pete watched him and they talked.

I also saw Tyler's vehicle driving down the road very slowly. It was pretty muddy, both the truck and the road. The two brothers and their wives piled out of the truck and turned to look at the llama ranch. I needed to start thinking of it as a bed and breakfast instead of a working ranch of any type. Waving from the window, I wondered if they saw me. They didn't wave back, so probably not. I could see them watching the spiders cross the road. It didn't look like any of them flinched, but I was far away with a limited view.

I glanced left and right, looking for a blonde head, just in case. Nothing. A mere mortal would have been jumpier because of the events of the past few days, but I'm a private eye. I don't scare as easily as the average woman. I chuckled to myself and turned from the window.

"Whatcha doin'?" my mother asked.

I jumped about a foot and my heart pounded. "Mother, if you keep sneaking up on me, I'll – "

"I didn't sneak up on you. You were so busy watching the neighbors that you didn't hear me." The grin on her face told me I was right; she'd tippy-toed into the living room, trying to scare me.

So much for nerves of steel, I thought.

"Do you believe me?" she asked.

"No. And I'm telling you here and now, I hope you've got a good, strong heart because I'll have you shivering in your shoes. Soon."

She raised her eyebrows and tried to look innocent. "Oh? You think you can frighten me? Give it your best shot." Her words belied her expression. She turned and walked away, laughing to herself.

This was a side of my mother I'd never seen before, a side that might mean she was a bit eccentric. She was having fun trying to frighten me. She was playing with me, and probably just waiting for me to try to scare her back. I'd have to plan carefully… Plan what? How to put my mother in an early grave? No, nothing like that.

I walked out of the living room and into the family room realizing the house had given her a mission which was to have a good time while we worked so hard. I'd just have to take her up on her quest to make life interesting.

After my father passed away we'd both been so busy trying to make a life for ourselves that we never had time for fun. The time had finally arrived to let go and enjoy each other. I smiled, ready to take her up on her challenge. It would all be in the timing.

I joined our small group in the apartment. Stanley and Felicity decided they could paint the bedroom without our help, while my mother and I painted things like the bathroom, linen closet and hallway.

"We make quite a team," I said. "Look how much we're accomplishing."

Mother glanced over her shoulder at me. "Sandi, have I ever told you I wouldn't trade you for anyone else in the whole wide world?"

My grin was huge and wouldn't go away. "Nor I you, Mom."

Felicity stuck her head out of the bedroom. "I love you both." And she disappeared again.

"You can be my second daughter," my mother called out.

Felicity had been adopted as a baby and had no idea who her real parents were. Unfortunately, her adoptive parents had passed away years before their time should have been over. She considered us her family now, and we returned the feeling.

Something must have set me off because I was spending too much time thinking about the past; my father, Felicity's background, and whatever wanted to interrupt my normal thoughts.

"A penny for your thoughts," Mother said after a few too many quiet moments.

"For some reason I'm thinking about what we've all been through. Did I ever tell you that Stanley's mother was a fortuneteller in a circus for most of her life? He had a strange childhood. I don't think he ever knew his father. I hope to meet his mother someday."

"I'd like to meet her, too. I'll bet she's a hoot."

"Hoot? When did you start using words like that?"

Mom shrugged her shoulders. "Maybe I've spent too much time around older people lately. Frank and I have been volunteering at the local senior center. Did you know they eat desert before they eat their lunch?"

"Why?" I asked. "I don't get it."

"One day I asked one of the elderly men why they do that and he said because at their age they didn't know if they'd still be around for desert if they ate it last."

Her story made me laugh. I couldn't help but wonder what her reply might have been.

Stanley stuck his head around the doorframe. "Sweetums told me what you two were talking about. We both love you. Just thought you'd like to know."

His head disappeared before we could respond.

What had started out as a typical day was turning into something different, and maybe a little special. I couldn't help but wonder what might happen next. On the other hand, with the blonde around maybe I didn't want to know. I shook my head and continued painting.

We were working on the hallway when Mom glanced at her watch. "I think we'd better start thinking about lunch."

"Why don't you whip something up and I'll keep painting?"

"Okay. I'll call everyone when lunch is ready."

She carried her paint brush to the sink and cleaned it before washing her hands.

While she did that, Pete and Frank came into the apartment bearing a refrigerator on a dolly. No one spoke a word while they got it hooked up and started it cooling.

Without a word they left, returning with a dining set and chairs.

Frank looked from the last chair to my mother. "I know we can't really set things up yet, but until the company comes out to put in new tile, we'll use this. We can't keep eating off of our laps, and when the weather is bad we can't eat at the barbeque table outside."

My mother set down the knife she was spreading mayonnaise with and gave her husband a hug and a kiss before finishing the sandwiches.

Pete watched them with interest before turning to smile

at me. I knew that he knew exactly what they were feeling. I smiled back, knowing I'd be on the receiving end of a hug, too.

"Come on for lunch everyone," my mother called out. "Felicity? Stanley? Can you hear me?"

"Yes," Fel replied.

She and Stanley walked out of the bedroom looking like someone had thrown paint at them.

"I think maybe enough spiders are gone that Stan can start helping the men," she said, taking a paper towel and trying to wipe paint off of her face.

"Oh, you." Stanley washed his hands in the sink.

After the sandwiches disappeared, the men, including Stanley, left to work on Frank's workshop. I could hear their voices disappear into the distance.

We cleared away the lunch trash and my mother picked up the dish soap. There weren't that many utensils to wash.

I glanced at my mother and Felicity. "You two go ahead and finish what you were doing and I'll wash up the dishes. Okay?"

"Trying to get out of painting?" my mother asked.

"Yes."

They returned to their jobs while I washed paint out of the sink and filled it with soapy water.

I was whistling to myself when I glanced out the window and saw the back of a blonde head on a woman standing near the swimming pool.

"Uh oh."

I grabbed a paper towel and dried my hands while I ran outside.

Chapter Twenty-Five

She was gone! In the time it took me to run from the sink past the breakfast bar and out the sliding glass doors, Blondie had disappeared. There were still a few tarantulas, but no blonde.

Would I ever find out who she was and what she wanted?

Tarantulas? The *ick* factor reared its ugly head.

"Sandi? What are you doing out there with all the creepy critters?" My mother stood at the sliding glass door watching me.

"She was here again."

She knew exactly who I meant. "You know, sweetie, if you were anyone else I'd begin to wonder if your imagination was working overtime. However, you're my daughter and I know better."

"Was that your way of saying if it was anyone else you'd think they'd mentally jumped off a cliff? Gone around the bend? Lost their marbles?"

Mother laughed. "Yes, that's about the gist of it, but in your case I have a feeling this is really happening. I don't get it, but you're for real and so is your blonde."

"She's not my blonde, but thank you, Mom. You have no idea how much I appreciate your confidence in me."

"I'm confident you'll figure this out before you leave for your honeymoon. Right?"

"I sure hope so."

"With no furniture, voices echo in here," Felicity said, walking out of the bedroom. "I couldn't help but hear your conversation. I have confidence in you, too, and I'd be more than happy to help you figure out what's going on. In all honesty, I don't believe in ghosts either."

Before we could discuss the situation, a voice travelled down the stairs. "Hello, are you down there?" It was Tyler.

"Come on down. We're here," my mother replied.

We heard his footsteps on the short flight of stairs before he stepped into the apartment. "I didn't just walk in," he said apologetically. "Frank said to come on inside when I told him I wanted to talk to you."

"That's okay," Mom said. "Until we get moved in, don't worry about just walking in. After we move in you can start knocking. And when we become a B&B, you can walk in without knocking most of the time." She grinned.

"Thanks, but I'll knock from now on. Anyway, I want to talk to all of you for a minute. I just heard from Zetta Ellison. I told her you were going to go over to talk to her and she said to let you know she's waiting."

"Hmm. We need a break anyway," I said. "Why don't we go talk to her right now?" I looked from my mother to Felicity and they both nodded.

Turning to Tyler, I asked, "Which house does she live in?"

"She and Bill live across the road in the green mobile home. Living out here means they don't have company often, so they're anxious to meet you all. You in particular, Livvie. They want to know who their new neighbor is."

"As soon as we clean up a little, we'll head over there." My mother held out her paint-spattered hands.

Taking note of my clean hands, he said, "Sandi, can I talk to you about my writing for a few minutes? Maybe while the others are washing up?"

"Sure. Let's go upstairs."

Tyler asked a few questions about what it was really like to be a private investigator.

"Overall? Kind of humdrum," I said. "We spend plenty of time watching people on behalf of insurance companies and we do a lot of research. As a writer I guess you'd say I go on stakeouts. I call it surveillance. Just about the time we're comfortable, some bigger case comes along and we fall all over ourselves trying to find information, or clues. We're sometimes very protective of clients, too."

"Have you ever been involved in solving a murder?" he asked.

I almost laughed. Me, the one Rick Mason calls a body magnet? "Yes."

"Would you elaborate?"

I gave him the basics about a few cases, leaving out all the gory details. He could use his imagination if he wanted to beef up his mysteries.

"Do you feel you're involved in a mystery here at the llama ranch?"

I thought for a moment. "In a way, yes. Let me ask *you* a question. Has there ever been anyone around here who had long, blonde hair? Your wife mentioned that the women don't try to keep their hair blonde because the sun just bleaches it out here in the desert."

He tipped his head, looking at me with curiosity. "Why do you ask?"

"To be honest, because I keep seeing a woman with long, blonde hair in the oddest places. I never have the opportunity to see her face though. And no one else has seen her."

"I only remember one blonde who lived out here. I mean, really, there aren't that many homes this far out of town. I remember all the neighbors. Some not so well, but I remember them all to one degree or another." He sat quietly for a moment, looking introspective.

"Tyler? Who was it?" I asked. "Who do you remember?"

"Francine."

"Francine? A neighbor?"

"No. Francine Stockholm. She was Harry's wife and she died when I was quite young. Or maybe I hadn't even been born yet. I don't really remember her except for the hair color. My parents have pictures of her in a photo album. Maybe that's where I remember her from, because I can't recall actually seeing her."

"Do you know anything about her that might have some bearing on seeing a blonde? Well, never mind. That's silly. She's been dead for many years."

He grinned. "You realize that most people out here believe this house is haunted, don't you?"

Mentally, I squirmed. "I don't believe in ghosts."

"Ah."

"Why would she be showing herself to me and no one else? Answer that."

"Where have you seen her?"

I thought for a moment. "When we first pulled up to the house I thought I saw someone watching us out of one of the bedroom windows. When I was cleaning I saw a blonde watching me through the window. She was outside the house during yesterday's storm." I sighed. "And, lastly, I saw her standing by the pool today."

"But you don't believe in ghosts." It wasn't a question. He was mimicking what I'd said.

"No." *At least, I don't think I do*, I thought to myself.

His grin grew larger and he chuckled. "I don't either, but you never know about these things. Now let me ask you a few more questions about your job." He tactfully changed the subject, which I whole-heartedly appreciated.

Tyler asked questions and I told him about some of the more complicated things I do, like searching for people and questioning them in depth, and he took notes on a pad of paper he'd brought with him.

"This is great, Sandi. I'll be able to create more realistic situations and characters in future books. Would you mind if I call you with questions from time to time?"

"Of course not." I gave him my phone number.

I walked him to the front door and he stopped with his hand on the doorknob. "You said you've never seen the woman's face?"

"That's right."

"But you saw her general build."

"Yes."

"I'm going to drive in to my parents' place and I'll borrow their photo albums."

"I'd appreciate that."

He left and I headed for the stairs leading down to the apartment, but my mother and friend were already climbing up to meet me.

It was time to meet the Ellisons and ask some questions. I hoped they had some answers.

Chapter Twenty-Six

Once outside, we saw the sun was still shining brightly and things were beginning to dry out. Unfortunately, not enough. Two steps out onto the dirt road and our shoes were wet and muddy.

"Oh, well," my mother said, lifting her foot and surveying her shoe. "We can wash these off and change into something else when we get home. I think we'd better take our shoes off and leave them on the porch before we enter the Ellison's house."

Felicity nodded and I kept walking. We'd been so busy painting that we'd almost forgotten about our challenge to find out more about what happened in the llama ranch house. I wouldn't turn my nose up at a short break, either.

Glancing over my shoulder, I saw Pete step out of the workshop and watch us. He was probably wondering what we were up to.

I turned back to discover a pothole in the road, but I was too late to step around it. My mother reached for my hand, but she missed. My shoes filled with rainwater and mud.

Felicity snickered. "That could only happen to you."

That's when she found her own pothole. She tripped and fell in, only to stand up and discover she had mud covering her jeans and shirt.

"That's my Felicity," I said, laughing.

She laughed with me. "It's a good thing I'm used to these little *accidents*."

Felicity and Stanley were the two most accident-prone people I knew. They were perfect for each other because they just laughed it off or ignored what they'd done, except for offering apologies.

My mother, walking in front of us, delicately stepped around a mud puddle and *tsked* at us. "You girls should be more careful."

I glanced up and noticed an elderly man standing on a porch in front of the green mobile home. He was grinning and shaking his head. I had to assume he'd seen our antics, and he waved us over.

"Come in, come in," he said.

Mother smiled at him. "Just let us take off our shoes first."

"My wife will appreciate that."

"Your wife is Zetta?" Mother asked, balancing on one foot and taking off her left shoe.

I reached over and steadied her before following suit and taking off my own shoes.

"Yes, I'm Bill. We heard you had questions about the old llama ranch and what happened there."

"We do, but just say something if we're intruding," I said.

He shook his head, indicating we were welcome and not intruding.

After we'd taken care of the shoe situation, we followed Bill inside. Zetta was waiting for us with tea and cookies. A younger woman sat next to her.

Felicity and I stood by the door on a small area rug, trying not to drip mud on the floor.

"Ladies, come on in." Zetta waved her hand at us.

"Thank you, but we'll stay over here. We don't want to bring our muddy clothes into your house." Felicity swept her hand in front of herself, calling attention to our state of muddy dress.

"Nonsense. Believe me, this house has seen its share of mud."

I briefly studied the group. Zetta and Bill were both thin and somewhat haggard looking. Zetta had her hair pulled up in an old-fashioned bun, and Bill's hair was nothing more than a few wisps. Both seniors were of average height, and apparently Arizona's normally arid weather was the reason for their overly wrinkled faces.

The woman sitting on the couch had a passing resemblance to Zetta, although she wasn't thin, and I had a feeling she was related to the Ellisons.

Zetta stood and held out her hand. She was taller than I'd realized. "We just love having company," she said, taking my mother's hand. I noticed she didn't shake it, but simply held on to it for a moment.

"I'm delighted to start meeting some of my neighbors," my mother said, pulling her hand back. She glanced around. "Love your home. You've got some wonderful antiques here."

Zetta frowned. "We used to have more wood furniture, but the heat and dry air ruined it." Her smile returned. "Oh, well, what were we to do?"

She pointed to the woman on the couch. "This is my granddaughter, Marion. She was here when the tragedy took place across the street." Zetta frowned again and shook her head. "Heartbreaking, just heartbreaking." She sat down next to her granddaughter.

Marion appeared to be around forty-five or fifty. She was relatively average looking, although she had strikingly beautiful and intense green eyes shadowed by long, lush lashes.

"It's nice to meet all of you," my mother said, seating herself on a chair. "Do you live with your grandparents, Marion?"

She spoke and I was surprised at how deep her voice was. A smoker maybe? "Only temporarily. I was laid off from my job so I'm going to help Gram and Gramps out for a while."

"You're a good granddaughter." My mother pointed in my direction. "I'm Livvie, and this is my daughter, Sandi. Little Bit over there is Felicity." She nodded towards Fel. "I'll be totally honest with you. My daughter is a private investigator, and so is her husband. We've heard the story about what happened at the llama ranch, but not the whole story. So the men in our lives challenged us to find out what really happened. That's why we're asking questions. I realize it sounds like we're on a lark, but we're not. We all have investigative experience."

A lark? Was Mother trying to put it in terms they'd understand? That wasn't a word I'd ever heard her use before. And we *all* had investigative experience? I stifled a laugh.

"I understand," Bill said. "The murders took place a long time ago. Time passes, but curiosity doesn't. And, after all, you're moving into what some people think is a haunted house. I'd want to know the details, if I were you. We know a lot. We were the Stockholms' best friends and the police were kind enough to keep us informed when they investigated."

"Thank you for understanding." My mother crossed her legs and swung her foot – slightly. I recognized that she might be feeling a little uncomfortable. Bill had revealed more about the relationship between the two families.

"So what do you want to question us about?" Zetta asked. "Would everyone like some tea and cookies?"

We said we would, and while she poured the tea, her

granddaughter watched me intently.

Glancing first down, and then at Felicity, I noticed the mud had already dried on our clothing.

I sat forward, on the edge of my chair and spoke to Marion. "Your grandfather said the police filled you in while they investigated. Was there anything about the situation that you felt they should have investigated further?"

Marion looked from Zetta to Bill and back at me. "Yes. They seemed to think it was cut and dried, but we always felt there was more to it."

"Like what?" I asked.

Zetta patted her granddaughter's knee, looking thoughtful. "I can't explain it, other than to say it was just a feeling, but Harry became really cranky after his wife's death. I think he took it out on his daughter, to some extent, and I believe that's why she didn't come home for so long. My woman's intuition told me, at the time, that he had something to do with those two men arguing all the time. Does that make sense?"

"Yes," I said. "You were here and you saw and heard what was going on. I'm sure you know what you're talking about."

"Oh, Gram, Harry was *always* cranky. You and Gramps kept making excuses for him. He was a mean son-of-a-gun *before* Francine died. He was never nice to me. I can't believe you considered him your best friend."

Marion looked down at her lap, then back up at me through her eye lashes.

"Gram won't tell you this, but there were times I saw bruises on Francine's arms, like Harry had squeezed them. She had a black eye once, too, but she said she'd fallen down the stairs. Likely story. I don't know why my grandparents made excuses for that old buzzard."

"*Marion!* You stop that kind of talk right now." Zetta looked distressed.

Bill shook his head. "Harry was my friend, but not my closest friend. He had too many bad habits. We're a good family, with morals, and Harry didn't have much respect for anyone he knew. He cussed like a sailor and spoke down to everyone. He thought he was better than the rest of us."

So Bill was changing his story about being close friends with Harry.

Zetta looked surprised. "Bill? I never knew you felt that way."

"Francine was your best friend and I figgered it was best to keep my lips zipped. There weren't that many of us out here and you needed a good friend." He sat down and, clamping his lips together, he was quiet. He looked like there was a lot more he wanted to say, but he kept it to himself.

Zetta's eyes teared up and she glanced from Marion to Bill. "Oh, my. I shouldn't have forced Harry's friendship on my family. I had no idea he was such a bugger."

"There's more," Marion said.

An *uh oh* feeling swept over me.

Chapter Twenty-Seven

Zetta's eyes widened and she clutched a napkin tightly in her hand. "More? Oh, dear. Maybe we shouldn't have said we'd answer questions."

"It needs to come out, Gram. Trust me." Marion looked deeply into her grandmother's eyes.

My mother leaned forward, studying Zetta's face. "Maybe we should leave. I think we're upsetting your grandmother."

The old woman looked from my mother's face to her granddaughter's and shook her head. "No. You stay. If Marion says there's more, then there's more. I just don't know how things like bruises could have gotten past me."

Marion began her story. "My father was in the army. He was stationed overseas and my mother went with him, while I stayed here with Gram and Gramps. I missed them so much, and the people around here took me under their wings – except Harry. He made me feel like a dirty little leech."

Zetta sucked in her breath and coughed.

"By the way, I wasn't a kid. I was in my twenties and fresh out of college. Gram had a bout with pneumonia and I came along to help out. I hadn't found a job yet.

"Harry treated me like something you'd hide in the back of your closet. I hated him, and the only reason I didn't say something was because of Francine. I'll never understand why she didn't divorce that horrible man." Her facial muscles tightened while she talked. "He was just a nasty old... When Barbara came home to take care of the ranch, I think she might have threatened him with a nursing home. He'd never treated her well either, but I never saw bruises on her. She said something one time when I came to visit that made me think the nursing home was her plan."

"What does this have to do with the murders?" I asked.

"I believe that to get even with her, Harry started dropping little hints to Clyde about Barbara having an affair with the neighbor. What was his name?"

"Mike Hamilton," Bill said.

"Yeah, Mike. He was quite a hunk. Too bad he didn't notice *me*." She sounded bitter. "He might still be alive. They *all* might still be alive. Anyways, I overheard things from time to time. Hey! I'm a Plain Jane and people don't always notice I'm within hearing distance." She'd anticipated our thoughts, or at least what she assumed we were thinking.

"You're no Plain Jane," Zetta said.

We all shook our heads. She had a low opinion of herself. She wasn't a beauty queen, but she wasn't bad looking. Maybe her attitude was her downfall.

She ignored us. "I used to go for walks in the evening, when it was cooler. I'd hear things, and sometimes I'd see things. I heard Clyde the Killer and Mike arguing about Barbara more than once."

Clyde the Killer? She given him a title. Somehow I had a vision of Marion hunkered down by a window, eavesdropping on her neighbors.

She gave me a quick glance and I could have sworn she'd read my mind.

"Maybe I'm making something out of nothing, but I don't believe what happened was based solely on jealousy. I think there was more to it, but I don't know for sure what it could be." Her expression was one of frustration, and yet there was something else.

I had a feeling she knew more than she was telling, but I didn't think she was going to elaborate. I got the impression she thought she'd said too much already, and yet she hadn't really said anything pertinent. Harry was mean and could have been abusive, but that was just a guess. Barbara may have hated her father, or at least that's what I was taking away from Marion's comments. The issue between Mike and Clyde may not have been jealousy. The information Marion gave us was too *iffy*.

I noticed that Zetta's hands had begun to shake.

"I think we'd better get back to work," I said.

"Hmm. I think so, too." Felicity stood and smiled at Zetta.

"Thank you so much for tea and cookies," my mother said. "I'm sorry we can't stay longer. Since we're going to be neighbors, next time I come over we won't even talk about the Stockholms. We'll talk about something more pleasant."

"Good idea," Bill said, standing and approaching us.

When we turned to leave, I glanced over my shoulder and saw Marion hug her grandmother. It appeared she realized how much she'd upset the old woman.

Bill saw us to the door. "We're glad you came for a visit. I hope you come again. Zetta enjoys company." I had a feeling he was simply being polite. His wife was upset.

I picked up my shoes and headed for the road. "I'm not putting these soggy things back on my feet."

"Me, either," Fel said, picking up her own shoes.

"Wait for me." Mother stopped us while she tried to put on her shoes, giving up because they were such a mess.

We crossed the road without more mud incidents.

"Ouch!" Felicity started hopping around on one foot.

Mother studied the ground. "Tarantula?"

Fel flinched. "*No!* I stepped on a sticker." She pulled it out of her foot. "Oh. It's a bull head sticker."

"A what?" I asked.

"A sticker that looks like a bull's head. At least, that's what I've always called them."

We studied the ground and walked carefully on our way back to the house, making sure we didn't step on anything else.

"What did you think of Marion's story?" my mother asked.

"I got the feeling she knows more than she's telling," I replied. "I'm not sure she was completely honest with us."

"I got the same sense from what she said." Felicity stepped up on the porch.

"I wonder if I might be able to get her to talk to me without her grandparents around. Maybe she doesn't want them to hear what she has to say." Considering where we were and what we were doing, I was having trouble coming up with a plan.

"I see the plumber and the electrician are back." Mother pointed at their trucks. "I wonder how much more work they have to do. I'm going to change into clean shoes and go talk to Frank."

I nodded and opened the screen door, once again taking note of the bullet hole. The door was what they call a security door. If I stood inside the house, I could see out, but anyone standing on the porch couldn't see in. There was a lock on the door handle, and a dead bolt had been installed, too.

Felicity followed my gaze. "That hole kind of creeps me out."

"Me, too," I said.

My mother touched the outside edges of the hole.

"Since the door is slightly rusted, we're going to paint it, but we're going to leave the bullet hole. After all, it seems appropriate for a Dude Ranch."

"It's not the O.K. Corral, and this was a llama ranch." I thought she was getting a little carried away.

"Not by the time I'm through with it." She chuckled to herself and walked into the house. "Oh, I've got to go to the motorhome. That's where I left my other shoes."

She turned and walked back outside, down the steps and toward the motorhome.

Felicity and I looked at each other. I rolled my eyes and she started to laugh.

"Your mother cracks me up," she said. "Leave it to her to want to leave the bullet hole intact."

"Yeah. Typical Livvie Brewster thinking." I left Fel to go upstairs for another pair of shoes.

I saw her heading for the stairs to go down to the apartment.

"I'll meet you downstairs," she called over her shoulder.

I found the plumber on his knees in the upstairs bathroom, checking the pipes. His flashlight slowly swung back and forth.

"Do you think it's going to take much longer to get everything working?" I asked.

"I'll finish up today, ma'am. I want to do some last minute pipe checks. We're just about ready to go live, as they say. Oh!" He leaned inside the cupboard under the sink.

"What's wrong?"

"Uh, I think you'd better take a look at this."

"I sure hope this isn't another *Uh Oh* moment."

"What?" He backed out of the cupboard and banged his head.

"Nothing. What'd you find under there?"

"You're not going to believe it."

He rubbed the back of his head where he'd bumped it.

Chapter Twenty-Eight

"*I*'m not going to believe what?" I asked.

"Take a look." The plumber moved out of my way so I could look in the cupboard.

I knelt down and stuck my head inside. "I don't see anything." And I didn't. Nothing looked out of place.

"Take a gander behind the pipes. A *good* gander."

It was dark. There were no lights in the bathroom yet, and the window was dirty, blocking out the sunlight.

The plumber tapped me on my back. "Here. Use my flashlight."

I reached back and he placed it in my hand.

Swinging the light back and forth and into the corners, I still didn't see anything. I was about to ask him what he was talking about when the light beam picked up something out-of-place. Tucked into the u-trap part of the pipe was a gun. It was partially wrapped in a cloth and jammed up against the wall so it wouldn't fall, but I could see most of the barrel.

"Have you got something I can use to lift this out? Never mind. It's obviously been here a long time." I reached forward and plucked the gun from its hiding place.

Backing out of the cupboard, I cracked my head, just like the plumber had.

"What's your name?" I asked, rubbing my skull.

"Frank, just like your father."

I didn't bother to correct him about Frank's status of stepfather.

"Well, Frank, would you do me a favor and send my husband up here?"

"Sure will. Knowing the history of this old house, I'd just as soon get out of here." He left in a hurry. I had a feeling he'd finish his work on the house in a hurry, too.

While I waited I stood and unwrapped the gun, opening the cylinder on the .22 revolver after I set the cloth on the sink. It was loaded and ready to fire. No bullets missing. That was something, anyway. Taking a closer look, I noticed a slightly reddish-brown stain on the grip. There were a couple of marks on the stain which looked like water from the pipes might have dripped on the gun. I unloaded it – no sense in taking chances.

Things were, once again, becoming interesting. Since the police would have already taken possession of both Clyde's and Harry's guns at the time of the crimes, this one wouldn't have been used in the multiple murders. Was it used for anything? What was the stain on the grip? Maybe it was rust from the sink since it had been resting in the trap of the plumbing.

It wasn't long before Pete showed up at the bathroom door. "What's up? Frank said something about a gun?"

"Yes. He found one under the sink. With everything that's happened in this house, finding the gun made my imagination start working double-time. Take a look at this and see what you think."

I handed him the revolver.

He studied it for a moment. "It's definitely an older pistol. And you say it was under the sink in the cabinet?"

"*Hidden* under the sink. It was wrapped in cloth and jammed in the pipes, not just casually tossed into the cupboard."

"Hmm. Interesting." He studied the grip of the revolver. "This could be rusty water, but it could also be a blood stain. I'd say we should turn it over to the local police, but there haven't been any crimes committed here in about twenty years. And they took the guns used in the murders as evidence already." He set the gun on the sink. "I don't think we need to worry about this. I have no idea who hid the gun, but obviously it wasn't used in any known crime. Think about it. It's an old gun to begin with, and no one has lived here for years."

"You're right. It's probably no big deal. I guess it just surprised me when Frank found it. It curdled his cream though. I have a feeling he's going to finish up as fast as he can and be done with this job. I don't think he wants to come back."

"What were you doing at the mobile home across the street? Meeting the neighbors?" He deftly changed the subject. Had he forgotten about our challenge?

Worked for me.

"Yes, they wanted to meet my mother and find out a little about their new neighbor."

"Uh huh." His tone sounded suspicious. "So you weren't asking questions about the murders?"

"Okay, ya got me. We were doing a full-blown investigation. Twenty years after the fact, we were grilling them about what happened."

"I suppose you think I'd forgotten about our bet." He grinned. "Not gonna happen. The boys, as you call us, have already spoken to one of the other neighbors. Maybe you need to keep an eye on us."

I sighed. "I should have known. We're in here working our little brains out and you're out socializing in the neighborhood."

"Yeah, socializing. There are so many people around here. Have you even bothered to count the houses? What are there? Half a dozen?"

"Gotcha," I said. "There are eight houses out here, and two of them are vacant."

Pete laughed. "That's my girl, always on top of things. Now I'm going back to work."

"Give me a kiss first." I fluttered my eyelashes at him and he responded, oh, so lovingly.

"How much longer are we going to stay here?" he asked.

"As long as it takes."

He nodded and turned, limping as he walked away. Was he that tired? Or looking for my sympathy? He got my sympathy. I wondered if he'd ever fully recover from his broken bones.

I set the gun and the ammunition on the bathroom sink, thinking I'd figure out what to do with them later. Before I could exit the bathroom, I heard footsteps thudding up the stairs.

"Sandi? Sandi?" My mother must have heard about the revolver.

"I'm in here," I said, stepping outside the small room and into the hallway.

She climbed up the last step and stopped in front of me. "I heard you found a gun. Do you think it was used in the murders?"

"No, Mom, the police took the other weapons in as evidence. This one had nothing to do with any killings – as far as I know." Stifling a grin, I egged her on, unable to stop myself.

She knew what I was doing. "You just never know. Remember, we have to check some suspicious places in this house. Which reminds me, you were going to pour some water down the back of the fireplace to see if it would run down the wall in the basement."

I snapped my fingers. "That's right. I forgot all about that. Why don't we do that right now? We'll take the gun with us and you can hide it in the motorhome. I wouldn't want Blondie to find it."

She nodded, picked up the gun and stuck the ammunition in her pocket before following me downstairs and snatching up a bucket for me to use. It still had some fresh water in it from when we'd been cleaning.

"Okay," I said. "You go downstairs and watch to see if the water runs down the wall after I pour it in the fireplace."

She nodded and took off to stand watch in the basement, leaving the door open so we could yell back and forth to each other.

Removing the foil I'd lined the fireplace with, I waited in the living room until I was sure she was downstairs. I tipped the bucket and ran water down the back of the fireplace.

"*Anything yet?*" I yelled.

"*No,*" she replied at the top of her lungs.

"What's all the hollering about?" Felicity stuck her head around the corner of the wall leading from the family room.

"I'm testing the fireplace to see if the stains on the wall in the basement could be from someone pouring water on a fire to put it out. Maybe it ran down the back, but so far it doesn't seem to be running off."

"Oh. Well, why not take something and clear the back of the fireplace. Maybe there was dirt and debris under the foil you used."

"Good idea." I picked up a piece of wood that was lying on the floor and began to scrape the back of the fireplace.

"*I'm waiting, dear,*" my mother yelled.

"*Give me a minute,*" I yelled back.

Felicity made a face. "I'll go stand between the basement door and fireplace so you two don't have to keep screaming at each other."

I nodded and tipped the bucket again, waiting for a moment before I said anything.

"Ask her if she sees running water yet." I knew Felicity would be able to hear me.

Before she could ask, I heard my mother's voice coming from the stairs.

"Phooey! I saw water running down the wall. We'll have to make sure to fix the fireplace so we don't start a fire in the basement with hot ashes falling through the space."

She reached the top of the stairs and walked over to stand beside me.

"Okay," Felicity said. "That means there's probably no body behind the block wall."

Was it my imagination or did my mother look disappointed?

Chapter Twenty-Nine

"*M*om, be *glad* there aren't any bodies hidden in this house. What are the odds of finding a body? Slim to none. I can hardly believe you're reacting this way."

"I don't think I'm *over*reacting. I just kind of got carried away because of everything that's happened here. You'll think I'm nuts, but I figured adding to the existing story might make people want to stay here if for no other reason than because they're nosey or curious."

"Ah."

"Honestly? I think this house has enough of a story already," Felicity said. "If you find another body, it's more than likely going to keep people *away* from your bed and breakfast."

My mother looked thoughtful. "Maybe you're right," she said slowly. "I don't really want to think someone else was murdered here. Besides, if someone was killed a long time ago and the body was hidden here, all we'd find would be a skeleton."

She was treating death too lightly, and yet I knew it would be a different matter if she was face to face with a body.

After all, it had happened. She's seen a dead body up close and personal. She was a bit eccentric, maybe, but not cold-hearted. My mother is a diehard mystery fan and she frequently wanted to know what my latest case was. She'd become involved in a couple of them and it seemed to whet her appetite for more.

"You don't want to find another body, but you sure seem to want to investigate the crimes that took place here. Is that right? Actually, I think you want to add to what's already happened here. You want even more of a story than we already have. Right?"

She nodded slowly. "Maybe I'm becoming a ghoul in my old age."

"You're not a ghoul," I said. "You're just a very curious woman. Sometimes you need to let things go and not pursue them."

"Yes, but you – "

"I'm a private investigator. It's my job, not yours. Now why don't we get back to work? If you want to imagine there are bodies hidden around the house, go ahead. But remember, although there were murders here, anything else is fiction. We're just trying to win a bet with the men about what really happened twenty years ago. Okay?"

"You're right, Sandi. I just got too carried away."

Felicity watched us talk, wide-eyed and surprised. "You two crack me up," she said. "One minute you're trying to scare each other, and the next you're rationalizing what's going on. Oh, and by the way, Livvie, you're not a ghoul. Far from it."

A sudden thought struck me. "By the way, Mom, are you and Frank going to sleep in the house again tonight?"

"Why? Are you going to try to scare me?" She narrowed her eyes and grinned.

"No. Would I do that?"

"Yes and yes. We're going to sleep by the fireplace

again, and yes you'd try to scare me. Remember, I'm no spring chicken anymore. You wouldn't want to give your mother a heart attack, would you?"

"Uh uh. Sometimes I think you're younger than I am, at least mentally."

"Well, Frank and I decided – or *I* decided – we'd rather sleep in the house where you're all within calling distance. It'll be more comfy."

"Yeah, it's gonna be real comfortable sleeping on the floor." I had a feeling she had something up her sleeve, but no idea what it could be.

The three of us laughed our comments off and, after some discussion, decided to work in the main kitchen upstairs for a while instead of going back to the apartment.

"What color are you going to paint the kitchen?" Fel asked. "Will it be yellow, too?"

"No, I've decided to go with pale blues and off whites up here."

I glanced at my watch. "Oh, my gosh! It's four o'clock. Do you realize we never ate lunch? The men must be starving. We'd better forget about painting for now and think about dinner."

"We didn't have lunch? I could swear we did." Mom looked chagrined, to say the least.

"I'm hungry, and other than cookies at Zetta's, I don't remember eating," I said.

"We ate. You've just got too much on your mind. I'll go out and check on the guys," Felicity said. "I'm half surprised they didn't come nag us about dinner already."

"Okay," my mother said. "While you talk to them Sandi and I will put something together." She was already heading toward the door and I knew she was going to the motorhome to see what we had to eat.

I followed her. "Wait a minute. Felicity's right. We had lunch before we walked over to see Zetta and Bill. I feel like we've crammed forty-eight hours into one day today. Even our memories are playing tricks on us. Maybe we should send the boys into town for pizza or something."

She stopped in her tracks. "Good idea, but why don't *we* drive in. I wouldn't mind getting away from here for a while."

I was about to turn and head for the shop where the men had been working when I noticed they were sitting outside relaxing, in front of the motorhome. Felicity sat on Stanley's lap. They were so cute together.

Mom explained her dinner plan to everyone.

"I have a better idea," Frank said. "Let's all go and we'll eat in town. I saw a couple of restaurants that looked pretty good. Can everyone clean up in a hurry?"

Stanley stood and dumped Felicity on the ground.

She raised her eyebrows at him. "Thanks a lot, precious. Is this the way you're going to treat me for the rest of our lives?" She looked up and smiled, knowing he hadn't meant to drop her.

"Oh, sugar dumpling, I didn't mean to do that. The idea of dinner just overwhelmed me. I wasn't thinking when I stood."

He helped her up and she brushed off her jeans. "I've never seen you take dinner quite this seriously before."

"Honestly, I've never worked this hard before. It builds up quite an appetite."

I noticed he kept glancing around at the ground.

"Yeah, you just want to get away from the tarantulas," Pete said.

"Well, there is that." Stanley took a step back, almost as though he thought another herd of tarantulas would arrive shortly.

We'd worked hard all day, but it hadn't been as hot as previous days. Instead of showering we all changed clothes and hoped for the best.

The drive into town seemed to take forever, although it couldn't have been much more than half an hour. The electrician and plumber left just before we did so we ended up following them out of the desert. I laughed to myself. We were following them out of the desert to a town that was in the desert. High desert, but still the desert. Of course, the llama ranch was in the high desert, too.

We had a wonderful home-cooked type dinner at an established restaurant. Feeling satiated, we made a stop at the grocery store to pick up a few things and then headed home.

Pete put his arm around me and pulled me close. The atmosphere inside the car was so quiet that I dozed off for several miles. I awoke when we turned onto the rutted dirt road leading to the house. With each bump we hit it felt like my insides were doing a tap dance.

Automatically and without meaning to, I glanced up at the second story window when we pulled onto the driveway. It was too dark by then to determine if a blonde-headed woman was watching us.

I patted Pete's knee. "It's good to be home. It's also good to put today and the work we've done behind us."

He leaned down to whisper in my ear "That honeymoon is looking better and better."

"I heard that," my mother said. "You have no idea how much Frank and I appreciate all of you helping us. I was going to tell you this later, but we've decided to help all of you out with a little spending money for your honeymoons."

"Oh, no, Livvie. We'll be fine," Felicity said.

I chuckled when I saw Stanley poke her in the ribs. I guessed he thought that was a great idea.

"Mother, that's very generous of you. I think we can all graciously accept your gift, and thank you." I gave Stanley a very pointed look.

I knew my mother wouldn't be happy if she couldn't help out a little. That was her way.

"Of course," I said, "you might change your mind if I manage to turn tonight into Fright Night for you."

I cackled maliciously and in a joking way but choked on my cackle when the car light briefly highlighted a blonde watching us out of the living room window.

Chapter Thirty

*P*ulling away from Pete, I glanced at everyone in the car. No one's head was pointed in the direction of the house.

I quietly sighed. Was no one but me ever going to see the apparition? Uh, woman? I shivered over my use of the word apparition. Pete thought I was cold and pulled me back against his chest, putting his arms around me. I wasn't cold, but his embrace was comforting.

I had to come up with a plan to take Blondie by surprise, and to see what she looked like. Picturing her in my mind, there was something familiar about her, but I couldn't place what it was.

When we parked, Stanley studied the ground closely before climbing out of the car. Apparently there were no snakes or crawly critters waiting for our return.

Mother and Frank headed for the motorhome and I heard him say, "Why would we want to sleep on the floor in the..."

I didn't hear the rest of what he said after a loud, "Shhhh!" from my mother.

Stanley and Felicity walked inside the house with us

and headed downstairs while we climbed upstairs to our bedroom. On our way to the stairs I made a point of studying the living room. Blondie had disappeared again.

"I wonder if the plumber finished today," I said.

"One way to find out," Pete replied, turning and walking into the bathroom.

He turned the knob at the sink and water bubbled out of the faucet. It took a minute or two before the air in the lines disappeared and we had real honest to goodness water.

"We'll still have to shower downstairs," he said. "This tub needs to be cleaned and we'll have to put up a shower curtain."

"Too bad," I said, not looking at him. "We could have had a nice shower together." I knew I'd start laughing if I saw the look on his face.

Pete gave me a loving pat on the rump. "All good things come to those who're patient, or something like that."

"Works for me. At least we may be near a working toilet now."

He walked over and flushed the commode, laughing when it sounded like a waterfall. "Uh, it works."

"Then all we need to do is clean it. But not tonight."

"Enough potty talk. Let's go to bed. Or let's go to sleeping bag, as the case may be."

"I'm going downstairs and bring a glass of water up here. I'll be back in a minute."

Pete yawned. "Okay, but don't take too long. Take a flashlight."

"I'll take one of the lanterns we've been using."

He gave me one of his looks, the kind that reminds me of rolling one's eyes. "You're just into the idea that this might be a haunted house."

"Yeah, that's right." I turned and headed downstairs, hoping my sarcasm wasn't lost on him.

I didn't really need the lantern. There was moonlight

streaming through the window in the living room and I could see quite well. The door that led to the Arizona room opened and closed and I figured it was probably my mother and Frank.

"Mother?"

"I'm coming," she replied.

We met in the kitchen.

"Frank wants to stay in the motorhome tonight. He's into comfort, not floors. I guess he's right. We should get a good night's sleep."

"Okay. I just came down to get a glass. That dinner was good, but it must have had a lot of salt in it. I'm really thirsty."

"Me, too. I hadn't thought about salt. You're probably right."

We found glasses we'd used during the day on the sink and filled them with water from the faucet.

"I'm glad there's water inside now," my mother said. "Maybe tomorrow we can concentrate on cleaning the bathrooms before we paint."

Mother took a drink and made a face. "The plumber had a good suggestion about putting in a filtration system. This is terrible."

I took a sip. "You're right. I think there's some bottled water left in the cooler."

I popped the top of the cooler and took out two full bottles, handing one to my mother.

Tipping my head, I watched Mom pour water into her glass. "You're definitely not giving anyone a chance to get bored with all of your hidden body talk, but I love you anyway."

"You're a good daughter."

We hugged each other before she walked out the door and I headed back upstairs.

Pete was already sound asleep. He was snoring softly. I gently kissed his cheek before I tried to follow suit and sleep. I say *tried* because something kept me awake. Have you ever been so tired that sleep wouldn't come? And, just to aggravate the situation, you couldn't turn your thoughts off? It had been a very long day and I couldn't stop thinking about all the things we'd accomplished. Of course, Blondie never entered my thoughts. Ha!

I'd finally drifted off, but came awake suddenly. Had I heard a sound? Was someone in the house besides the four newlyweds? I listened, but all I could hear was the sound of a hoot owl and crickets. Deciding to get up and investigate, I picked up the flashlight and tip-toed toward the stairs.

I heard loud snoring coming from in front of the fireplace. My mother must have talked Frank into sleeping in the house. She could talk the flea off a dog if she tried hard enough.

That's when it struck me. Now was the time to give her a good scare. I'd slip down the stairs, one step at a time, hold the flashlight under my chin so my face would look freaky, and wake her up. I knew I shouldn't do it because I'd scare Frank in the process, but I'd do it anyway.

The moon had moved, or the earth had turned, and the house was dark.

One of the steps creaked so I moved closer to the bannister – less creaking that way. I stopped to see if I'd awakened anyone. Nothing but silence greeted me. Two more steps and I was mid-stairway. I stopped again and listened.

My breath caught when I head a stair creak below me. Blondie? Maybe now was my chance to catch her. I listened again and thought I heard someone breathing. Do ghosts breathe?

Carefully, I took another step down. It sounded like the breathing was right in front of me.

I quickly flipped on the flashlight but before I could point it toward the bottom of the stairs, I ran into someone.

I tried to scream but all that came out was a gurgle. My

grip on the bannister tightened.

My *mother* screamed and immediately clamped her hand over her mouth. I should have figured that's who I'd bumped into.

We both turned and looked toward Frank. He continued to snore. The house could have fallen down around him and he'd have slept right through it. Looking up the stairs, we didn't see Pete's silhouette at the top of the stairs.

"Sandi!" mother whispered, reaching for my hand.

"Shhh."

We headed for the Arizona room where we wouldn't bother anyone.

"I was going to scare you," she said.

"Uh, I was going to scare *you*."

We started to giggle.

"What's the matter with us? Can you believe our timing?" Mom sat down on a chair she'd temporarily stored in the room and patted another one, indicating I should sit, too.

"We couldn't have planned the timing any better," I said. "Like mother, like daughter?"

She nodded. "Great minds and all that rot."

"Do you think we'll ever get to sleep tonight?"

"No. Let's just sit here and relax. You got my heart pumping. Oh, this is too funny."

Bubba *woofed* from the doorway and we both jumped out of our chairs.

"Bubba wins," I said. "He got us both."

My mother looked at the flashlight and started to laugh, barely able to talk through the guffaws. "It was bumping into you and the flashlight going on that startled me. That and the fact that I couldn't see who was holding it."

I couldn't answer her for a moment. I was laughing so hard that tears ran down my cheeks. "I was going to…" I snorted. "…hold it under my chin so I'd look evil…" Snort. "…and wake you up."

"It worked without the chin thing. And Bubba put an exclamation point on the whole thing."

The laughter finally died down. We chatted for a few minutes before I yawned.

Bubba must have been tired of us because he stood and walked into the house, glancing back over his shoulder at us.

They say laughter is the best medicine. I guess I'm living proof because the next thing I knew, someone was shaking my shoulder, trying to wake me up. I opened my eyes and saw my mother sleeping in the other chair.

Changing directions, I looked up in time to see the blonde leaving by the back door, rear view, as usual.

Can a ghost shake your shoulder?

Chapter Thirty-one

I was so tired. I couldn't even jump out of my chair to chase the elusive woman. "She didn't look like a ghost to me. She looked pretty solid. I sure wish I could see her face though."

"Are you talking to yourself?" my mother asked.

"Well, I wasn't talking to you."

"You sound a little cranky this morning. Get over it. You probably dreamed you saw the blonde."

Morning? I turned my gaze to the window. The sun was just beginning to rise. It reminded me of the morning I'd let Bubba outside so early.

Bubba. Where was he? Probably down in the apartment with the Hawks. Traitor. Oh! I remembered him leaving the room to get away from my mother and me.

"I didn't dream I saw Blondie. She was here. Why she woke me up, I have no idea. I need chocolate. I was trying to cut back, but I've held off long enough. I'm going upstairs to get more sleep, and then I'm going to eat chocolate. A lot of chocolate. Mega amounts of chocolate. It's a comfort food thing."

"I'll probably join you for chocolate. In fact, I'll make some chocolate chip muffins in the motorhome. I brought a mix for emergencies."

"Love you, Mom."

Standing, I headed into the house. Halfway up the stairs, I met Pete coming down.

"You disappeared again," he said, half accusingly.

"I tried to scare my mother, she tried to scare me, and we ended up sleeping on chairs in the Arizona room. Got a problem with that?" Uh oh. I *was* cranky.

He looked nonplussed. "Nope. Go on upstairs and take a nap. I'll leave you alone until you pull yourself together."

I wasn't letting him have a happy start to the day. "I'm sorry, Pete. The sun is barely up and I've already had a blonde sighting. I got very little sleep last night. And I'm even too tired to go in search of chocolate."

"I'll find you some. You sound like your mother this morning except she needs hormone pills to set her straight. In your case, it's chocolate."

"Don't bother. Mom is going to make some chocolate chip muffins."

I hugged him and headed for our bedroom. He hugged me back and held his tongue.

Waking up a couple of hours later, I didn't even remember my head hitting the pillow. Voices floated up from downstairs.

I could hear Felicity's sweet little voice as she sang to herself. It sounded like she was nearby, maybe in the bathroom. She was awfully cheerful for so early in the morning.

Groaning, I rolled out of the sleeping bag and stood, stretching as much as I could, trying to make my muscles obey me. Sore doesn't even begin to describe how I felt. Over the past few days I'd used muscles I'd forgotten I had.

The singing led me to Fel who was finishing a cleaning

job in the bathroom. She's just finished scrubbing the tub and groaned when she stood up.

"I know just how you feel," I said. "That same sad sound came out of me just moments ago."

She smiled. "All I have to do is hang this shower curtain and you can have a long hot shower. I had one, and I feel so much better."

"I'll hang the curtain. You've done enough, and thank you."

"You sound a lot more chipper than the way your mother and Pete described you." She tucked some cleaning products out of sight in the cupboard under the sink. "Did you know that before I became a model I earned a few extra bucks cleaning houses?"

"Get out of here. You're kidding. I can't imagine you spending your days that way."

"I did. A person will do whatever they have to do to make ends meet. That was *my* way."

"Have I told you how much I admire you, Fel?"

"No, but thanks."

"I'm going to take that shower you mentioned. Would you tell Pete I'll be down in a few minutes?"

She nodded and carried the rags she'd been using downstairs.

I put up rings and hung the shower curtain before climbing into the tub and turning on the shower. Felicity had left some towels and washcloths on the edge of the sink so I was ready for heat and relaxation. Bath soap sat on the edge of the tub, too. Ah, and thankfully, so did shampoo and conditioner.

I was momentarily in heaven, but it didn't last long. There was a knock at the door.

"Yes?" I called out.

My mother answered me. "Hurry up. Breakfast will be ready in about fifteen minutes."

"Thanks. I'll be down soon."

Felicity was right. I felt like a new person when I finished my shower. Fresh clothes made me feel renewed. Back in the bedroom, I brushed my wet hair into a ponytail.

Felicity frequently wore her hair in a French braid. I'd have to ask her to show me how to do my hair that way. I loved the look. I'd been meaning to ask her for a long time.

After one last look in the bathroom mirror, and shrugging my shoulders, I found my way to the apartment kitchen. My mother was setting things on the table the men had so graciously brought in for us.

"Sandi thinks she saw the blonde again," she said to anyone who would listen.

Sighing had become a bad habit with me, and I exhaled slowly. "I *did* see her. She woke me up this morning. Of course, I once again saw her from the back as she was leaving. You know, I've seen her so many times now that it's not worth getting excited about anymore. I'm getting used to her."

"She woke you up?" Stanley asked.

"She did."

"Would you like me to assist you while you put a plan together to catch her?"

"Stan, you just made my day. Honestly. I'd like nothing more than to talk to her and for someone else to see her. After breakfast we'll talk about it."

Without realizing it, he'd become my hero. No one else seemed to either believe me or want to get involved – including my new husband.

I smacked said husband on the arm.

"What?" he said.

"Nothing."

He shook his head and dished some fried potatoes out of a bowl.

Mumbling had also become a bad habit and I did so as I sat at the table. Apparently my mood hadn't improved much

– that is, until I saw a plate of chocolate chip muffins sitting on the sink.

My chair screeched when I shoved it back and made a beeline for the sink.

"After breakfast," my mother said.

"Not on your life," I replied. "These will go well with bacon and eggs."

"Whatever you do, don't get between her and the sink," Frank said. He grinned. "She's beginning to remind me of Livvie when..." The rest of his comment was left unsaid when he realized my mother was glaring at him.

It promises to be a fun day, I thought. *Yeah, right.*

"Maybe we need a break today," Pete said. "We're all tired, and it looks like there are plenty of places to explore around here."

"We could take the ATV into the hills," Frank suggested.

"As long as we don't tip it over," Pete replied. That's how he'd broken one leg and one ankle. An ATV accident. "And we'll take Bubba with us."

"He'd like that," I said.

My mother nudged Felicity. "We could talk to more neighbors."

Felicity nodded.

"I'll stay here with Sandi and we'll hatch a plan. That's the right word, isn't it? Hatch?"

"It sure is."

I winked at Stanley and took a huge bite out of a muffin, groaning again. This time it was a chocolate ecstasy groan.

Chapter Thirty-two

Although I knew there was a lot of work ahead of us, I liked the idea of taking the day, or some part of it, off to goof around. Each to their own brand of entertainment.

Mother packed sandwiches and drinks in a cooler so Pete and Frank wouldn't feel like they were on a schedule. They could investigate the small mountain all they wanted to, and the rest of us would keep ourselves busy. She included some treats for Bubba, and a small bag of kibble just in case they were late getting home.

"That should hold the bugger," Frank said.

Felicity and my mother left Stanley and me to do the dishes while they walked to Tyler's house to ask about the other neighbors.

"Okay, Sandi, you're a private investigator. You have the skills with which to catch the blonde woman. You and I really do need to devise a plan." Stanley dried a plate while I washed another one.

Sometimes Stanley spoke more formally than the rest of us, although he often tried to be one of the guys nowadays, and it endeared him to me. The cutesy names he'd been calling Felicity were so out of character, but I loved that side of him, too.

"Okay, we'll devise a plan. Let's finish the dishes, and then we'll sit down and I'll tell you everything that's happened so far. I don't think you're aware of all my blonde sightings."

The look on his face told me he was taking it very seriously. And, truth be told, I was thrilled that someone was taking *me* seriously.

We finished the dishes and sat at the table, ready to plan how to catch a blonde woman who seemed to want to remain anonymous.

"I have no idea what this woman wants, but it's obvious to me that she wants *something*," I said. "Don't you think it's odd she only shows herself to me?"

"I do. I know you don't believe in ghosts, but there is something decidedly odd about this entire situation. Is there any specific place where she shows herself? What I mean is, could she be trying to lead you to something?"

"So far I've seen her in several places. Last night, when we pulled in, I'm sure I saw her at the living room window. I think she might have been in the upstairs bedroom and we came home and scared her off. I have a gut feeling there's something about that bedroom that she wants us to see."

"Alright," Stanley said, "then let's start with the bedroom. We'll search it to see if anything out of the ordinary rears its head at us. Is it the room you and Pete are using?"

"No, it's at the front of the house. Pete and I are in the rear bedroom. You've been upstairs, haven't you?"

"Just once, and it was only a brief look at that part of the house."

I glanced toward the stairway. "Shall we get started?"

"Lead the way," he replied. "No, as a gentleman, I should lead the way."

"No, if she sees you first, she may hide. Follow me." I

stood and found that as I climbed the stairs, Stanley stayed a short distance behind me. He'd taken my comment seriously and apparently hoped she wouldn't notice him.

I smiled, realizing how happy it made me that my friend was taking an interest in my dilemma. My dilemma stemmed from the fact that I had no idea what this woman was up to and why no one had seen her except me.

Pointing at the side of the stairs nearest the wall, I let Stanley know there was less chance of creaking if we walked there. He understood and gently placed his feet on each step.

We reached the front bedroom and found the door closed. I was fairly sure it had been open the day before, but I wouldn't swear to it. Maybe Pete had closed it. I pushed it open.

A small piece of paper rested on the floor in front of the window. I approached it slowly, looking inside the open closet and in the corners as I moved.

Stanley marched past me and picked it up. "It's a photograph."

So much for keeping quiet. Oh, well, she wasn't in the bedroom anyway.

"Let me see it," I said, reaching out.

Instead of handing it to me, he motioned me to his side to look at it with him. I tried to give him a questioning look, but he was concentrating on the photo.

"What is it?" I asked.

"Surprise, surprise. It's a photograph of a blonde woman."

I hurried to his side, all pretense of being quiet set aside.

"Is this the woman you've been spying around the house?" Stanley asked.

I studied the picture. It was old and the colors were fading. There were three people in the photo, and their style of dress could have been from the late sixties, or maybe the early seventies. There was a man, a woman and a child. They appeared very serious, not like they were out having fun in the sun.

"It looks like the same hairdo, and she appears to be about the same size, but I've never seen the woman's face. I don't know if it's her or not. I wonder who the other two people are."

"What type of clothing is the woman wearing when you see her?"

"Why, Stan, you're turning into quite a private eye. You're asking the right questions. She always has on the same clothes. They're rather nondescript, but if I had to guess I'd say they're from about the same time period as what the people in this picture are wearing."

"Anything else?" he asked.

"I've only had glimpses of the blonde, but you're making me remember things with your line of questioning. Her slacks are a bit too short for her, although they could be capri pants, and they've got vertical stripes. Her blouse is long-sleeved and white with a large collar. That's all I can remember."

"Something else will come to you. And if you see her again, you'll be more conscious of her mannerisms and the little details. So many times the story is in the smaller details." Stanley handed me the photo. "Obviously she wanted you to see this."

"Stan?"

"I've been reading everything I can find on detecting, and I've been considering taking a class at the community college."

"You have a lot of hours in, working for us, and with the right credentials you could become a P.I. Are you sure that's what you want to do?"

He'd accompanied Pete on a few investigations, but mostly he'd done research for us. He was a computer wiz.

"It is what I want to do. It makes me feel wonderful to figure things out. Each case and each piece of information is like solving one of life's puzzles. Although, I don't believe I'd become involved in some of the cases you and Pete have handled."

"You've already been involved in some of our more insidious cases," I reminded him. "Remember the thugs who were after me because they thought I knew where a buried treasure was located? And what about the time you accompanied Pete on a murder investigation at Lake Tahoe? Then there was the time – "

"Yes, Sandi, you're right. I can handle myself." There was a note of pride in his voice.

I smiled at him. "Sometimes your methods are a little off the wall, but you manage."

He grinned in return. "I have my moments."

The picture we'd found was important. I could feel it in my bones. It weighed heavy in my hand simply because I knew I should be able to figure something out based on the significance of it being left in this bedroom, in front of the window.

I studied each person in the photo, the blonde in particular. There was definitely something about her that seemed familiar. There was a niggling thought in my head that I couldn't quite make sense of, but I'd figure it out in time. I shook my head, almost as though I was trying to shake the thought out of the shadows.

Stanley raised his eyebrows at me without asking why I was shaking my head.

"I know I should be putting things together, based on the photo," I explained. "But I can't quite put the sightings and this picture together. I know there should be a connection, and yet there's not. Yes, the blonde I've seen reminds me of this woman, and yet she doesn't. Does that make sense?"

"It does. You'll figure it out. In the meantime, did you

notice there's a handprint in the dust on the window? It looks like someone leaned against it, maybe while they watched us pull in last night."

"Why, Stan, I'm astonished at how savvy you've become." I turned from him and studied the window. He was right. Someone had leaned against the window and left a right handprint. Too bad I didn't have the means to check the fingerprints. I could call the police, but for what purpose?

No, I couldn't involve the police because I was pretty sure they didn't believe in ghosts either.

Chapter Thirty-three

"What now?" Stanley asked.

"Let's go downstairs and I'll show you every location where I've seen Blondie. Maybe something will come to me."

"Is there any pattern to the places she's shown herself?"

"Not that I can figure out." After taking another quick glance at the photo, I carefully placed it in my jeans pocket. I didn't want to lose it, and next time I saw her I wanted something to compare her to.

"Any other ideas?"

"Yes," I replied, "I'll show the photo to Tyler. Maybe he'll recognize her. He was going to borrow his mother's photo albums, so I'll see if he's done that yet."

"Let's take a look at the locations and when we're done, we'll go see Tyler. You're right, it would be beneficial for us to meet with him and have him examine the photograph."

"I have a feeling this bedroom is somehow involved in what's going on. I've seen her here twice, and she left the photo. I need to sit quietly and try to use logic to put it together. I guess I'd better gather more information first."

Stanley nodded his agreement.

We visited each place where Blondie had shown herself, which didn't take long. It didn't spark any ideas on Stanley's part, but he reminded me about our visit to Tyler.

On our way to his home I saw my mother and Felicity knocking on the door of a neighbor's house. I waved but, of course, they didn't see me.

We approached Tyler and Racheal's door and heard laughter coming from inside.

I knocked on the door. "It sounds like they're having a good time."

Stanley smiled. "We're the individuals having a grand time."

Zoë opened the door and when she saw us she pushed open the screen door. "Come on in. We're looking at some old family photos."

"I guess we're just in time," I said. "It sounds like Tyler must have picked up the photo albums from his parents."

"He did, and he and Micah were a couple of dufuses when they were kids. You've got to see some of these pictures."

Stanley and I entered the house with smiles on our faces. The good moods of these people were catching.

Tyler glanced up. "Sandi! Come on in and see what we've found." He nodded at Stanley. "Good to see you, man."

Stanley nodded back, grinning. Tyler sounded so welcoming.

"I take it these are the pictures you were going to pick up from your mother?" I stepped over to the couch and glanced down at one of the albums.

"Yes, and I'm glad I picked them up. Check this out." He turned the album toward me and tapped one of the pictures. There were two little boys – one on a bicycle and one on a tricycle.

"I don't know how the heck you two could ride bikes on these dirt roads," Stanley said.

"It wasn't easy. Our dad put a cement trail through the yard for us," Micah said. "And he'd drive into town to the park for the day. Well, he drove me in. Tyler was too young." He slapped his brother on the back of the head.

It was good-natured and Tyler didn't look annoyed. He simply reached back and swatted at his brother over his shoulder.

"Would you two like some iced tea?" Racheal asked.

"Please," I said.

"And thank you," Stanley added.

I sat down on one side of Tyler and Stanley sat on his left. He began turning pages, showing us other pictures of an earlier time, including photos of his parents.

"Now they're a good-looking couple," I said.

"Thanks," Tyler said.

Micah picked up another album and handed it to his brother. "Ty, get down to business. You know she wants to see the pictures of Francine Stockholm."

"I'm enjoying seeing you and your brother as kids," I said.

He had a half smile on his face. "I want to see the look on your face when you see Francine." Did he have something up his sleeve or would it turn out to be morbid curiosity?

Tyler grabbed the album from his brother. "You're right, bro. I'm keeping her waiting for nothing."

There was a piece of paper marking a page. He pulled out the paper and handed me the album. There were five pictures which included a pretty blonde.

I glanced from the pictures to Tyler and back again, and then up at Micah. "Are the man and child in the pictures Harry and Barbara?"

"They are," Micah said in his loud, deep voice. "Is this the woman – "

I held up my index finger, cutting him off and indicating he might want to wait a moment. Standing up, I pulled the picture we'd found under the window out of my pocket.

I took a quick look at Stanley and he had a knowing look on his face as he watched.

Micah looked over my shoulder at the photo. "Where'd you get that?"

"Someone, apparently the blonde, conveniently left it in the upstairs bedroom under the window. She's been in that bedroom at least twice now."

Tyler sat up straighter. "I think you're on to a real mystery." He took the picture out of my hands and laid it on the page of the album. "This is definitely Francine."

I hadn't noticed Racheal and Zoë return with the tea. They set the glasses in front of Stanley and me along with a sugar bowl and spoons.

Zoë picked up the picture from the album page. "Well, this is eerie. Who would have left this in your house?" She looked me in the eyes. "Are you sure you don't believe in ghosts? Ahh, there's no such thing as a ghost. Someone is putting you on, trying to get your goat. I don't know why, but that's got to be the case."

"I agree." Stanley spoke a little too quickly. "Why, I'll bet your mother found it and left it there as a joke. You know your mother. She's been trying to scare you since we first got here."

Racheal's eyes were opened in surprise while she studied the picture. "He's probably right. It must be your mother just fooling around." She didn't sound convincing or convinced.

I studied the pictures without replying. There was a definite resemblance between my blonde and the one in the pictures. "I can't swear this is the woman I've seen because I've only caught glimpses of her from behind, but the hair style, color and general build are about the same."

"And no one else has seen her?" Micah asked.

"No."

"Well, hell, it's probably just your imagination." He patted my back but the look on his face belied his words.

"Okay," Tyler said. "We're going to keep a closer watch. Micah and Zoë are going to be here all week."

Racheal nodded her head. "If you see us watching you, just remember we're not being nosey or spying. We're trying to help."

I almost laughed, but it caught in my throat. "I know this woman wants something. I just can't figure out what it could be. And I didn't mean to drag all of you into this situation."

"No, she didn't, but if you'd be kind enough to keep your eyes open we'd certainly appreciate it." Stanley seemed to feel he had my back.

I stood and handed the album to Tyler, holding back the picture we'd found under the window. "I guess we'd better get moving. At least, thanks to all of you, I have some ideas rolling around in my head. I still don't believe in ghosts, but there does seem to be some connection between Francine and my blonde."

"Don't leave yet," Racheal said. "I'll copy this page of pictures for you on our printer so you can study them later."

"Thanks. That might help."

"So you and your mother are trying to scare each other?" Micah asked.

"I know it sounds silly, but yeah. Just for fun."

"Come back later and talk to me. I think I've got just the thing to make you the winner."

Tyler looked at his brother and grinned. "I know what he's talking about, and he's right. Now where is Racheal with those pictures?"

"Sandi will have them as a frame of reference," Stanley said. "We'll work this out. She and her mother can frighten each other, but I'm not going to let some ghost harass Sandi."

Micah grinned down at Stanley and slapped him on the back, almost knocking him over.

Stanley did kind of a two-step to keep his balance.

"Sorry, pal, but you're the man. You're kind of a little guy and yet you're ready to come to your friend's defense."

"I do my best." Stanley's chest puffed out, just a little. Or maybe he just stood straighter.

"Let's find this ghost," Zoë said.

I sighed. Why wouldn't people believe me?

"I don't believe in ghosts."

Chapter Thirty-four

Stanley and I returned to the llama ranch. I'd have to ask my mother if she'd come up with a name for the place yet. "Llama Ranch" wouldn't be fitting for the bed and breakfast/dude ranch she'd planned.

We stood in the living room and I called out, but apparently she and Felicity hadn't returned from the neighbor's house yet. Maybe they'd moved on to another one. Pete and Frank were still gone, too, out ATVing. I hoped they were having a good time.

"What now?" Stanley asked.

"I simply don't know. This is so different from any other case I've ever handled that I feel kind of lost. I think we need to figure out a way to catch the blonde. Any ideas?"

Stanley looked at me, at the ceiling, and at the floor. You could almost hear the wheels turning in his head. "We need some kind of signal. You only see her when you're alone or the others aren't looking. You need to be able to signal me so I can come in a hurry."

"I have no idea what we can use for a signal. If I yell, it'll scare her off. It's too bad we didn't bring those walkie talkies with us. They would have come in handy."

Stanley snapped his fingers. "Wait here." He ran out of the house like the tarantulas were after him, or the snake.

I waited. And waited. What on earth could he be doing?

He returned in a few minutes with his hands behind his back and grinning like the Cheshire cat.

"No," I said. "It can't be."

"Yes, indeed, I brought the walkie talkies with us. I have no idea why, but it seemed like the prudent thing to do. I guess because I'd heard how spacious the property is. I placed them in the glove box and quickly forgot about them."

He continued to grin and I joined him.

"I never would have thought of bringing them along." I reached out and he handed me one of the little black contraptions.

"The next time you see the woman, call me on the walkie talkie and I'll get here as fast as I can. We're in like Flynn, as the saying goes."

"Stan, Micah was right. You're the man. You come through for me at the darnedest times."

"These might come in handy for other things, too. You never know when we might need them. For instance, your mother won't have to yell across the property when a meal is ready for consumption."

"That's true, but she'll have to come to me because I'm not letting this little sweetie out of my possession."

We heard my mother and Felicity talking as they entered the house, and they sounded like they'd had a good time.

"I've got some great neighbors," my mother said. "They're older people, but they're sweethearts. They were thrilled to pieces to find out their new neighbor is younger than they are. I guess they'll be calling on us for help with things, but that's okay. Shirley and Jeff Shaw said Tyler's been helping them when they need things done. Now they won't feel like such a burden when they need something. At least that's what they said. And I sure wouldn't think of them as a burden. They were delightful." My mother sounded pretty wound up.

"Jeff sure has a great sense of humor," Felicity said. "He about had us rolling on the floor. Shirley just looks at him. I guess she's used to him, but we're a new audience."

"I'm glad you had so much fun and I'd like to meet them, but did they have any new information?" I asked.

Felicity sobered up quickly. "Not really. They had neighborhood barbeques and things like that from time to time, but their property used to be a chicken farm. They had other animals, too, and they were busy most of the time. All they knew about the murders was what we've already heard."

"That's it? It's not helpful," I said. I'd hoped we'd learn more.

My mother held up her hand as though silencing us. "There was one other thing. Shirley said she had a feeling that Harry didn't treat his family well. I asked what she meant and she beat around the bush.

"So I asked her if she'd ever noticed bruises on the mother or daughter. Her cheeks turned bright pink and then she told me that, yes, she'd seen bruises on both of them, but just on their arms. She said it looked like Harry had grabbed them and squeezed. She felt bad because she thought she should have told someone."

"Did her husband add any information to her revelation?" Stanley appeared to be quite interested.

Felicity tipped her head back and thought about the conversation. "No. He was surprised and chastised Shirley for not mentioning it to him at the time. He said he'd have 'run ol' Harry ragged' for mistreating the woman and their child. Shirley added something about not being sure he'd actually done anything to his daughter. Her bruises could have just been from playing outside."

"It sounds like you had quite a visit. Stanley and I have some news, too." I held out the page of pictures Racheal made for me along with the photo I'd found under the window. "Take a look."

My mother and friend studied the pictures.

My mother's head snapped up like she'd heard a gunshot. "Don't tell me this is the blonde you've been seeing." She sounded almost hopeful.

"I can't say for sure. There's a definite resemblance, but I've only seen my stalker from the back, from a distance, and when I was half asleep."

Felicity started to laugh. "Your stalker?"

I shrugged. "I don't know what else to call her. I'm the only one she shows herself to, and she shows up when I least expect her. What would you call her?"

"I have no idea. I guess that's as good of a name as anything I could come up with right now."

"Let's go eat lunch and we'll talk about it more while we eat." My mother waved her hand at us and walked toward the stairs.

We followed like a herd of hungry wildebeests and chatted along the way. Felicity said Shirley put her hand on Jeff's arm while he was talking and he said, "I told you not to touch me" and kept talking. She chuckled about it and said it was obviously a joke and Shirley just ignored him.

She put her hand on Stanley's back and he said, "I thought I told you not to touch me."

His comment turned Fel's chuckle into a laugh. "That's the idea."

I tried to help my mother fix some sandwiches, but she waved me off and told me to go sit down.

"What? Two women in the kitchen is one too many?" I asked.

She waved her hand at me again and I sat down with

Felicity and Stanley.

"It sure is quiet around here without Bubba walking underfoot and woofing." I was glad he'd gone with Pete and Frank. He needed a day off, too.

"Let me take another look at those pictures," Felicity said. "Where'd you put them, Livvie?"

"On the sink. Here, Sandi." She reached toward me with the pictures in hand.

I stood and took them from her, handing them in turn to Fel. She studied the photographs closely with Stanley looking at them with her.

"She definitely doesn't look like a happy woman," she said. "Their daughter doesn't appear to be happy either. It really makes me appreciate my own childhood. My adoptive parents treated me with love and kindness."

"It makes you wonder what's wrong with some people, doesn't it?" I asked. "I remember working on a case where people's actions stemmed from abuse. It broke my heart."

"As I recall, didn't someone say Francine died in the middle of the night?" Stanley asked.

"Yes. Harry told the neighbors she got sick and he had to drive her to the hospital. No one ever saw her again."

"Interesting." My mother set a glass of iced tea and a paper plate with a sandwich in front of me. "Maybe we should be looking into what happened to Francine instead of the four murders."

I took a bite of my sandwich. "Then again, you'd think if something bad happened to her, somehow the neighbors or Barbara would have known about it."

Of course, their daughter may have gone off to college by then.

"I have a feeling we're letting our imaginations run away with us," my mother said. "Think about it. Her ghost wouldn't come back and follow *you* around, now would she? What could you do?"

"Set the record straight?" I asked. "No, I think you're right. We're so used to odd cases that we're reading something into this that isn't there."

Chapter Thirty-five

We discussed the idea of something sinister happening to Francine and finally came to the conclusion that the four murders were kicking our brains into overdrive.

"Aren't we the ones," my mother said. "Give us a couple of oddball possibilities and we try to turn them into something. Silly us."

Stanley swallowed a bite of sandwich and choked. After drinking some tea he spoke up. "I think we've become suspicious people because of the nature of our jobs. I don't know if that's good or not."

I studied him for a moment. "I think you're right. As private investigators we tend to be suspicious. If you think about it, we've learned a lot about people's facial expressions and the way they posture. We have some idea if they're lying or covering something up. At least we generally know when to ask more questions and be more watchful."

"Do you want to do this for the rest of your life?" Felicity asked. "I mean, is being distrustful a fun way to live?"

"Not really, but I think Pete and Stanley and I have learned to balance reality with wishful thinking. Do I want to do this for the rest of my life? I don't know. I sure don't want to go back to a regular nine-to-five job. I like being my own boss. I guess only time will tell."

My mother smiled. "Maybe someday you'll find another buried treasure."

"Yeah, like that's going to happen. Although, one can always hope. I've heard there's plenty of treasure buried in the Ozarks. Maybe I'll take a vacation there some day."

"Maybe we'll all go with you," my mother said.

I sighed. It was fun to dream about that kind of adventure.

"So, back to our discussion about Francine. If Harry did her in, I think we would have found her body by now with all the digging we've been doing. The boys broke up and dug out that cement slab in the yard, and it didn't seem to have any real purpose, other than it covered up a lot of trash. And look at all the work they've done in and around the stable. We've done so much around the house that I think we'd have found something out of the ordinary by now. Remember, too, the block wall and stains turned out to be nothing."

"You're right, sweetie." My mother ate the last bite of her sandwich and stood, taking both of our paper plates to the trash. "We're out in the middle of the desert, so to speak, in an area with not much going on. It's quiet all the time. It's given us too much time to let our imaginations work overtime. The only crimes committed here were the four murders, even if one may have been self-defense. Let's forget this nonsense and concentrate on doing as much as we can to the house before you leave."

"You're right, Livvie." Felicity stood and carried her own plate to the trash. "Tomorrow we'll get back to work. In fact, I think I'll do a few things this afternoon. Why don't you and I make a list of what needs to be done and what we can do before we leave? I mean, I know we can't do everything, but we can sure get a start on putting this house in order."

"Good idea."

I took Stanley's paper plate to the trash can. "You two go ahead and start your project. I'll wash the glasses."

Felicity kissed Stanley's cheek and told him she'd make up for not spending the day with him that evening.

His eyes widened and he grinned from ear to ear.

Our day off wasn't quite the way it should be. Instead of Pete and me spending time together, and Stanley and Fel doing something, we were paired off wrong. Oh, well, it didn't matter. It wouldn't be too long before we went on our honeymoon. In the meantime we were each doing something we enjoyed.

"So what's next?" I asked, turning to Stanley.

He still had a smile on his face and there was a faraway look in his eyes. He shook his head, clearing away whatever thoughts he was having. "That's an excellent question. Why don't we sit outside since the weather is nice and we can discuss the issue?"

"I'm surprised you want to sit outside with the bugs and snakes."

"Oh, there's been so much activity around here. I'm sure we've scared most of the, uh, animals and bugs away. I've come to a decision. I'm determined not to let them bother me."

"Well, good for you. Let's go outside right now."

I poured us each more iced tea and we left by the sliding glass door, strolling around the house and out to the motorhome. We sat down at the outdoor table and relaxed.

"You know," I said, "we really should spend the rest of the day unwinding. It's been a busy week, beginning with our weddings."

"No wonder I've been so tired." Stanley stretched and leaned back against the table. "It really doesn't seem like we've had any quiet time except when we sleep. I have to admit all the hustle and bustle has invigorated me though. I feel like a new man."

"You are. You're a new man embarking on a new life with an adorable wife." I looked off into the distance, realizing I was speaking for myself, too. "I hope Pete and Frank don't spend all day out there."

"No more lollygagging," he said. "We can rest and relax, but I believe we should put our plan together while we do so. If we can face the blonde, we can find out what her agenda is and put it all behind us. We can finally discover what she looks like and who she is."

"You're absolutely right. Your idea to use the walkie talkies was inspired, too. Be on your toes and ready for a call from me at all times."

"I'll try to keep track of you so I have a general idea of your whereabouts each day in order to be Johnny-on-the-spot. Should I tell Pete what we're doing?"

"I'll tell him tonight," I replied. "Even though you're helping me, I don't want to put you in an uncomfortable position. I think Pete will understand. Maybe he'll even help us."

"He may decide we're handling this correctly."

"I'm sure he will. And thanks again, Stan."

He nodded. "I'm going to try to start talking less formally, too. I should be just one of the guys."

"How about just being yourself? That works."

"Maybe I can combine the old me and the new me into something completely different."

He looked past me with an expression of disconcertion on his face.

"Stan? What's wrong?"

He narrowed his eyes and stared off into the distance. "Either my eyes are playing tricks or I just saw your blonde stalker."

"*What?*" My head whipped around so fast it almost made me dizzy.

I followed the direction of his intense gaze. I couldn't see anything.

"Where did you see her?"

"It looked like she was entering the house through the front door." He jumped up and headed toward the house.

I followed him.

"Be quiet and don't let her know we're coming," I whispered.

He nodded, slowing down and taking soft steps. I followed his example and tread softly.

We reached the front of the house and saw the screen door was ajar. We quietly climbed the steps and stopped. We couldn't peek inside because it was a security screen.

I reached forward and wrapped my fingers around the edge of the screen door, pulling it open and trying to be quiet. It screeched.

How could she have gone in without causing the same noise? I crossed my eyes and quickly pulled it open.

We stepped inside and scanned the living room. No blonde. I pointed toward the family room and motioned Stanley to check it out.

While he headed in that direction, I ran to the stairs. The basement door was open. I grabbed a flashlight we'd taken to leaving by the stairs so I could see into the dark corners of the rooms.

I moved to the top step and stood quietly, listening for any telltale noises. Nothing. I descended a few more steps and cocked my head, listening again. Still nothing. Taking the last couple of steps quietly, I stopped at the bottom and heard what I really *didn't* want to hear. The door to the garage clicked behind someone as they left the basement.

I ran across the room to the door and threw it open, only to find absolutely nothing. She'd disappeared again, but she'd had plenty of time. And do ghosts use doors, or do they walk through them? Once again I reminded myself that I don't believe in apparitions.

I had a sudden silly thought about a ghost trying to grip a door handle and her hand sliding right through it.

Chapter Thirty-six

The sound of footsteps on the stairs reached me and I turned to find Stanley joining me.

"She was here," I said.

He raised his eyebrows. "She was? How can you tell?" His gaze travelled around the basement.

"I heard the door leading to the garage close. She left as soon as I reached the bottom of the stairs. I can't believe whoever this is can be so crafty. She manages to be seen when she wants to be and still she manages to disappear. It's really frustrating."

"Well, at least now you have a witness. I didn't get a good look at her, but at least I saw her."

"Yeah. You saw her. Now everyone will have to believe me. I'd be willing to bet they'll all help now. She's not going to have a chance to get away next time." His observation had brightened my mood tremendously. "Let's go take a look at the screen door and try to figure out how she entered the house without making a lot of noise."

"That's an excellent… Good idea, Sandi."

I took one last look around the basement before we

ascended the stairs, but nothing seemed out of order and there was, of course, no blonde hiding in the shadows.

My question about the screen door was answered by my mother who opened the right side of the door instead of the left before we reached it. It didn't make a sound.

"What are you two up to?" she asked.

"Sandi's right about the blonde. She does exist," Stanley said. "I saw her. We tried to catch her, but to no avail."

"She went down to the basement and left by the door leading to the garage," I said. "She's slippery, I'll give her that."

"You saw her, Stanley?" My mother pursed her lips and shook her head. "I just don't get it. Why haven't any of the rest of us seen her?"

I almost laughed because she sounded like she felt left out.

"I believe my sighting was accidental. I'm not even sure she intended to show herself to Sandi this time."

"He's right," I said. "She probably didn't see us sitting by the motorhome. I can't imagine what she wanted in the house though. And what led her to visit the basement? You know, we found the photo in the upstairs bedroom. Maybe I should go downstairs and take a second look. Maybe she left another clue down there."

Mother looked thoughtful. "Perhaps she did. I think I'll just wander down there with you."

I smiled. "Okay. Let's go."

"Where's my wife?" Stanley asked.

"She's sitting at the table in the apartment kitchen making a list of things we talked about doing while you're all here. I went outside to walk and stretch my legs a little."

He nodded and walked toward the stairs that led to the apartment. "I'll see you in the basement in a few minutes."

We waved and headed for the door to the basement. Descending the stairs quickly, we began searching for a sign from the elusive woman.

"Mom, now that Stan's seen Blondie, you want in on the action, too, don't you?" He'd been with me when we found the photo and he'd finally seen the woman. I knew that would drive her nuts. She wanted to be a part of it.

"Well…" She was hesitant. I figured she didn't want to admit how she felt.

"Come on," I wheedled. "You can be honest about it."

She stopped walking and looked me in the eye. "Okay. Yes, I want to be a part of all of this. Obviously something isn't right. Since we're going to be living here, I want to know what's going on. What if, after you all leave, I begin seeing this woman around every corner? I could develop a bad case of nerves."

"You?" I laughed. "You'd probably find a way to scare her off. Hey! That's not a bad idea. We keep trying to scare each other when maybe we should be trying to scare *her*."

"Sandra, how can we frighten her if we never know when she'll show up?"

"Good point." I started walking again. "Come on. Let's see if she left anything behind."

I still held the flashlight so I began shining it in the corners, hoping to find something. "When is the electrician coming back? We could sure use some lights down here."

"He'll be back tomorrow. In the meantime, I know some of the lights are working." She flipped a switch on the wall and a dim light came on in a ceiling light with fixtures for four lights. "Well, I guess that was a *duh* moment, wasn't it? Why didn't we just try the switch to begin with?"

"I guess we weren't expecting it to work. You're right. We've had a few *duh* moments around here."

"I'll find more light bulbs." She looked around the basement. "I don't see anything to stand on, so I'll bring back a ladder, too."

"You get the bulbs and I'll bring in a ladder from the

garage."

"That's where the bulbs are," she said. "Follow me."

We traipsed up the short staircase and into the garage, which was only at a little higher level than the basement. It seemed like the whole house was made up of levels.

My mother knew exactly where she'd left the bulbs and she found three sixty watt lights.

I had to search for a ladder. They'd brought three, and one was in the house with the second set up in the barn. The third one rested behind some boxes.

"Look at this," I said. "It seems Frank moved some boxes in front of the hole in the wall. What are the odds he thought you'd forget about the hidden staircase?"

She started to laugh. "Oh, that Frank! You're probably right, but honestly, I didn't forget about it. I'm still going to talk him into opening the wall so we can see where the stairs lead. Who knows? Maybe we can put them to use if they lead somewhere interesting."

"Uh huh. You'd make him tear out a wall? I'm sure they're probably just something the builder used temporarily."

"Hmm. You're most likely right. Maybe I'll let it go. I'll think about it."

We carted the bulbs and ladder down to the basement and I replaced the lights as she handed them to me.

"I'll take the ladder back upstairs and we can get busy searching this place. I simply can't imagine why she'd have sneaked into the house and ended up in the basement."

I was almost to the stairs when I tripped and dropped the ladder. "Oh, for crying out loud." Glancing down I realized I'd tripped on a long crack in the cement flooring. I reached down to get another grip on the ladder when something caught my eye. I stooped down and examined the crack. Something sparkled.

"What are you doing?" My mother walked over to join

me.

"There's something here. Look."

Although I could see the sparkle, whatever it was had dirt covering it. I must have disturbed it when I dropped the ladder.

"What's that?"

I shoved the ladder aside. "I don't know." I tried to pull whatever it was out of the crack, but it was stuck. "I'm going to need something to pry it out."

My mother glanced around the basement, realizing we didn't have any tools to work with nearby. "Give me a minute. I know where there's a screwdriver in the garage. Maybe we can pry it up. Do you think it's something important?"

"Probably not, but the way things have been going, I think it's worth a look."

"Be right back." She scampered up the stairs and returned within a couple of minutes with a small screwdriver, handing it to me.

"Thanks." I sat on the floor and began working.

"I brought a small one."

"I see that."

She sighed. "What I mean is, it will probably fit better than a big one would."

"Of course."

I shoved the screwdriver into the crack and began trying to pry the object out. It was stuck tight and I had to struggle. After a couple of grunts, and when I least expected it, the object flew out of the crack and across the room with the screwdriver not far behind.

My mother ran after the object and found it quickly. After picking it up, she rubbed it, apparently trying to get rid of the dirt.

"Well, will you look at this!"

She looked from the object in her hand to me and back again.

Chapter Thirty-seven

"What is it?" I stood and walked over to my mother. What could have possibly been hiding in the crack in the cement floor?

"A wedding ring, and I think it might match that engagement ring we found upstairs." She turned the ring over in her hand and studied it.

"Okay, this is weird. Why would there be an engagement ring upstairs under the molding, and a wedding ring down here in a crack?"

"I think we have more mysteries than we could have anticipated." Mother handed me the ring.

"You're right. We found an engagement ring upstairs, the wedding ring down here, and a gun in the bathroom. Somehow I think they're all connected, but I can't put it together. We've also got neighbors telling us stories about the people who lived here. Marion, from across the street, really didn't like Harry."

My mother nodded. "I can see why, considering the way he treated her. Imagine how he treated his own family. It seems everyone around here noticed bruises on Francine's and Barbara's arms. It makes me wonder if there were bruises in places covered by their clothes."

"Yeah. Me, too. Something wasn't right in this house and it involves more than just Clyde the Killer, as Marion likes to call him."

I had a feeling Zetta's granddaughter knew more than she was telling. It was just a feeling with nothing concrete to base the thought on. "We need to start asking more questions."

"Whom do you think we should talk to?"

"Marion, of course. She knows something. It's only a gut feeling, but it's a strong one. I think she'd like to tell us everything she knows, but something is holding her back. We need to, let's say, *encourage* her to talk."

"What're you going to do? Get out the rubber hose?"

"Oh, Mom, sometimes you just crack me up. I left the rubber hose at home."

"Har de har har, Sandi. How are we going to get her to open up?"

I looked at the floor and thought for a moment. "Maybe she wouldn't tell everything because her grandparents were there. I've seen her take walks down the road. If I happen to take a walk at the same time, she might talk to me. It's worth a try. I'll keep my eyes open for her."

"That's a good idea. Maybe I'll go with you. Sometimes people will talk to a mother before they'll talk to a private eye."

Looking into her eyes, I said, "You may be right. I could lag behind while the two of you talk."

"In the meantime, I think I hear the ATV. I guess the boys decided it was time to come home." My mother headed through the kitchen and toward the Arizona room door.

I followed. As it happens, as busy as we'd been, I still missed Pete. We sure weren't acting like newlyweds. It was time to change a few things around the llama ranch. Instead of working with my mother and Felicity, I'd work beside Pete. Felicity could work with her husband for a while, doing his jobs. I'd mention my idea to the two men, and my mother.

We headed for the ATV where Frank had parked it, next to the stable.

"Mother, I think Pete and I should spend more time together, and – "

"Funny, but I was thinking the same thing. For two people who just got married, you've hardly seen each other at all. Do you want him to help you paint or do you want to work on the stable?"

I started to laugh. "If I can talk him into painting, I'd be surprised. On the other hand, with his leg bothering him, maybe he'd rather do that for a while. I can't picture Felicity and Stanley being much help with the stable though. Well, maybe Stanley, but Fel is so small and delicate."

"Tell you what. You and Pete paint and I'll help outside. With Frank and the three of us we should be able to get a few things accomplished. Besides, we don't have to work on the barn."

Before we could discuss it further, Pete climbed out of the ATV and walked toward us. He was grinning from ear to ear, although I did notice he was limping again. Maybe it had something to do with sitting for too long and the bumpy ride through the hills.

He stopped in front of my mother. "That was an amazing ride. Frank is going to want to take more rides, Livvie, and he'll want you to go with him. There's so much to see."

"I've been out with him before, and you're right. What was out there today? Snakes? Tarantulas? One-eyed mountain lions?"

Pete chuckled. "We saw a snake, but the sound of the ATV made it slither away in a hurry. It was too far away to tell if it was a rattler. And we saw a couple of Big Horn sheep, along with a few wild burros. The vultures were circling something, but we didn't bother to find out what it was. It was too far away. Oh, and we found an abandoned mine shaft."

"Did you go into the mine shaft?" I asked.

"No. There's no telling what condition it's in. Frank's going to ask Tyler if he knows anything about it."

"It sounds like you had a good time," Livvie said.

"We did. Bubba did, too. And don't worry, Sandi, we kept an eye on him. There was plenty for him to sniff up in the hills. He really wanted to take out after the burros, but we kept him close to us."

I smiled, knowing he wouldn't let my – our – mangy mutt get in trouble.

"Mom and I have a plan, if you're willing to go along with us."

"What's that?"

"Tomorrow why don't you help me paint instead of working on the stable? We need to spend some time together, and so do Stanley and Felicity. Mom says she wants to work with Frank, too. What do you think?"

"Sounds like a good plan to me. Are we going to do anything else today?"

I glanced at my mother for an answer.

"No," she said. "We decided this would be a day off, and we'll keep it that way." She touched Pete's arm before walking away from us to go talk to Frank.

"It sounds like you really did have a good time." In a way I was sorry I hadn't gone with them. "Maybe before we go home you can take me for a ride?"

"Sure, baby, we'll do that. Did I miss anything around here?"

"You bet your sweet patootie. There was another Blondie sighting, and this time Stanley saw her. Oh, and we checked out the upstairs bedroom because I thought I saw her up there when we came home last night. Whoever she is, she left an old photo of a woman with long blonde hair under the window. I think she was hoping we'd find it."

"You – "

"There's more. Stanley and I went over to Tyler's house. He borrowed some photo albums from his mother, and there was a picture of the same woman in the album. She was Barbara's mother."

"And you think this is the same woman you've been seeing around here? I thought you didn't believe in ghosts."

"I don't. And I have no idea if it's the same woman or not. I've never seen the face of my blonde. One other thing, Pete. I said Stanley saw her. She was sneaking into the house. We followed her inside and I saw the basement door was open, so I followed her. I was sure that's where she'd gone. Anyway, she left by the door that leads to the garage before I could catch her."

"Anything else?"

"Yes."

He looked surprised.

"Mom and I decided to search the basement to see if she'd left anything behind, like another photo. To make a long story short, we found a wedding ring stuck in a crack in the cement. I think it matches the engagement ring we found in the living room."

"What engagement ring?" He crossed his arms across his chest, showing more interest.

"We found the ring when we were cleaning the floors in the living room. It had been stuck behind the molding. I realize you probably think I overreact to things, but in this case I honestly believe we've stumbled on to a mystery. There's something strange about this house, and its former occupants."

"I'm starting to believe you."

"You didn't before?"

"Not really. I figured your imagination was working overtime."

"It figures."

I rolled my eyes and sighed, making a quiet statement.

Chapter Thirty-eight

*P*ete and I wandered over to my mother and Frank to talk about switching jobs. She'd already told him, and he was fine with the plan.

Felicity and Stanley soon joined us and we explained it to them.

"Works for me," Felicity said. "How about you, puddin' pop?" She looked up into Stanley's eyes and grinned.

"I have no issue with this, snookums, except maybe it would be too difficult for you. You're quite small, you know."

"Believe me, punkin', I know my size and I'm a lot stronger than I look." Her grin disappeared and she sounded tense.

Stanley backpedaled before she could say more. "Now, you little munchkin, I know you can do it. I thought maybe – "

"End of story, *sugar lump.*"

Bubba glanced back and forth, from one to the other, almost like he was at a tennis match. It must have been their tone of voice.

Pete looked Stanley in the eyes. "Good. I don't know how much more I could have taken with the cutesy names."

"Oh, you know you really like the way we talk, hunkie man," Fel said.

"Okay, I can live with that one." It was my husband's turn to grin.

"Hunkie man? I'll have to file that one away in my memory bank for when I need a favor." I poked Pete's arm.

"Uh huh."

Frank glanced at his watch. "It's later than I realized. Maybe we should start thinking about dinner. Today has flown by."

Mother patted his arm. "Yes, dear, we'll start putting something together right now. Come along, girls." She waved at Felicity and me, motioning us to follow her.

We fell in step with her and strolled to the house.

"I think they should fix dinner once in a while, but what do I know?" I asked.

Mom looked over her shoulder and smiled at me. "We'll have them barbeque something soon."

She'd bought some thinly sliced roast beef from the grocery store deli when we were in town the night before along with macaroni salad and hamburger buns. She had barbeque sauce in the refrigerator so she tore the beef into pieces placed it in a pot and added the sauce.

While she did that I set up the little outdoor cook stove, making it ready to heat the meat.

Felicity put butter on the hamburger buns and toasted them in the tiny little oven.

Mother put the pot on top of the stove and I opened some pork and beans and started those heating, too.

Felicity sat down at the table. "Come sit down, Livvie. This is turning out to be an easy peasy dinner."

"I know. I didn't really need the two of you to help me get dinner ready, but I thought Sandi and I should fill you in on what we've found."

Fel sat up straighter, looking expectant. "What's going

on?"

We told her about our afternoon and the wedding ring. She leaned her elbows on the table, looking interested in hearing more.

"My, my. You've had a busy day for what we decided would be a day off. Stan told me about the picture you found and going over to Tyler's house. So you think your blonde is the woman in the picture?"

"Not unless she's risen from the dead. No, there's something else going on here," I said. "Whatever it is eludes me and I need everyone's help to figure this out. Pete seems more interested now that I've told him about our day. If we're all on alert, I think we'll catch her."

"Yeah, Sandi's bringing the rubber hose to talk to Marion from across the street. Maybe she'll use it on the blonde, too."

"You're a riot, Mother."

Felicity snickered.

"Look. I want to catch this woman and find out what she's up to. It's obvious, at least to me, that she wants something from me. She's been so careful not to let anyone else see her. She might have gotten away with it if she'd realized Stan and I were sitting out by the motorhome, but I don't think she saw us."

"She's a sneaky little thing." My mother stood and walked to the cook stove to stir the meat and beans.

"I haven't had a barbequed beef sandwich in years," Felicity said. "It smells wonderful, and the aroma is making me hungry."

"About five more minutes," my mother said.

My friend got out some paper plates and cheese slices, in case anyone wanted cheese on their sandwich, and I brought out the iced tea and glasses.

"I'll go tell the men to come for dinner." Fel wandered out the sliding glass doors and headed around the house.

I heard a thud and Felicity yelled, "*Hey!*"

Without glancing at my mother, I ran out the door to see what was wrong.

"Felicity?" She was sitting on the ground. "Are you okay? Did you trip or something?"

"Or something would be more like it." She reached up, wanting me to help her stand.

I took hold of her hand and pulled.

"What happened?" My mother followed me out the door.

"Your blonde is getting sloppy," she said. "Now I've seen her, too. I came out the door and she was hiding, listening to us. Unfortunately, I didn't see her until it was too late. She shoved me and ran away, right past me."

Excitement overtook me. "You saw her face? What did she look like?"

"No. By the time I looked up, all I saw was her back before she ran around the side of the house." She wiped dirt off the seat of her pants. "I honestly don't think she meant to hurt me. I think I scared her."

"Which way did she go?" I asked.

Fel pointed toward the corner of the apartment.

"That's the same area where I saw her when she watched me through the bedroom window, when we were cleaning. I guess there's no point in trying to find her. She'll be long gone by now."

"All right, girls, this could become dangerous. I mean, she pushed Felicity. She could have sprained an ankle or something." My mother crossed her arms and watched me intently. "It seemed like a game in the beginning, but if she was listening to us and getting pushy, then it sounds like things have changed."

Felicity looked thoughtful. "I don't think so. I agree with Sandi about her wanting something, but I have a feeling she was in the wrong place at the wrong time when I came out here. I think the sight of me scared her because there's no good reason for her to come out of hiding to shove me. She could have stayed where she was until I was gone."

"Honestly? I think my mother's right. Listening to us talk puts a different light on things. And shoving you? It wasn't necessary. She could have run away without getting physical. I have a feeling there's something she really wants us to know, or see, or do. No one's lived here in years, so I can't imagine what it could be, but…"

"So what do we do?" Felicity turned and glanced in the direction the woman had fled.

"Stanley brought four walkie talkies with him. I'm going to pass them out. If anyone sees her, then quietly call to the rest of us. With all of us on guard I'm pretty sure Blondie's days are numbered."

My mother lifted her hand in a *hold on a second* motion. "There are four walkie talkies and six people. Who are you going to pass them out to?"

"Anyone who's within running distance." I wanted each of us to have easy access to the others. "You know, Blondie knows this house like the back of her hand or she wouldn't be able to come and go, and disappear, as easily as she does."

My mother nodded. "I've thought about that very thing. This house has been vacant a long time. She's had years, apparently, to discover all the ins and outs of this place."

She was quiet for a moment.

"Did you know the Powers that Be have declared hormone pills are a controlled substance?"

"Well, that was out of the blue," I said.

"It's because they have testosterone in them. I have to get the prescription renewed every month."

I watched Felicity as she stepped away from my mother.

Mom started laugh. "I just got to thinking, if I couldn't

get my hormone pills Blondie wouldn't stand a chance against me."

"Neither would anyone else," I mumbled under my breath.

"What, dear?"

"Nothing."

Chapter Thirty-nine

This had begun to feel like one of the longest weeks of my life. Pete and I were newlyweds and how were we spending our time? I didn't want to think about it. Looking ahead at my life with Pete, it really was only one week out of our lives. Or maybe a week and a half. I had a feeling Felicity probably felt the same way I did.

This time when Fel left to call the men for dinner, I went with her. We found them sitting at the table by the motorhome, drinking a beer and talking.

"Stan? Are you drinking beer?" Felicity knew Stanley couldn't hold his liquor very well.

He turned the can around and tapped it, showing her he'd opted for a soft drink. "No beer, but we'll still have a wild time at the llama ranch tonight."

She grinned. "Why, Stan, whatever do you mean? No, don't answer that in mixed company."

His face turned pink when he realized what he'd said. It was so out of character for him. "Well…"

"Come on," I said. "Dinner's ready and waiting. Remind me to ask Racheal for the dinner triangle bell thingy she said she had."

They threw their empty cans in the trash and headed for the house. I held back and took a good long look around the property. It was dusk, and even with all the work that needed to be done, the place looked like it would eventually belong on the front of a brochure. Which reminded me, I wanted to ask my mother and Frank what they'd decided to call their bed and breakfast.

I glanced up and saw Pete standing by the corner of the house, watching me. He looked happy.

I smiled. I was happy, too, even if we weren't on our honeymoon. I stopped wasting time and headed in his direction.

We walked hand in hand to the apartment and dished up our dinner. Mother had set everything on the small breakfast bar, buffet style.

"Pete?" I looked up at him and smiled again. "Why don't you and I take our food outside and eat by the motorhome? Just you and me."

He nodded while he continued to pile barbequed beef on his hamburger bun. "What more could I ask for than dinner and you?"

I laughed to myself. What a romantic! Uh huh.

No one followed us outside. I had to assume they realized we wanted some alone time. I only gave one thought to Marion taking her walk and quickly dismissed the idea of watching for her.

There were no insects bothering us, no snakes rattled at us, and I didn't see even one tarantula. Any lurking scorpions kept their distance, too.

Pete excused himself and headed for the garage. Returning, he lit a hurricane lamp he'd found earlier in the garage. The sun dipped behind the hills and we had the closest thing to a romantic dinner possible.

I knew in my heart that good things were waiting for

us, no farther away than a trip up the stairs.

Turned out I was right.

~ * ~

We slept well and didn't wake up as early as we had earlier in the week. The extra sleep made a difference in the way I felt, thankfully.

Blondie hadn't bothered us and my mother and I hadn't tried to scare each other. I'd have to come up with a plan. We'd been having fun throwing the scare factor into the mix. I'd have to find out what Micah was talking about when he'd said he had something that would serve my purpose.

Pete took his shower first while I relaxed and almost fell back to sleep. It promised to be a productive day, and we'd make a great husband and wife team. I had a feeling with him working beside me, we'd accomplish a lot.

I didn't have enough time to doze off before Pete came in and dressed, letting me know the shower was ready and waiting.

Breakfast turned out to be a "roll your own" meal.

"We've got plenty of work to do today and cooking isn't on my To Do List this morning." Mom sat at the table and ate cereal.

I joined her.

So did Pete. "I don't think I'm going to work up the same type of appetite as usual today."

"Are you saying that painting is easy?" I asked.

"No, but it's not as demanding as working in the stable or the yard. I think Frank is planning on tearing out some dead trees and bushes today."

"Ah."

Pete poured a second bowl of cereal.

He asked the question I'd been meaning to ask. "Livvie, what did you and Frank decide to call this place? I'm sure it needs a name if it's going to be a B&B."

"We haven't figured it out. I've got a couple of ideas,

but Frank and I haven't agreed on anything yet."

"You'll come up with something unique." I spooned a bite of cereal and ate it.

Mother finished her cereal. "See ya. Everyone else is already outside, looking things over and figuring out what we need to do. Oh, and your walkie talkie is sitting on the counter."

She looked in both directions before stepping outside. Blondie wouldn't get the best of her.

"What part of the house are we going to work on?" Pete sat back in his chair and watched me finish eating.

"The apartment. If we can get it done before we leave, Mom and Frank can live here while they work on the rest of the house. I think she said someone is coming tomorrow to start installing tile, so we should probably try to get as much done today as we can."

"Works for me. Where's the paint? It's in the Arizona room, isn't it?"

I nodded. "Let's get busy."

The morning passed quickly. Working with Pete sure wasn't like working with my mother and Felicity. He was a no-nonsense guy and we finished the two bathrooms. That left one bedroom and the living room.

"What color is your mother using on the living room?" Pete asked.

"Off-white. Since she did the kitchen in yellow, nothing else would look quite right. Actually, the whole apartment will be off-white except for the kitchen."

"Off-white it is, just like the bathrooms. We need more paint. Back in a minute." He left the apartment and headed for the Arizona room.

I'd just sat down at the kitchen table when I heard a voice.

"Sandi, are you down there?" It sounded like either Tyler or Micah. My guess would be Tyler. Micah had a booming voice.

"Down here," I called.

Both Tyler and Micah strolled down the stairs.

"How are you guys, this morning?" I asked.

"Good," Micah said. "We decided to come on over and see if there's anything we can do to help. The wives will be here shortly."

"Thank you. We can use all the help we can get. Mom and Frank want to live in this apartment while they work on the rest of the house. If y'all want to help me and Pete paint the living room, we can do the rest ourselves."

"Y'all?" Micah grinned.

I grinned back. "I'm not from the south, so I'm not sure where that came from."

"Never end a sentence in a preposition," Tyler said, "at least in a book. I have trouble remembering all the rules when I write, but sometimes I can make exceptions in dialogue."

"Not the time or the place, bro," Micah said. "And don't ever correct me when we talk."

I could see where these brothers might get on each other's nerves from time to time.

I stood up and the walkie talkie fell out of my pocket.

"What's that?" Micah picked it up for me. "Oh, a walkie talkie. What's this for?"

"Four of us have them," I replied. "If anyone sees the elusive blonde, we'll call the others. My goal has become to catch her and figure out what's going on."

Tyler nodded. "I think I may have to use her in one of my books unless it turns out she's some nutcase. Well, even if she is, she might make a good character. Especially after we figure out what she's up to."

Micah studied his brother for a moment. "Yeah, I think we ought to help these good people. Maybe we can stake this place out one night. Isn't that what you call it in your books? Staking things out?"

Tyler looked shocked. "Uh, are you telling me you've actually read one of my books? I'm shocked."

I could tell he was teasing his brother by his tone of voice.

Micah gave him a withering look. "Yeah, I've read them all. But only because Zoë said I should and she said they were good."

"And are they?" I asked.

"If you like mysteries, I guess they are. And the blonde would fit right into one of his puzzles."

"I think I just got a glimpse of her," Pete said from the doorway, "but you've got the walkie talkie, and she disappeared around the house. She's got a lot of guts, I'll give her that."

Chapter Forty

"**Y**ou could have dropped the paint can and given chase," Tyler said.

Pete set down his load. "The paint can isn't closed. She'll be back, and we'll be ready for her. I heard what you said about staking out the place, Micah. If we do that it might give your brother some real experience for his books."

"Cool!" Tyler said. "I'd like to have some experiences for the books."

His brother slapped him on the back. "You're a real piece of work sometimes. What are you? Thirteen?"

"If I ever make the bestseller list, you'll be talking out of the other side of your mouth."

Did I need to break up this interaction? "Okay, okay, guys, let's get busy. If we get the living room painted and you're still in a helpful mood, maybe you can see Frank outside and work off some of your... Uh, *feelings* toward each other."

"Now you sound like my wife." Micah picked up a paint roller.

Pete headed for the door. "Back in a minute. I'll go grab

a couple more brushes and rollers." And he was gone.

Tyler picked up a paint tray and filled it while Micah scoped out the living room. "We'll have this done in no time with four of us working on it."

"Make that six," came a female voice from the stairs.

I smiled at Racheal and Zoë. "Welcome to the painting party."

Pete stuck his head inside, saw the two wives and turned around. "Back in a minute."

Racheal looked around the room. "If we each take a wall – "

"Six of us and four walls," Tyler said.

"Yes, but two of the walls are longer, so we can get this done in no time." She smiled sweetly at her husband.

"Have any of you noticed how much smiling and laughing goes on around this place?" I asked.

"No, we haven't been here that much," Zoë said. "But it'll be what you make of it – hard work or a lot of fun."

Micah gave his wife a hug. "Love your attitude."

Pete returned once again. "Okay, grab a brush or a roller and let's get this done. And thanks for the help."

Pete and I took a longer wall while the Hansens divided up the rest of the room. At first there wasn't very much conversation, but once we got into it we started talking.

"So what do you think the blonde is up to?" Zoë asked. "Are you sure she's not a ghost?"

"I'm sure," I said, "but I have no idea what she wants. From the back she resembles the woman who used to live here, but you already heard that. Maybe the resemblance is on purpose. I just don't know. Thanks to Stan, we're using some walkie talkies. If anyone sees her, they'll send out an alarm and hopefully we can catch her."

"Don't we have some walkie talkies in the truck?" Zoë tapped her husband on the shoulder and dropped her hand to her side. Unfortunately, she forgot she had a paint brush in her hand and his dark blue shirt suddenly had an off white stripe down the arm.

He looked from the stripe to her and shook his head. "Yes, dear, we have walkie talkies in the truck. I'll fetch them for you when I go back to my brother's house to change shirts – after we're through painting."

"I didn't mean – "

Before she could say any more, the walkie talkie in my pocket buzzed. I set down the roller and pulled it out.

"Yes?"

"No sightings," my mother said. "I just wanted to check to make sure it was working. Things have been so quiet."

"Pete thought he saw her, but she disappeared. As usual."

"We need to sit down as a group and discuss her knowledge of this house."

"Sounds good to me, Mom. The Hansens are here, too, and they want to get involved."

"Good. It'll be better with more people."

"We'll talk later," I said. "Now I'm going back to work."

"Roger and out," she said.

I looked up and everyone was watching me. I hadn't realized how quiet it had become.

"Roger and out?" Zoë was chuckling to herself.

"Yeah, my mother likes to play the role."

Pete started painting again. "She likes to be involved, you mean."

"Well, sure. She doesn't like sitting on the sidelines."

"Sounds like my mother-in-law," Micah said.

Zoë poked his side. "Be careful what you say about my mother."

"I was only joking, honey." He hunched his shoulders before relaxing them and going back to work.

It didn't happen in mere minutes, but we finished painting the living room quicker than I'd hoped we would.

"What's next?" Racheal asked.

"Pete and I are going to work on the last bedroom. If you're still up for it, why don't you head outside and talk to Frank. I know he's got plenty of outdoor work just waiting to be done."

They walked outside as a group while Pete and I made our way to the bedroom.

"It looks like everything will be ready when the tile guy comes tomorrow," he said.

"I can hardly believe how much difference painting the rooms has made. This house is going to be gorgeous when it's finished." Sometimes a person doesn't realize how much things have changed until they stand back and take a good, long look.

"The cupboards in the kitchen are going to have to be cleaned up, or maybe refinished."

"Mom and Frank can take care of that when they move inside. They must be tired of the motorhome by now."

"Frank tells me it's actually comfortable for the short term. I don't think I'd want to live in one though. I like a good, solid house."

"Yes, Pete, I know you do."

The walkie talkie buzzed. Actually, it was static, not a buzz.

"Sandi?" It was my mother.

"I'm here," I replied.

"In about half an hour you need to take a break and come eat lunch. Racheal and Zoë are bringing a pizza over along with some breadsticks and salads."

I glanced at my watch. "Okay, we'll be out in half an hour."

Pete smiled. "Pizza it is. Love that stuff."

"Maybe we can talk about Blondie while we eat. We

really need to come up with a plan. I'm feeling less like a private detective with every sighting."

"We'll figure it out." He filled his paint pan and began working.

We were quiet for about ten minutes.

"Someday we'll have to take a vacation and stay here at the B & B," I said.

"Sounds like a plan to me. You can have the B & B part and I'll take the Dude Ranch part. Win-win."

We finished one wall before I glanced at my watch and saw it was time for lunch.

"Come on, Pete. Let's go eat."

"Wash your brush out first or the paint will dry."

I nodded and headed for the kitchen and the sink. He was right. He put the lid on the paint can, loosely, and followed me.

After traipsing around the house, we found everyone already seated at the barbeque table and in extra chairs.

Tyler was filling everyone in on the surrounding area and what other things they could find in the hills.

Pete and I picked up paper plates and dished up salad and pizza.

Before I could sit down I saw Felicity suck in her breath and point toward the house. "I saw her! Just now. Blondie's at it again."

Stanley fairly leaped out of his chair. "Where?"

She sighed. "She's gone. She waited until we were all together and stood by the house watching us."

"What did she look like?" I asked. "Did she look like the photograph?"

"She was too far away. I have no idea. It's too bad I didn't have a pair of binoculars."

"I'm going to drive into town and buy some," Stanley said.

"Don't bother," Tyler said. "I've got a couple of pairs at

home. I'll bring them over."

Frank looked around at the group. "I'll say one thing. That Blondie of yours sure keeps everyone on their toes – especially my wife. She's constantly watching the area, and even though she tries to be inconspicuous, I see it."

"Like mother, like daughter." Pete took a bite of his pizza.

I ignored his comment. "Okay, we said we were going to come up with a plan, and I may have one. At first I thought she wanted me to see something. I've had second thoughts. Now I believe she's looking for something."

"Like a set of wedding rings?" my mother asked.

"Could be. There's really nothing else in the house to search for, unless there's a secret compartment or something."

"Don't fantasize too much," Pete said. "We've had a good look around the house. I don't think we've missed much."

"Except the hidden staircase in the garage." Mother studied the table while she talked. "Has anyone seen her near the hidden staircase?"

Chapter Forty-one

"What hidden staircase?" Zoë asked.

The rest of the Hansens watched my mother, waiting for an answer.

"A box fell and knocked a hole in the wall of the garage, near the door to the basement. If you look through the hole you can see a wooden staircase, but we can't see where it leads."

"I'd like to see it," Tyler said. "You know, just in case I can use it in a story."

Micah shook his head and took a bite of pizza.

My mother glanced from face to face. "Let me repeat my question. Has anyone seen her near the hidden staircase?"

Frank answered for all of us. "No, Livvie, no one has seen her near the garage or the staircase."

"Well, we know she ran *through* the garage," I said, "but she didn't stop to look around. She'd disappeared by the time I opened the door between the basement and the garage."

"I wish I could get a good look at her." Tyler sounded almost wistful.

Micah shook his head again. "Sure you do. You write mysteries, and here's a real one right in front of your nose. Actually, I wish you could see her, too. You know everyone around here. If you recognize her, it might answer a lot of questions."

"He's right," I said. "You're the one who needs to keep the binoculars handy. Realistically, you and Racheal should both keep a pair with you."

"What if it's not someone from around here?" Racheal asked.

"We'll deal with that if you see her," I said.

"Here's a plan." Pete spoke slowly and set down the paper plate with the pizza on it. "If she's looking for something, she needs the house to herself. What if she thought we were all gone for a while? We could leave in the late afternoon tomorrow. I mean all of us, the Hansens included. We can park somewhere down the road and quietly come back here – and wait for her."

It was a good idea.

I told him so. "Great idea, Pete, but instead of everyone leaving, let's just make it look that way. A few of us could hide out in the house or the motorhome until the rest of you come back."

Before we could discuss it any further, everyone started to talk at once.

Pete and I sat quietly and listened.

Apparently they thought he'd come up with a good plan, too.

"One last thing," I said. "I'm going to leave the wedding rings on the counter in the apartment. If that's what she's after, let's give them to her."

"What rings?" Tyler asked.

"Oh. I keep forgetting, you don't know everything that's happened." I explained about the rings and finding them in separate places. "We also found a gun hidden under the bathroom sink upstairs. I don't know if it has anything to do with, well, anything. It was hidden though, not out in plain sight."

That last bit of information started another round of chatter. It took everyone by surprise and, of course, they all figured it must have something to do with... That's when things got quiet. No one had a guess about what the gun might have to do with anything.

Thankfully, I wasn't the only one feeling stumped.

"Sandi," Pete said, "when some of you leave the house tomorrow, you need to be in that group. She's always watching you for some reason. My guess would be because you're an investigator and she wants something from you. I haven't figured out how you'll sneak back yet, but that's the way it's got to be."

"I know. You're right. If she doesn't see me leave, she probably won't take advantage of trying to search the house again. I think she's looking for the wedding rings, because other than the gun, there's nothing here out of the ordinary."

"I don't know about that." My mother sounded thoughtful. "Think about it. We've found the rings, the gun, and the hidden staircase. It stands to reason there may be other things we haven't found yet."

"Are you saying you think we should actively search the house and grounds?" Frank looked dubious, to put it mildly. "We've got a lot to do around here without having a treasure hunt."

"We could search while we work," she replied.

"Uh huh. And all the work will take longer to accomplish. We can't expect the kids to stay here, working their fingers to the bone, indefinitely."

"We'll talk later." Mother seemed to have made up her mind.

"But – "

"Later, dear."

I noticed a look that involved clenched jaws on his face, but he didn't say anything else.

The Hansens looked uncomfortable and concentrated on their food. So did Felicity and Stanley.

Pete surprised me and started to laugh.

All eyes immediately turned to him.

"Oh, come on. You know Livvie's going to have her way. She always does."

Frank started to laugh with him. "You're right, Pete. She just lets me *think* I'm getting my way from time to time. Let's finish eating and get back to work. If we find something in the process, we'll let everyone know."

I glanced toward the front of the house and saw they'd pulled up some of the dead trees. Others seemed to be okay now that we'd started watering them.

"What's next?" Stanley asked.

Frank smiled. "I want to plant a hibiscus bush by the side of the house."

It was my turn to laugh, but I couldn't explain why, at least not with my mother sitting next to me. When she was in the throes of menopause Frank planted a hibiscus bush in their back yard. When one of her moods struck, she'd take the broom outside and beat the bush half to death. It helped her get her menopausal anxiety out of her system. She never realized the broom beating was the exact reason he'd planted the bush.

"I'll help you with that, honey. I do love hibiscus bushes." My mother was trying to stay on Frank's good side, or so I thought.

I picked up my plate and threw it in the trash before turning to head back to the house, trying to hold back another guffaw. Pete followed suit and when I looked up at him he had a huge grin on his face.

We walked around the back of the house and headed for the apartment. The walkie talkie hissed at me. I pulled it out of my pocket.

"Yes?"

"It's your mother. I *know* why Frank keeps planting hibiscus bushes, but don't let *him* know I know." She clicked off before I could answer her.

Pete and I both started to laugh. Sometimes you have to deal with the crazy, the eccentric, and the drama all in the same day. This was one of those days.

"What now?" Pete asked.

"Let's finish painting the room and do a quick survey of the apartment to see if we've missed anything."

Pete saluted me. Uh huh, like I was the boss in the family. He'd known what we had to do without asking.

"I had an idea," I said. "Something we should have thought about is nighttime. If we make out like we're all leaving after dark, Blondie will believe she's safely hidden in the dark, and we can sneak back without worrying too much about being seen."

Pete held his paint brush mid-air for a moment. "Now why didn't I think of that? I must be too relaxed to come to logical conclusions like that one."

I placed my hand on his and started moving it up and down so he'd get back to work. The look on his face told me he'd already considered carrying out our plan at night.

"I'm going outside to mention this part of the plan to everyone. I think we've been too excited to think about details. If we hadn't thought of it, someone else would have."

Pete nodded and continued to paint while I climbed the stairs and left the house by the front door.

I stood on the porch for a moment, watching everyone work. Yes, they definitely had the harder jobs at the moment.

I watched my mother struggle to lift a pot with a young tree in it. Zoë saw her, too, and helped her lift it and move it to the area where it would be planted.

It suddenly struck me that my mother wasn't twenty-five anymore. She certainly wasn't old, but she probably shouldn't be working so hard. I was pretty sure she wouldn't agree with me, but I thought she deserved a rest. After we all went home, she'd have plenty left to do.

I hurried down the steps and took her side of the pot, nudging her out of the way.

Sandi to the rescue.

Or did she want to be rescued?

We'd talk.

Chapter Forty-two

$\mathcal{M}$iraculously, the trees were all planted, and the painting in the apartment was finished.

Pete and I headed upstairs and, after talking to my mother about colors, we started working on the living room. She still had us using an off-white. We finished one wall and almost replaced the baseboards, but after a little discussion we decided they should all be done at the same time. That reminded us that the ones in the apartment hadn't been replaced, but by that time we were tired. It would have to wait.

I glanced out one of the bay windows and saw Frank shaking first Tyler's hand and then Micah's, apparently thanking them for their hard work.

My mother gave the two women a hug before the Hansens headed home.

"I think you and I should take care of dinner tonight," I said. "Everyone else has worked so hard."

"You're right. We've got some steaks in the refrigerator. Why don't I barbeque while you put together a salad? We can figure out what else we want later."

"Do we have enough steaks for the Hansens, too?"

"I think so. I'll go downstairs and take a look."

While he did that I headed outdoors to let everyone know what we'd planned. Once I knew we had enough steaks, I'd go over to Tyler's house and ask them back to dinner.

Pete met me outside. "There's plenty of food for everyone. In fact, I'm not sure how we ended up with so many steaks."

"In that case, I'm heading to the Hansen's to invite them over."

"I'll go with you," Felicity said.

I nodded and we walked down the road, back to the Hansen's house, with Bubba following.

I knocked and Racheal answered the door. She glanced past me, at Bubba, and grinned.

"We wondered if you'd all like to come back to my parents' house for a barbeque. We've got plenty of steaks, and I'll make a salad. I'll have to think about what else we'll have."

She turned to her sister-in-law who'd joined her at the door. Zoë nodded her assent. "Thank you. We'd love to. And I've got several ears of corn we can barbeque, too."

"Really?" Felicity seemed surprised. "I didn't know you could barbeque corn. Sounds good."

"We'll be down as soon as we clean up a little. Micah wants to get rid of the stripe I painted on his shirt. I kinda like it myself." She pointed behind me. "I see you brought the big brute with you, and he's grinning as usual."

"He doesn't like being left out," I said, offering my own grin.

Felicity and started home and I saw Marion headed in our direction. When she saw us, she started to turn back.

"Marion," I called loudly. "Wait and we'll walk with you."

Her back hunched a little, but she turned back to us. "I

was out for a walk and decided it was time to go back to Gram and Gramp's house."

"What's up?" Felicity whispered out of the side of her mouth.

"Wait and see."

She didn't know about the conversation I'd had with my mother.

We caught up to Marion. I noticed she didn't look happy.

"What do you want?" she asked. "And why'd you bring that big dog with you?"

"Nothing. We're just being neighborly."

She tipped her head and watched me, giving me a nonverbal, *Yeah, right.* She started walking and we fell in step with her. Bubba walked beside her and she patted his head.

I was surprised. She didn't seem afraid of him at all, and he acted like she was an old friend.

"I'll get right to the point," I said. "I got the feeling you wanted to tell us more than what you said in front of your grandparents. Is there something you'd like to tell us?"

"No."

"Oh, I'm sorry. I really felt like you wanted to talk."

Felicity shifted her look back and forth between us. I could tell by her expression that she was beginning to understand what I was doing.

"No, I don't want to talk. I don't have anything else to tell you. You're imagining things."

"Okay, but can you tell us more about Harry Stockholm? I definitely got the feeling from the other neighbors that he was a real piece of work. It sounds like you might have been right. I think he was abusive to his wife, and maybe to his daughter, too."

"What does it matter now? They're all dead and gone anyway." Marion sounded petulant, but I didn't understand why.

"They may be dead and gone, but some stories need an ending. I think there's more to what happened in that house than anyone knows."

Marion stopped and turned on me. "You could be right, but is it any of your business? I know you're a private investigator, but what do you care about something that happened so long ago? It's over and done with, and it should stay that way."

"But..."

Bubba backed away from her, not sure how to process her attitude.

She turned and stomped away from us in the direction of her grandparents' house before I could ask more questions. When she reached their yard she didn't turn in, but kept going – and she continued to stomp her way down the road.

Felicity turned to me and looked up, into my eyes. "What was that all about? Explain."

"I can't really. It's just a hunch, but my mother and I believe she knows more about what happened in that house. We both got the feeling she didn't tell us everything she knows about the past."

"I got that same feeling when we first met her. I think you're right." She chuckled. "Your investigative skills sure didn't come through for you this time."

"They will. I'm simply getting a feel for Marion right now."

"Oh. I see." Felicity sounded like she thought I was making excuses.

I wasn't – not really.

"Bubba seemed to like her."

Shrugging, I watched Marion walk away. "There's no accounting for a dog's tastes. I'm telling you, I've seen her somewhere before. She looks so familiar. I might think she's been showing up wearing a blonde wig, but she's taller than Blondie. No, shorter. Maybe a little heavier. I'll figure it out."

It's something I couldn't explain, but my shoulders tightened up. There was something about her that set my teeth on edge. I had no idea what was going on.

Felicity stopped walking. "Okay, let's say she's Blondie. What could she possibly want? Why would she go to all the trouble to wear dated clothing and a wig? What's in it for her?"

"I honestly can't give you an answer. I have no idea about what's going on, but it'll come to me. I need to quit being on vacation and start wearing my private eye fedora."

"Oh, you're so funny sometimes. You watch too many old movies. Fedora? Maybe we can dig up a fedora in one of the closets."

"Let's hope we don't dig up anything else, except maybe a few clues. Know what I mean?"

"I sure do." Felicity scrunched up her face. "I don't know what it is, but you're right when you say there's something about Marion that doesn't feel right. Maybe she wanted to tell us something but changed her mind."

I shrugged my shoulders, which was becoming a habit like sighing, and we headed up the dirt driveway. Dinner was starting to sound pretty good. I hadn't realized how hungry I was until I smelled the barbeque heating.

Bubba trotted off in the direction of Pete and the barbeque grill.

"I'll go inside and make the salad," I said. "For as primitively as we're living, we sure have a lot of food on hand. Between the refrigerator in the motor home and what we've bought and put in the one in the apartment, we're set for a while."

"We bought more than we realized when we first got here and when we stopped after our dinner out. Maybe we duplicated what your mother bought."

I quickly changed the subject, simply because the amount of food we had wasn't an issue. "Okay, back to

Marion. I just know there's something going on with her. I seriously wonder if she's playing the role of Blondie, but why? Is she nuts or does she have a hidden agenda?"

"My preference would be a hidden agenda." Felicity smiled at me. "I don't want to think some crazy woman is living across the street and she's able to get in and out of this house at will."

"I'm with you. Besides, if it's her, then there's no ghost."

Chapter Forty-three

"*T*he idea of no ghost works for me," Felicity said. "My mind is made up. It's got to be Marion playing the part of Blondie."

I didn't respond because I simply wasn't sure.

We made our way around the house and to the apartment where we found my mother busily spreading butter on French bread. "I'm assuming everyone will want garlic salt and parmesan cheese on their bread?"

Nodding, I said, "I think so. We've got a pretty hungry group for dinner tonight. I think we'd eat anything that made its way to the table. I'm going to put the salad together."

I passed my mother and opened the refrigerator, pulling out a fresh head of lettuce, tomatoes, some sliced jicama I'd found at the store and a can of black olives. I searched for anything else I could find, but that was it. Thankfully we had a couple of bottles of salad dressing, although I would have preferred homemade.

When I turned to the sink, I realized Felicity was already telling Mother about meeting Marion out on the road.

"...and she said she has nothing more to tell us. I don't

believe her, and I don't think Sandi does either. And we think she might be Blondie."

Mother put the lid on the tub of butter and returned it to the refrigerator. "Well, that's a possibility. I hadn't thought about someone actually wearing a wig. We talked about it, but I didn't really believe it." She looked thoughtful for a moment. "You know, we only saw her sitting on the couch at the Ellison's house. I never thought about what she might look like if she stood up. I didn't notice what she was wearing either. Of course, why would she be wearing vintage clothing?"

"If it is her," I said, "she'd probably save the sixties outfit to wear when she had the wig on. I have to assume she's been trying to look like Barbara's mother. What was her name? Oh, yeah. Francine."

"But why?" my mother asked. "What's the deal about her wanting to look like Francine?"

Mother brought a large bowl in to use for the salad, so after washing it, I started picking the lettuce apart and putting the pieces in it. "I've been thinking about the photo Stan and I found in the bedroom. I think she knows about something that happened here and she wants us to figure it out without having to tell us. I don't get it, but... Hmm. Maybe she wants us to think Barbara's mother tried to look out for her and it didn't work. Both the mother *and* the daughter are in the picture."

"Yeah, maybe she saw something the police don't know about from when the murders took place. Who knows? Maybe the ranch hand didn't really kill those people. Marion takes walks. Maybe she saw what really happened."

"You might be on to something," I said.

We stopped talking and I thought about that scenario while I cut the jicama sticks into pieces.

My mother grinned. "You know, girls, we make pretty good detectives. Why, I'll bet the men aren't even thinking about what could have happened."

"Of course, they don't know our latest theory about Marion. Let's put it to them and see what they think."

Felicity sliced the tomatoes. "What about our competition to find the details of the murders?"

"The heck with the competition. I think we need to work together. My gut feeling is something a lot bigger than we think happened here." I dropped the jicama pieces in the salad and tossed it, knocking some salad on the floor.

"When they say *toss a salad*, I don't think that's what they mean." Mother picked up a couple of pieces of lettuce and jicama.

"Sorry. I guess I got a little too excited. You know, the more I think about it, the more I believe Marion knows something. And I mean something big."

Felicity carefully laid the tomato slices on top of the salad. "Don't you think the police probably had all the facts? Maybe we could get a copy of the police report and see if something seems wrong. We talked about doing that once before, if I remember right."

"That's a good idea. Mom, do you think Frank would drive into town and see if he can get the report?"

"He's so anxious to get as much done on this place as possible while he's got help. I don't think I want to ask him. We'll figure something out though."

"Are there any more neighbors left to talk to?" Felicity asked.

I almost slapped my forehead. "What about Tyler's parents? If we can't talk to them, he can. I'll ask him about it over dinner."

"Knock, knock." Racheal stood at the sliding glass door. "What about Tyler? Sorry, I wasn't eavesdropping, but I couldn't help hearing his name."

"Come on in," I said.

She opened the screen door and joined us. "Zoë stayed

outside with the guys. So what about Tyler?"

"I was just thinking about his parents." I shoved the salad bowl to the side. "We've talked to the other neighbors, but we haven't spoken to the Hansens. I thought if he knew the questions I have, maybe he'd talk to them for me. What do you think?"

She grinned. "Are you kidding? He'd like nothing more than to become involved in this. I know we're going to help catch the blonde, but he wants to do something else, too."

"Good. We'll talk about it over dinner." Mother wrapped the bread in foil. "I'm going to use the oven in the motorhome to heat this. I'll meet you outside."

I nodded and picked up the salad, grabbing a couple of paper towels to set on top of it so the flies wouldn't land on it, and followed my mother out the door.

Felicity and Racheal were right behind me.

We walked past the barbeque and heard Zoë telling Pete how to barbeque the corn on the cob.

I stopped for a moment and gave Pete a quick kiss.

As we walked away, I heard Zoë giving him some other barbequing tips. I glanced over my shoulder and saw him nodding, but not responding. She soon caught up to us.

I glanced at Pete again and there was no doubt in my mind he was doing the corn her way, but the steaks were *his* way.

Bubba had himself firmly planted next to the barbeque, his nose in the air, sniffing for all he was worth.

"We brought an extra table," Racheal said.

"I see that." I set the salad on one of the tables.

Frank was setting out paper plates, plastic utensils and steak knives.

Stanley was walking a few steps behind him, setting out napkins and moving the forks to the left side of plates since Frank had put everything on the right.

I heard Felicity chuckling. "Frank doesn't even see

what Stan is doing."

"That's probably a good thing," I said.

My mother brought out the toasted bread and Pete appeared with a plate stacked with steaks.

"They're all medium since I didn't know how everyone likes them," he said. His tone almost sounded like he was daring anyone to argue with him. He left for a moment and returned with two plates, one bearing baked potatoes and the other loaded with corn on the cob.

"Very good," I said.

For the next few minutes there wasn't a sound except that of food being dished up.

"Pssst."

I looked and saw Stanley sitting directly across from me.

"I decided to sit here so I can keep an eye on the house. If Blondie shows up, I'll know it," he whispered.

"You don't need to whisper," I said. "Not only that, but you've brought up a subject we want to talk to everyone about."

"Oh."

While we ate I explained out ideas about Marion and Blondie. I didn't have much detail, but I told them what I could.

Tyler scratched his chin. "You know, you could be right. There's always been something about Marion that didn't quite settle right with me. She always made me feel like she was secretive, but I couldn't figure out what she might need to hide. I'll ask my parents if they remember anything about her."

"Ask what they think about the ghost stories, too," I said.

Pete reached under the table and squeezed my knee. "There's no such thing as a ghost. Only nuts like the woman across the road."

Chapter Forty-four

*I*gnoring Pete, I turned to Tyler. "That's another thing. I was hoping either you'd talk to your parents about what's been going on or maybe I could. What do *they* remember about the murders? Can they tell us anything about Marion? Can they think of anything that might explain why she seems to be directing us toward Francine? You know, that kind of thing."

"Sure. Not a problem. I'll give them a call tonight." He turned to his brother. "I know you were young, but do you remember anything from when the murders happened? Or do you remember Francine?"

"I was too young, bro. Mom and Dad shielded me from everything that happened. I don't really remember Francine, either. I'm not even sure I'd been born when *she* died."

"What about Marion?" Tyler forked a piece of steak and popped it in his mouth.

"Marion wasn't living with her grandparents the whole time I was at home. I don't know her very well. She didn't seem to like kids that much, either. I vaguely remember her shooing us away from her grandparents' house. Oh, yeah, and she wanted us to stay away from the llama ranch. She made a point of telling us what a bas... Uh, what a piece of garbage Harry was." He glanced at the ladies sitting around the table and then pointedly stared at his plate before digging into his baked potato.

Bubba sat politely next to the table, staring intently at Micah, almost as though he was willing the man to read his mind. *Give steak. Give dog steak. Good dog want meat.* I had a feeling I was pretty close to Bubba's thoughts and the corners of my mouth turned up.

"Okay," I said. "I guess that tells us at least a little about Marion."

"She's odd. At least, that's always been my opinion of her." Racheal reached for another piece of garlic bread. "She comes and goes, sometimes staying with her grandparents and sometimes just visiting, but she's not social at all. She ignores the neighbors, which is a shame because Zetta is a real sweetheart and loves to visit with them, but when Marion is there everyone keeps their distance."

"Interesting." My mother turned and looked toward the Ellison house.

"If you're right about her posing as Blondie, I don't believe we have to worry about her making an appearance while we eat." Stanley pointed toward the road. "She's taking another one of her walks."

We each turned and looked, and she was watching us, but abruptly turned and walked the other way.

Pete shook his head. "I just don't get her. What are the odds she's Blondie?"

"I'd say they're pretty good." I believed more and more that we were right.

We spent the rest of the dinner hour eating and making plans for the next night. Since Micah's car had tinted windows, he'd pick me up after dark and drive off. No one would know the truck was empty except for me.

My mother would park their car in the back where no one could see who climbed in it, and leave right after us.

Again, by being in the dark no one would be able to see if the car was full of people or not. Pete would do the same thing with our Jeep, and turn the radio up so it would sound like a noisy crowd.

Then we'd all sneak back to the house, where the rest of the group would be waiting.

"I've got to remember to leave the wedding rings somewhere conspicuous. I was thinking of leaving them on the sink, but she might not look there. I'll figure it out."

"Yeah, where would you look if you'd been searching for years?" Zoë asked.

Stanley sat up straighter. "I'd look in one of two places. The upstairs bedroom where we found the photo, or the basement where she seemed to be looking for something." He was proud of himself.

"The basement," I said. "That's the last place I saw her, and she only left because she heard me coming. Of course, I have no idea if she's really looking for the wedding rings, but what else could it be?"

"I guess we'll find out," Zoë said. "And I think I'll be hiding in the basement, waiting for her."

Micah leaned forward and stared into her eyes. "Not by yourself. I'll have Tyler drive my truck and I'll wait in the basement with you."

Zoë looked surprised. "You know I can take care of myself. I've *always* taken care of myself."

He looked uncomfortable. "This is different. We don't know what that broad is up to and I'm not taking any chances."

Pete and I looked at each other. We'd had similar conversations regarding some of our cases. He winked at me. I reached under the table and patted his knee.

"Well, okay Mic, if you put it that way." Zoë's voice

had wonder in it and I guessed he'd never been protective like this before. "But I get first shot at her."

Her last comment burst my little bubble. She was humoring him, not admiring his protectiveness.

"Not if I get to her first," Micah said.

"Honestly, I think I should be in the basement with Sandi." Pete gave the couple a meaningful look. "You two haven't had experience in situations like this. I was a cop, and I have, and so has Sandi. So here's the deal. Micah can drive my Jeep out of here and I'll wait in the basement. Sandi can climb into the truck with Tyler, but let her out right away so she can sneak into the house. If Marion is doing the search, she's going to wait until she's certain we aren't coming right back."

"Good point," Micah said. "You were a cop? Interesting."

The conversation took a turn and the men spent considerable time talking about Pete's experiences with the L.A.P.D.

The women cleaned up the now empty paper plates before we adjourned to the chairs we'd set out by the swimming pool. My mother and I assured them we'd clean up everything else later.

"I honestly can't figure out what Marion is up to," I said. "I've looked at several scenarios, but nothing seems to fit."

"I think you were right when you mentioned thinking she knows something about the murders that the police never figured out." My mother took a sip of her iced tea.

"I'm sure they did a thorough investigation though. I can't imagine what they could have missed." I opened a chocolate candy bar – dessert.

Zoë leaned forward in her chair. "She could have seen something that would change everyone's perception of the murders, although for the life of me I can't imagine why she wouldn't have ratted everybody out. They were all dead. What would, or what could, the police do after the fact?"

"And how would it have impacted her if she told what she knew when it was a done deal? Unless she was involved, there wouldn't be anyone left to punish. Like you said, they were all dead." Felicity seemed taken with the idea that Marion had seen or heard something.

She, Zoë and Racheal began dreaming up scenarios that could have changed the outcome of the police investigation. My mother and I listened, but some of their ideas were pretty far-fetched.

"Livvie, what do *you* think?" Felicity asked.

My mother didn't hesitate with her answer. "I think she knows where the bodies are buried, so to speak. She knows something, but I think she's afraid to come forward. She just needs a little encouragement – the kind Sandi can give her."

"Felicity and I tried that earlier. She'll come around though. I think maybe we opened a door for her. I'll bet she's thinking about talking to us right now." At least I hoped so.

Mother glanced at her watch. "Well, it's getting late. I'm about done in for the day. This barbeque was a lot of fun and we'll have to do it again."

We stood and my mother gave the Hansen women a hug.

So did Felicity and I.

Mother smiled. "It's been fun getting to know you better, and putting together a scheme. We'll catch Blondie before she knows what happened to her."

We strolled back to the tables where the men sat and chatted. I guess men don't call it chatting, but that's okay. I was glad they'd formed friendships.

Stanley looked so happy to be a part of it all. The expression on his face did my heart good.

Bubba sat by Pete, grinning. Oh, that grin was something to see.

"Okay, gentlemen," my mother said. "The tile people will be here bright and early tomorrow morning, so I'm thinking we'd better call it a night."

Everyone stood and began collecting their belongings.

Micah stepped in front of me. "Why don't you walk us out," he said softly, which was unusual for him. He and Zoë were outgoing, not the type to whisper or act secretive.

"Sure."

"I mentioned something in storage at my brother's house. I wanted to tell you about it." He glanced in my mother's direction. "Remember? You wanted to scare your mother."

He had an evil grin on his face.

So did I.

Chapter Forty-five

"*B*ack in a minute," I said to no one in particular. "I want to ask Micah a couple of questions about the neighborhood, if you can call it a neighborhood."

That should throw everyone off. I walked as far as the gate with him.

"I have something that will... Well, you'd have to see them. Come over in the morning and I'll show you what I'm talking about. They're silly, but they'll make your mom watch over her shoulder."

"What are they?" I asked. "Give me a hint."

He told me what he was talking about and I laughed. "I don't know if she'll fall for that or not."

"Trust me," he said. "Do it right and it won't give her a heart attack, but it will make her start watching everyone with suspicion in her mind."

"You're on. I'll be over bright and early."

The rest of the Hansens caught up to us so we changed the subject and tried to act nonchalant.

"Have a good night." I waved at them.

They closed the gate and headed home.

I'd have to share my plan with Pete. I'd need someone heavier than me to make a dent in the Scare My Mother plan. I didn't think he'd have a problem with it. He'd probably think it was ridiculous, but I knew he'd go along with me.

I helped my mother and Felicity finish cleaning the tables before Pete and I headed for bed. It was late and we were tired, but we'd had a good day.

Before we went to sleep I told him about my dastardly plan to scare my mother. Under the circumstances, dastardly seemed like a good description.

He laughed. "Only you would think of something like that."

"Well, I had a little help from Micah."

~ * ~

The people from the tile company showed up bright and early the next day. Well, it wasn't really a bright day. Monsoon clouds had moved in again. It looked like we were in for more rain. Interesting, someone at dinner had said the monsoon season was over in September. Mother Nature hadn't been listening.

Frank called the boys together and suggested they finally get the trench dug before the rains came. Remembering the last rain, Pete and Stanley started digging as soon as we finished breakfast.

My mother filled the sink so she could wash a few pots and pans. "You realize that if it rains this afternoon we're going to have to postpone our plan to catch Blondie, don't you?"

"I do." I threw several paper plates in the trash.

Felicity collected the silverware and dropped it into the soapy dishwater. "It doesn't matter when we catch her, just as long as we do. Right? I mean, what difference is one more day going to make?"

"None that I can think of, and maybe we can get a little more work done around here." I really wanted to get as much done as possible before we left my mother and Frank alone.

Mom handed me a couple of forks to dry. "I asked the tile people to do the living room first so we can finish painting in there. The apartment is painted, but the rest of the house still needs work."

Felicity and I nodded, but my enthusiasm was waning. The house seemed like a never-ending job – a money pit, although we were saving my parents substantial funds by helping. Honestly, we were having fun, regardless of the work. I guess I still had a modicum of enthusiasm after all.

"I'm going to have to excuse myself for a few minutes." I wiped off the table and threw paper towels in the trash. "Tyler asked me to come by for a few minutes. He wants to ask some technical questions about the work I do."

"Oh? What kind of questions?" Mom looked curious, but not overly so.

"I don't know. I'll have to let you know later."

With any luck she'd forget about it.

I'd have to warn Tyler and the women not to let her know I'd actually met with Micah.

"Want me to go with you?" Felicity asked.

"No, this is one of those times you'd probably be bored. And I think Zoë and Racheal are leaving for town." I was turning into such a good little liar, but not without just cause.

Before anyone could ask another question, I left the house and headed for the Hansen place.

Surprisingly, Micah was waiting for me. "Follow me out to the shed."

I did, and you could have knocked me over with a feather.

"We used these as a Halloween joke, and they worked perfectly. I mean, it's not like they're big enough to belong in a circus or something."

I started to laugh. "Oh, Micah! These are perfect. She'll catch on, but not right away. I could try to explain it away, but

I can hear her already. She'll say, 'Welllll, you never know about these things.' She's always looking for a mystery to solve."

"Her and my brother. Stop in and see him before you leave. I'm sure he has questions about our plan. He's been worried all morning about the rain throwing a in a monkey wrench and wrecking things."

"I will. Maybe he's got a sack I can throw these props in, too. It would be just like my mother to come walking out and see them."

Micah shook his head. "Don't bother Tyler about it. I've got an old burlap bag you can use. I'll bring these up to the house in a few minutes."

I turned to head for the house, but stopped and turned back to him, grinning. "Has anyone ever told you that you're devious?"

"Many, and by the look on your face I'd have to guess you might be a devious woman on occasion."

I just laughed and walked to the house.

Tyler and I spent about half an hour together. As it turned out, I had unintentionally told the truth to my mother. He really did have some questions about being a private eye. I gladly answered them. Racheal and Zoë had gone to town, too, to pick up a few things at a department store.

"Did you talk to your parents last night?" I asked.

"Yes, but they didn't have anything of interest to add to what everyone else has told you."

"Well, I was hoping."

"I asked my mother about Marion, too. All she said was that she'd always thought of her as kind of an odd duck."

"That seems to be the general consensus."

Before I left, he handed me a book. "This is one of my masterpieces. Give it a try. I think you'll like it."

"I will, as soon as I can." I was curious about his writing. I loved a good mystery, but I wouldn't know if he could put one together until I read the story.

Returning to the house with my burlap bag, I talked Pete into taking a break. I set the bag down and opened it, letting him take a peek. Frank and Stanley walked over, curious about what we were looking at, but not wanting to be nosey.

"What have you got in there? Snakes? Tarantulas?"

Bubba sniffed every square inch of the bag, his curiosity in full control of him.

Pete just shook his head. "Sandi's got a hair-brained scheme to scare Livvie."

"Oh?" Frank looked in the bag. "I don't get it."

I explained the plan and that Micah had helped me.

"Pete is going to do the dirty work."

Frank scratched his chin. "Why don't you get Micah to do it? He's bigger, and you need big and heavy for this."

"What am I? Minced meat?" Pete sounded a little offended.

Frank laughed. "No, but he's well over six feet tall and muscular. You're not as tall or as heavy."

"But you're muscular," I said.

Pete and Frank both turned and gave me a look, one that didn't tell me much.

"Well, you are."

Frank grinned. "Back to my original thought. Let Micah do it."

I was surprised. "You're not going to try to stop me from scaring my mother?"

"Are you kidding? Livvie will remember this experience for years to come, and knowing her she'll tell anyone who'll listen. She likes nothing more than to tell a dramatic story, and end it with humor."

Picking up the bag, I ran back to see Micah.

Bubba followed along, unable to forget the bag. I wondered what had originally been inside, and I wasn't sure I really wanted to know. He watched Micah take the bag and walk away from us. I wouldn't let my dog follow, even though he whined.

It hadn't taken much to talk Micah into helping. He placed the burlap bag back in the shed.

~ * ~

The men spent most of the day digging trenches, ending them in the field of dirt and weeds. At least the areas around the house and barn wouldn't overflow with rain water again. Until they had horses, it probably wouldn't make much difference other than the weeds would be plentiful from all the watering.

Bubba didn't help, busily sticking his nose into piles of dirt and digging.

Pete tried to shoo him away, without much success.

I returned to the house.

The tile in the living room looked like old wood flooring. It made the house appear just a bit more rustic. I loved it. The tile company had sent a crew and the tile would be done before the end of the day.

Mother, Felicity and I worked on the living room until lunchtime. We accomplished quite a bit, but we still had a long way to go.

After a quick lunch we got back to work. While they painted the next to the last wall, I began installing the base boards.

Even though the air began to feel humid, indicating incoming rain, the paint dried quickly.

We finally put the paint away and washed our brushes, having finished the living room. It looked great!

"How much of the house is going to be tile?" I asked.

"All of it."

"All of it?" Felicity looked surprised.

"Yes. With strangers tramping in and out all the time, it'll be easier to keep clean. No carpet here, just nice, washable tile."

A light rain began to fall, and our plan to catch Blondie temporarily flew out the window.

Chapter Forty-six

"We've accomplished a lot today." My mother laid the brushes on paper towels to dry.

"We have." Felicity dropped onto a chair at the table. "We've accomplished a lot in the last *week*."

"It's been fun, hasn't it?" I looked from one woman to the other. "Just think. Instead of having such a great time, we could have been off having a whole different kind of fun. Maybe somewhere tropical. But honestly? I'm glad we spent our time here."

"It won't be much longer until you all leave." Mother sounded, well, maybe a little sad.

"We'll be back every chance we have."

I gave her a hug and she hugged me back with feeling.

"Don't leave me out," Felicity said.

She joined in and we made it a group hug.

I wanted to tell my mother that our adventures weren't over yet, but I didn't want to forewarn her that I had a plan to keep our Scare Game going.

I remembered Marion. "Oh, yeah. We still have our plan to catch Blondie. The adventure isn't over yet. It's only just begun, in a manner of speaking."

Felicity took a huge swig from a glass of iced tea my mother handed her. "Thanks, Livvie. I can't wait to find out what her story is."

Mother poured another glass of iced tea and held it out to me.

"Thanks." I was thirsty.

"It promises to be pretty interesting." She poured a glass for herself. "Too bad I didn't put the pitcher out in the sun this morning. This is almost gone. Sun tea tastes so much better than when I make it on the stove."

The boys came inside. Pete and Frank had beer, and Stanley took the last of the tea.

They sat down at the table and everyone was quiet for a few minutes.

Stanley was the first to speak. "I saw that woman, Marion, out for a walk with an umbrella. Nothing seems to stop her."

"It would appear that way." Everyone's eyes were on me, as though I had more to say. "That's all. Nothing seems to stop her. Stanley's right."

Frank looked outside. "The rain is coming down heavier. I don't think we'll be able to pull off your plan tonight."

I nodded. "I know."

"Do you think the Hansens will understand?" Mother was always worrying about something.

Pete stood and looked out the window. "Tell ya what. It's only sprinkling right now, so I'll go over there and make sure they know."

He left before anyone could stop him, and I noticed his limp was quite pronounced. Of course, he'd been digging trenches all day.

Bubba started to follow him.

"Stay," I said.

He sat down by the sliding glass door, apparently waiting for Pete to come back.

My mother pursed her lips. "Poor guy. I feel so bad when I see him limping. I don't understand why he wanted to go to the neighbor's house."

"He knows when walking will help and when it won't," I said. "Besides, I have a feeling the humidity is making things worse. He needs to move around. He says it helps, but I have my doubts. The doctor told him it'll get better over time."

Pete was gone for about an hour.

The rain was heavy again. I could hear it pounding on the roof, sounding like hail. I walked over to Bubba and looked out the window. It wasn't hail, just large raindrops.

My mangy mutt sat for a long time, finally lying down and relaxing, and then sitting up to wait again. Maybe he wasn't missing Pete as much as he'd wanted to go with him.

The rest of us sat quietly and vegetated, making small talk as the mood struck us.

Bubba continued to wait patiently. I knew Pete was returning when the dog stood and stared out the window. Apparently he and my husband had come to terms, after locking horns on many occasions. They both wanted to be the alpha in our little group.

Pete ran his fingers through his damp hair. "I stayed and talked with Tyler and Micah until the rain let up. Talk about two different personalities, and yet they seem to get along. Their wives are nice, too."

"I'm glad you enjoyed yourself," I said. "What did they say about our plan being delayed?"

"Not much. They'd already figured out it wasn't going to happen tonight."

My mother sat forward in her chair. "Tomorrow night we'll finally get to the bottom of this."

"I sure hope so." Stanley sounded excited.

Frank grabbed a bag of potato chips off the sink and brought it to the table. "I'm ready for a snack. I could go find a pack of cards and we could play poker for a while."

He glanced at each of us and didn't see any enthusiasm on our faces.

"Guess not." He ate a handful of chips.

"I think everyone is worn out, sweetie." My mother patted his hand. "Maybe another time."

Pete leaned back in his chair and glanced at Frank. "We'll play cards one night before we leave. You and me and Stanley, and maybe Tyler and Micah would want to join in."

"No women?" Stanley asked.

"Nope. Just us guys." Pete reached out and rubbed Bubba's head.

I moved the conversation back to Marion. "Let's go over our plan one more time. I don't want any mistakes tomorrow night."

This seemed to be the one subject that held everyone's interest. In a way, it almost felt like playing a game called Catch Blondie. At least it was something different, not work.

I fed Bubba, but the rest of us ate dinner a little later, discussed possible reasons for Marion's behavior, and went to bed. It had been another long day.

I had trouble sleeping that night. Consequently, I could hear the dog wandering around the house. His nails clicked on the tile, and he was so big that the sounds were fairly loud. And, I could hear him thumping around, pushing on doors to see if they were open. He finally settled down outside our bedroom door.

Pete was out in about thirty seconds, snoring lightly. Nothing seemed to keep him awake.

I heard Bubba bark once and run down the stairs, but he quieted down after what I assumed was a peek out the window. Ah. Micah must have come calling with...

I don't remember anything after that. Sleep finally

overtook me and I slept like I had no cares in the world.

~ * ~

Pete arose before me in the morning. I could hear the shower running, although the sleeping bag was still warm where he'd slept.

I wanted to look out the window to see if Micah had really been there, but our windows faced the wrong side of the house. I tiptoed to the other bedroom and looked out at the front yard. And there they were, in all their glory.

Great big, giant-sized footprints, settled deeply in the mud. I grinned. Now those were prowler footprints to be dealt with, and I wondered how long it would take my mother to find them.

Uh, not long.

She stood at the bottom of the stairs and called to me, sounding slightly panicky. "Sandi, you and Pete had better come down here. We had a visitor last night, and it wasn't Blondie. Someone has... Just come down here."

"Coming," I called. "Pete's in the shower. We'll be down in a minute."

I could hear voices and knew Frank was with her. I hoped he was able to keep a straight face.

I opened the bathroom door and stuck my head in, speaking just loud enough for my mother to hear me. "Pete, you're needed downstairs. Mom says there was an intruder here last night, and it wasn't Blondie."

I threw on a pair of jeans and a shirt and hurried downstairs with a pair of flip flops in my hand.

"What's up, Mom?"

"What's up? Didn't you hear me? We've had a prowler out in the yard."

"How can you tell?"

"He left some very distinctive footprints. I swear, this guy has to be a monster. The prints look like they're at least a size eighteen."

Frank stood behind my mother, covering his mouth with his hand. I could see the corners of his lips turning up, and he kept clearing his throat.

Mother turned and faced him. "What's the matter, Frank? Why do you keep clearing your throat? Are you coming down with something?"

He cleared his throat again. "Must be the weather. I woke up with a frog in my throat."

"Oh, dear, I didn't mean it. I hope you're not getting sick."

"I'll be fine, honey."

"Let's go take a look at those prints. I'm sure it's nothing," I said.

"I'm sure it's *something*." My mother crossed her arms across her chest. "And I sure don't get why Bubba didn't set off a ruckus last night. He must have heard something."

"He was upstairs with us. He probably didn't hear a thing."

"Sure. Like a dog with super hearing would have missed a prowler." Mother turned and headed for the front door.

"Shouldn't we check to make sure Felicity and Stanley are okay first?" I asked.

"We're fine," Felicity walked around the corner, into the living room, with Stanley trailing behind her. "What's going on?"

Chapter Forty-seven

"My mother says we had a prowler last night," I explained. "We're just about to go look at the huge footprints he left."

"What footprints?" Felicity sounded frightened. "You're saying they're big?"

Stanley tried to reassure her. "It's okay, sugar foot. Let's put on some clothing before we go outside."

He ushered her toward the stairs and I could hear him quietly talking to her.

I'd forgotten she wasn't in on the plan. Stanley would take care of that, and I hoped she didn't give it away.

Pete hurried down the stairs and joined us. He had a great poker face. "What's happening? Sandi said there was an intruder last night?"

"Follow me." My mother strode toward the front door and threw it open like the drama queen she can be sometimes. She also shoved the screen door open with gusto. It creaked loudly, adding to the moment.

I smiled at my mother's back.

The mud had fallen in on the prints, just a little, but

they were still discernable.

I made light of them. "Oh, Mom, these could be anything. Maybe they're not footprints at all."

"Of course they are. Those are gigantic footprints or I'll eat dirt. Take my word for it. They're from a prowler."

"They are pretty big, I have to admit. Maybe Marion has a partner in all of this. No, I think these are an anomaly. They could be something that just *looks* like footprints."

"Sandra, there's a trail of them. And look how far apart they are. This guy must be *huge!*"

"It's nothing, Mother. I'm sure of it."

Pete nodded his agreement.

She didn't look quite so sure of herself. "Weeeell, you never know about these things. But, Sandi – "

"Don't make something out of nothing. This is some strange kind of coincidence or something."

"I think you're wrong. I'm going to investigate and get to the bottom of this. And keep your eyes open." She narrowed her eyes and turned toward the Ellison house. "I'm going to be watching Marion very closely today. I have no doubt that she's involved with this person in some way."

"This doesn't scare you, does it?" Frank asked.

"Of course not. Well, maybe a little. I just don't know, but I'll get to the bottom of this. Trust me on this one."

"I'm sure you will, Mom."

Bubba sniffed the footprints. He didn't seem all that interested and only wagged his tail once before wandering off toward the barn.

I put my hand on Pete's arm and turned back to the house.

"I will," she said to my back. "Frank will help me."

"Uh huh."

I heard her speaking to Frank as we walked away. "Pete was a police officer. You'd think he'd be interested in those prints, wouldn't you?"

"Give him time to wake up. He's probably still half asleep."

Felicity and Stanley passed us when we walked inside. She was grinning, and Stanley stared at the ground. I had a feeling that was the only way he could keep a straight face.

I glanced out the front window and saw Felicity nodding while Mother talked, her hand flying through the air. She pointed toward the garage, indicating the prints went around the house.

Stanley continued to stare at the dirt.

"How long are you going to let this go on?" Pete asked.

"As long as it takes her to say Uncle. I want to win this scare game."

Pete shook his head and headed for the stairs to the apartment and the kitchen, meaning the coffee pot.

I climbed upstairs to take my shower.

When I was done and made my way to the apartment, I found my mother showing pictures she'd taken with her camera – of the footprints, of course. "You can see how big they are, even in this picture. I had Frank stand next to it so we could compare sizes."

I wondered what Micah had done so the footprints stopped at some point and didn't show him walking back to Tyler's.

"Where did the prints lead you, Mom?"

"Out to the field. With all those weeds I couldn't see where they went after that."

"Ah."

It was smart of Micah to head in that direction. She couldn't follow him. I had a feeling he probably stuck to the heavier weeds. Of course, with the rain and moisture, he may have tramped them down. I'd have to ask him what he did.

We ate breakfast, a serve yourself type of meal consisting mostly of cereal and toast, and went back to work. It was never-ending.

I noticed a conspicuous absence of the Hansens that morning, although I knew they'd be over later for one last discussion about our strategy for the evening.

The clouds had disappeared and I didn't think rain would be an issue again.

We were as back to normal as possible. No snakes, tarantulas or black widows were in sight, no Blondie sightings, but there were still the footprints.

My mother went outside no less than half a dozen times to take another look at them. She followed them to the weeds at least three times.

I began to worry when she was too quiet for the mother I know and love. Maybe I'd gone too far.

"Mother, I said it before and I'll say it again. I'm sure there's a reasonable explanation for the footprints."

"What are the odds that they're anything other than a prowler? I haven't seen any neighbors who might be big enough to wear shoes that large."

"I think the odds are good. We're way out here in the desert, and why would someone want to come all the way out here to prowl around?"

"Weeeeell, you never know. Maybe we haven't seen all the neighbors yet. Can ghosts leave footprints? Maybe Harry Stockholm was a big guy. No one ever really described him."

"Micah's a big guy, too, but I don't think his feet would fit those prints. Besides, we saw a picture of Harry and he wasn't all that big." I was pushing it.

"I'll be back in a minute." Felicity's voice was high pitched and she quickly turned her back on us, heading up the stairs.

I thought I heard a small giggle, but I wasn't sure.

Mother was too intent on looking at her photos again to notice any sounds out of the ordinary.

"Let's forget this for right now," I said. "I think we'll want to rest a little before our big night."

"Maybe Marion won't show up. Maybe Big Foot will come in her place."

"Mother, let it go!"

She turned off her camera. "For now, dear, but not forever."

I'd created a monster. She wasn't going to let anything go until she had answers, but I wasn't ready to provide them.

At around one o'clock we decided to call it quits for the day. We sat out by the pool and drank from a new batch of sun tea.

"It's too bad you don't have the pool ready to use yet," Pete said. "I could use a swim right now."

It had warmed up considerably. It was unseasonably warm for October.

"It's going to have to be redone." Frank stared at the pool. "The pool sat empty for too long. The bottom is stained from old water sitting in it for too long. Must have been rain water."

It was about twenty-five feet wide and fifty feet long, and it was going to have to be completely done over. It had been covered by wooden planks forming a protective covering, but the men had worked and finally pulled the covering away, revealing a pool filled with rain water and bugs.

"That would have been a good place to hide if you boys hadn't taken off the boards." Mother's forehead was creased with worry lines.

"Livvie – "

"Now, Frank, I can't help it. Why isn't anyone else worried about the intruder? This just doesn't make sense. Well, in a way it does. I mean, we've been inundated with bugs, creepy crawlies, snakes and… Wait a minute."

She turned to Stanley.

"Don't take offense, Stan, but if anyone should be as scared as I am, it's you. How come you're not having fits?"

"I guess I've come a long way since staying out here. If I can face a snake and those big arachnids, I can face anything."

Mother pursed her lips. "Uh huh."

I had a feeling she was beginning to catch on.

She left us and returned to take another look at the footprints, returning with a skeptical expression on her face, but she didn't say anything.

I smiled at her.

She didn't smile back. She was putting the pieces together.

"What did you...?" She stopped talking when we heard voices coming up the driveway.

"We figured we'd better make it look like we're making plans." Racheal pulled up a chair and sat down with us. She'd brought her own soft drink with her.

Zoë pulled up another chair. "I'd love some of that iced tea."

Mother poured her a glass and handed her a spoon and the sugar bowl.

Racheal dropped the bomb, so to speak. "I heard you had some problems over here last night."

"And where did you hear that?" Mother's back stiffened.

"Oh, uh..."

Racheal let her voice trail off.

Chapter Forty-eight

"*U*m, it's like this, Mom." I thought I'd better answer on Racheal's behalf since she and my mother would be neighbors. "You know how we kept trying to scare each other?"

Before I could say more my mother started laughing. "You almost had me, Sandi, but it just didn't make sense that no one else seemed concerned."

My turn to laugh. "I did have you, Mom. I saw how worried you've been all day. My little plan worked."

"And who's the culprit who left the prints?"

Zoë held her hand in the air like a kid in class. "That would be my culprit. In fact, Micah was the one who gave Sandi the idea. A friend of his named Al pulled this on him when he was a kid."

"Oh, my." Mother leaned back in her chair. "You really had me going. You win, Sandi. I can't think of anything to top this, unless Blondie turns out to be an honest-to-goodness ghost and not Marion."

"You just had to say that, didn't you? Ghost. I don't believe in ghosts, and you know it."

"We'll see." My mother gently nodded her head, her eyes looking far away as though she were watching something in her mind.

I sincerely hoped I hadn't given her any new ideas.

Zoë set her glass on the outdoor kitchen bar. It almost fell over and tea sloshed over onto the bar top. "It looks like you've still got your work cut out for you. This bar needs new tiles."

Mother handed her a napkin, for all the good it would do on the dirty bar. "You're right, there's lots to do, but we want to be done and open for business in about six months. Actually, we already have some soon-to-be newlyweds who want to be our first guests."

She was talking about Rick and Jessica, who'd mentioned at our wedding that they were going to be wed in about six months.

"Okay," Micah said, "let's get on with it. About tonight, what time do we want to start this shindig?"

"Let's make it about six o'clock." Pete looked at Tyler. "It should be dark by then, or at least almost dark. Pull in and let Sandi climb into the truck. Racheal can climb out to let her in so Marion will see her and think you have a full truck. Then drive to the back like you're going to turn around. Sandi can jump out by the garage and use the garage entrance to get to the basement."

Mother spoke up. "Frank can get in the car with me. Zoë, you come with us. We really need to make it look like we're all leaving. We'll drive down the road a way until we're out of sight, and then we can all sneak back to the house."

"Everyone can take a spot to watch from," I said. "Pete will be in the basement. Marion is going to have her eyes on me when we load up, not him. Actually, when I get to your truck, I'll point to the back and holler something about needing to pick him up. That should account for his whereabouts."

"You've got this pretty well planned out," Tyler said. "I think she's really going to think we're all leaving. And I'll remember to turn the radio up so we're making noise. That will throw her off."

"What about Stanley and me?" Felicity asked.

"You'll come with us." Frank turned to Stanley. "Don't worry, when we sneak back we shouldn't run into any snakes or anything." He was giving our friend a hard time.

"Are you sure?" Stanley had been fine until the mention of snakes.

"I'll take my snake gun, just in case. Remember, Marion walks these dirt roads all the time, and she doesn't seem any the worse for wear."

Frank was grinning and Stanley realized my stepfather was messin' with him.

"Whew! You had me going for a moment."

We walked down the driveway with the Hansens and made a show of looking like we were finalizing our plans. Bubba walked with us and sat next to Pete when we waved goodbye and stopped to talk.

Now, all we had to do was wait. Or, at least, I hoped that was the case.

"What if she doesn't come back to the house?" I looked up at Pete.

"Then we've made a lot of plans for nothing."

"What about Bubba?" Felicity asked. "If we're going out for a night on the town, or so we want her to think, we can't leave Bubba here."

"Sure we can," I said. "He's used to her comings and goings. He never alerts us when she's around. I'll bet you anything that she's been making friends with him all along, giving him treats or something. Remember how he walked with her when we approached her on the road? She wasn't afraid of him, either."

I looked at the dog and narrowed my eyes. "Traitor."

He grinned at me. You'd think he understood what we were talking about.

I sighed, again, for about the umpteenth time since our stay began at… "Mother, did you and Frank ever decide what you're going to name your B&B?"

She glanced at Frank and he nodded.

"We're naming it Legend Ranch. Between the history of the house and the things that have happened since we got here, we decided that's a good name."

I thought about it for a moment. "You're right. It's a perfect fit. Legend Ranch," I said, repeating the name.

Pete looked upward, at the sky, before turning to my parents. "It's perfect. People will find it intriguing. Just don't share everything with them. You don't want to scare them off."

"Good point," Frank said. "I can't explain it, but from everything I've heard I have a feeling there's more to this Marion situation than we know."

"I think you're right," I said.

"Let's get some rest." Mother turned toward the house. "It looks like it might be a long night."

No one actually took a nap. We settled out by the pool and leaned back in our chairs, once again making small talk.

It felt good to relax. My arms were sore from all the work I'd done, and I figured that was a good thing. I needed the exercise, although going up and down the stairs hadn't bothered me because I had stairs at home.

Stanley actually looked healthier since we'd been in Arizona. His color was good and he'd been eating bigger meals. Even though it had only been a week, I was pretty sure he might have put on a couple of pounds. With all the work he'd done, he was toning himself up. He seemed to have gotten used to wearing jeans instead of slacks, but I honestly couldn't say he looked more rugged.

I caught Felicity watching him with admiration in her

eyes.

After some time passed, my mother turned and said, "We need to eat. She may be watching, but that can't be helped. We'll just let her think we're going out for a night on the town, not dinner."

While she put something together, I fed Bubba and checked his water dish. It was almost empty so I filled it.

Over dinner I explained a variation on our plan. "I'm going to wait near the garage door so I can watch the Ellison's house. If I see her heading toward Legend Ranch, I'll hurry to the basement. Pete, you should probably stay out of sight, but upstairs, in case she doesn't come to the basement. Maybe you could relax in a corner of the Arizona room."

"That makes sense. Between everyone outside and us inside, we're bound to catch her in the act."

"I've decided to wait in the basement with you." My mother put her fork down and gave me a challenging look.

"Okay." I was fine with that.

She looked surprised, but picked up her fork and started eating again.

~ * ~

Six o'clock rolled around and everyone filled the roles they'd been assigned. When Tyler pulled around back to turn around, I slipped out of the truck and quietly moved to the corner of the garage where my mother was waiting for me. Tyler rolled the windows up and turned on the radio.

Frank started to follow him out of the driveway. Felicity made a point of making him stop so she could run back and get something she'd allegedly forgotten. She seemed to want Marion to be sure to see that she was in the car. Stanley stood by the car door until she returned.

It looked like things were going perfectly, as planned.

I watched the vehicles travel past the Ellis house. Marion was watching out the window. She turned her back and spoke to her grandparents, moving farther inside the house.

I waited.

Everyone had remembered their walkie talkies and each one checked in with me as they reached their assigned hidey hole, or actually, a bush, tree or fence to hide behind.

"No more talking," I said. "I don't want her to hear anyone." I glanced pointedly at my mother.

Dead silence followed my comment.

About half an hour passed before I saw Marion open the front door. She stepped out and I heard her say, "I'm going for a walk, Gram."

She shut the door, pulled a blonde wig out of somewhere – I couldn't see where it had been hidden – and headed in the direction of Legend Ranch.

I watched until I saw her heading for the garage before grabbing my mother's hand and hightailing it through the door and down to the basement.

Chapter Forty-nine

I pulled out my walkie talkie. "Don't answer me, but she's on her way to the garage. I think that means she'll come to the basement."

I heard some static and knew that was confirmation that they'd heard me and might be moving in.

Our wait wasn't long. Shortly after my message went out, the door to the basement opened. We watched from a dark corner.

Marion had a flashlight with her. She pointed the light at the floor of the basement and started searching, almost inch by inch.

The wedding rings we'd found rested on top of a small pile of wood. She worked her way in that direction and I watched, fascinated. Would she find them? And is that what she was looking for?

She pulled the wig off and scratched her head. It must have been warm with that thing on. Before long she put it back in place, tucking the ends of her own hair under it.

She rubbed her back and stretched, groaning in the process. All the bending to search the floor must have been getting to her. She shined the flashlight on the small pile of wood and headed for it, still holding her back. I assumed she needed to sit down for a few minutes.

And she saw the rings.

I was across the room from her and her eyes were as big as saucers. Her mouth formed a big "O", and she began to cry.

I stood and headed her way. Mother waited in the dark corner. She didn't seem to hear me coming, and she picked up the rings and sat down on the wood.

"Marion?"

Startled, she jumped up and turned to me. "What...?"

"Marion, we knew it was you with the blonde wig. I don't understand what's going on, but I'm sure you'll fill me in."

The panic on her face couldn't be missed. She turned and ran toward the door leading to the garage. Before she could leave, Pete opened the door and positioned himself on the steps leading down to the basement, with his arms folded across his chest.

Marion cried harder, dropping to the floor and staring at the rings.

I let her cry it out without saying a word.

She finally calmed down. "I've wanted to tell my story for years, but I couldn't do it. I don't know if I can, even now."

"You saw something the day of the murders, didn't you?" Pete asked.

"Yes, but that's not what this is all about. Well, not exactly." She wiped away tears and took a deep breath. "I suppose I have to tell someone."

I took hold of her arm and helped her up. "Let's go outside and sit at the barbeque table. We can talk there. I have a feeling you need some fresh air." I couldn't explain it, but I felt sorry for her. I knew she had some big things to talk about, maybe life-altering things, and I was pretty sure they were horrific. The pain on her face spoke volumes.

Mother stepped forward and gave Marion a reassuring look.

Pete and I helped Marion to the table and we sat down. Before long, the others joined us, but they stood behind Marion who faced the motorhome instead of the garage. She didn't seem to realize they were there until Felicity entered the motorhome and brought out a glass of water, setting it in front of her. My mother sat next to Marion with her arm across her shoulders.

"What happened, Marion? What's had you so upset for so long?" I asked.

And the story began.

"I told you what a creep Harry Stockholm was, but I've never told anyone the whole story. He had a mouth on him that would make a sailor blush. He was horrible, and mean. I know that Francine wanted to take Barbara and leave him, but he controlled all the money and she was afraid of him.

"One night I went out for one of my walks. Barbara was gone. She was staying with her grandmother for a week. I heard Harry yelling at Francine. He was saying horrible things. It was so loud that I could hear him out in the street. I looked up and saw him and his wife through the front bedroom window. I could see a gun in his hand. I thought he was trying to scare her – to dominate her."

She took a long drink of the water.

"I thought he was going to shoot her and I knew I'd better go call the police. But he didn't shoot her. She turned away from him – I think she was going to run – and he hit her over the head. It stunned her and she stood still for a second, and he hit her again. She dropped, never got up again, and there was no doubt in my mind, she was dead. I could see him drag her out of the the room. That was the night he told everyone she was sick and she died at the hospital, and I knew I was right about her death."

"Why didn't you report this to the police?" Pete asked.

"I stayed where I was, in shock. Harry came back to the bedroom and looked out the window and saw me. He pointed the gun at me and I figured it meant if I said anything he'd kill me, too."

"What happened next?" my mother asked.

"I went for my walk and tried to act like I hadn't seen anything. Remember, I was fairly young. If the same thing happened today, I wouldn't hesitate to report it. But things were different then, and I was scared half to death. I remember feeling like I had lead weights on my feet. I cried, but it was dark and no one was there to see me."

"I don't understand why you kept looking for the rings." I had to know what was going through her head.

"Harry was out the next day and I snuck into the house to see if Francine might be alive. He hadn't told anyone that she'd died yet. Her rings were sitting on the kitchen sink. That's when I knew she was gone. I don't know why, but I grabbed them. I guess because they were a statement about what happened to her.

"I heard Harry pull in and ran through the living room to the basement. I dropped one of the rings in the living room. I dropped the other one in the basement, but I could hear him moving around and I couldn't stop to look for it."

She glanced at the rings in her hand.

"And you people came here and found them with no problem. Where were they?"

I didn't take my eyes from her face. "One ended up behind the baseboard in the living room. The other one was in a crack in the basement floor. We found them by accident."

"There's more," Marion said.

I didn't reply, but waited for her to go on.

"First, I don't know what Harry did with her body. I watched the house, but I never saw him dig a hole or anything." She started to cry again. "I adored Francine. She always treated me like I was special. She was such a good woman. I don't know how she got hooked up with that... That murdering piece of scum."

I still held my comments to myself. She'd said there was more.

"That's why I wore the wig and snuck around the house. I figured you'd think it was Francine's ghost and you'd go snooping around and find her body. She deserves an ending, like a funeral."

Frank quietly entered the motorhome and turned on an outside light.

Marion flinched.

"Why did you keep this to yourself all these years?" I asked.

"Because I was afraid the police would arrest me for keeping it quiet. When Harry killed his daughter and the neighbor, I felt like he sealed my fate."

"*Harry* murdered them?" Pete asked. "I thought it was the ranchhand."

"No, it was Harry. I still can't believe it after all this time, but I witnessed the second murders, too. I saw Harry walkng through the yard with a shotgun and a pistol and I knew there was trouble. When he entered the house I snuck up to the front window and peeked inside.

"I saw that Harry had leaned the shotgun against the wall. He was screaming at his daughter. I don't know why, but he was angry that she was in love with Mike, the neighbor. Mike started to charge Harry to take the gun away from him, and the old man shot him in the head. Barbara screamed and he turned the gun on her, too. He killed them both."

She stopped talking and took another drink of water. Her hands were shaking so hard that water spilled on the table. She closed her eyes and rocked back and forth with her arms folded, holding onto her arms as though she were cold, before continuing the story.

"Clyde heard the shots and came running, tearing into the house like someone was chasing him. He saw the bodies on the floor and looked up at the old man. Harry started to cackle like he'd just played a funny joke.

"Clyde charged him and wrestled the gun away from him, but in the process he accidentally shot Harry. But Harry didn't go down. He grabbed the shotgun he'd leaned against the wall and killed Clyde. He picked up the pistol and wiped his fingerprints off of it. I don't understand it, but it went off. That's why there's a hole in the screen door. He put the gun in Cyde's hand and started to walk away, but he fell to the floor before he got very far."

She started to cry again.

Mother patted her back and squeezed her shoulders.

"I ran home and told Gram to call the police to tell them I'd heard shots fired at the house, but by the time they got here they were all dead."

"Why didn't you tell the police what happened?" my mother asked.

"Because I'd never told them what happened to Francine, and everyone had died. What good would it have done?"

Chapter Forty-nine

*P*ete took over the conversation. "If you'd told the authorities about Francine's murder, then Barbara, Mike and Clyde would still be alive, and Clyde's memory wouldn't be that he was a killer. I understand how afraid you were. Harry had threatened you, even if it was only by pointing a gun at you. However, by keeping your mouth shut, he got away with *four* murders."

Surprisingly, Pete didn't sound like he was sitting in judgment, even if his words did.

"I know, but I was so afraid. I really was."

"It wouldn't have made any difference if you'd told them everything after the multiple murders," I said.

"I might have been sent to jail."

"Unlikely," my mother said.

"They wouldn't have known where to look for Francine's body, and Harry would have come after me, even if it was just in my bad dreams. I'm getting sick to my stomach just thinking about it."

"That makes sense to me," Felicity said.

Marion started rocking back and forth again. "The guilt

has been too much to live with, so maybe your husband is right. Maybe I'd better finally talk to the police."

She looked deeply into my eyes.

I knew she wanted something.

"Would you come with me?"

"We'll call them and they'll send someone out to talk to you. Under the circumstances, and since it's been so long, I don't think you'll have anything to worry about. They've got too many current crimes to worry about."

"What about Francine's body?" she asked.

"Let me think about it."

In the next moment, I had the answer. I looked past Marion, toward the house, and I saw a glow in the garage. It came from in front of the hole in the wall where we'd found the hidden staircase. I didn't see a woman's figure standing by the wall, just the light. But I knew in my heart we had the answer.

So did Bubba. He sat quietly with his head up, listening to something none of us could hear.

I turned to Frank. "It's time to tear down the wall in the garage and see what's at the top of that hidden staircase."

"Hidden staircase?" Marion stopped rocking.

My mother rubbed her back. "Yes, dear, there's a staircase leading to who knows where? I've wanted to check it out all along, but no one would listen."

"I'll take care of it first thing in the morning." Apparently Frank had decided this would be the prudent thing to do. "We'll do everything in the morning, including calling the police."

I stood. "He's right. Tonight we need to get some rest."

Tyler stepped forward with Racheal. "We'll come over for moral support, Marion. That's what friends are for, right?"

She looked at him in wonder. "You're my friends?"

Racheal held out her hand. "You bet we are. Come on. We'll walk you home. You've been through enough for one lifetime, so once tomorrow is over you can get on with your life."

Micah and Zoë nodded and the Hansens walked Marion home.

~ * ~

Frank tore down the garage wall early the next morning, but we left it to the police to climb the stairs. They found Francine's body, or at least what we assumed was her body. They'd run tests to be sure.

Things worked out, although we'd had our doubts. The police took Marion's statement. Everything had happened so many years ago that the D.A. didn't prosecute her; they were just happy to update and close their files. We turned the gun that had been hidden under the bathroom sink over to them. Yes, it was blood on the grip of the gun.

Mother watched them take Francine's remains away and stood quietly, shaking her head. "So sad. What a horrible ending to a tragic life."

She headed into the house, up to the front bedroom.

I followed her.

"I think I'll have this entire room redone. Or *I'll* do it. I'm going to use cheerful colors in honor of Francine. By the way, what made you decide the staircase would lead to her body?"

"I saw a light in the garage, by the hole in the wall. I can't explain it, but I knew it was a message."

"But you don't believe in ghosts, sweetie."

"I didn't say it was a ghost. It was just a light, and it was purely coincidental that I saw it when I did."

"Uh huh."

EPILOGUE

Over the next week we worked with renewed vigor and did as much as we could around the yard and house. When we finally left there was still a lot to do, but Mom and Frank seemed to have things covered.

Felicity and Stanley left for a honeymoon in Australia. They had a fantastic time. An Australian friend, also a model, had taken the time to make sure the couple was able to do and see things that the average tourist wouldn't.

Pete and I decided to forego our honeymoon until we had the business up and running again. We were happy with the way things were and couldn't decide where we wanted to go anyway.

Tyler helped Frank find horses and they filled the stable with four geldings, part appaloosa and part quarter horse.

One horse was a solid bay with blanket markings. Although dark brown, he had a black tail and mane. The second horse was black with a snip, or a white marking between the nostrils. The third horse was a sorrel, a reddish colored horse with three white socks. Lastly, the fourth horse was gray with black spots. On a weekend trip back to see my parents, I went nuts over the sorrel and we developed a special bond. Yes, people and horses can become friends.

Mother bought some chickens, of all things, and said she wanted fresh eggs from her own chickens. I laughed. My mother would smother those chickens with affection. She'd probably name each and every one of them. And Racheal helped her start her own vegetable garden.

I have no idea why, but Frank set up a spot for them and bought four goats. Go figure.

I read Tyler's book and enjoyed it so much that I started recommending it to friends. He called me from time to time to ask technical questions.

Micah and Zoë left before we did, returning to their farm. They invited us to come for a visit.

Mom and I stopped trying to frighten each other. After we heard Marion's story, it wasn't so much fun anymore.

I still believe there's no such thing as a ghost, glow or no glow.

Legend Ranch

About the Author

Marja McGraw worked in both criminal and civil law enforcement for several years before relocating to Northern Nevada, where she worked for the Nevada Department of Transportation. She also lived in Oregon where she worked for the Jackson County Sheriff's Office and owned her own business, a Tea Room/Antique Store. Her next stop was Wasilla, Alaska. The draw to Northern Nevada was strong, and she eventually returned.

Marja wrote a weekly column for a small newspaper in No. Nevada and she was the editor for the Sisters in Crime Internet Newsletter for a year and a half. She belongs to several writer/reader groups.

She has appeared on the morning news in Reno, Nevada, and on KLBC-TV in Laughlin, Nevada. She's also been a guest on several radio and Internet radio shows.

Starting with *Secrets of Holt House, A Mystery*, Marja followed up with *A Well-Kept Family Secret - A Sandi Webster Mystery* and the beginning of a series.

Most recently, she began a new series beginning with *Bogey Nights – A Bogey Man Mystery*.

She says that each of her mysteries contains *a little humor, a little romance and A Little Murder!*, and that her books concentrate on the characters and solving the crime rather than the crime itself.

She and her husband currently live in No. Arizona.

Marja's website can be viewed at www.marjamcgraw.com.

Made in the USA
San Bernardino, CA
04 August 2014